About the Author

Romantic Book of the Year author, Kendall Talbot, writes action-packed romantic suspense loaded with sizzling heat and intriguing mysteries set in exotic locations. She hates cheating, loves a good happily ever after, and thrives on exciting adventures with kick-ass heroines and heroes with rippling abs and broken hearts.

Kendall has sought thrills in all 46 countries she's visited. She's rappelled down freezing waterfalls, catapulted out of a white-water raft, jumped off a mountain with a man who spoke little English, and got way too close to a sixteen-foot shark.

She lives in Brisbane, Australia with her very own hero and a fluffy little dog who specializes in hijacking her writing time. When she isn't writing or reading, she's enjoying wine and cheese with her crazy friends and planning her next international escape.

She loves to hear from her readers!

Find her books and chat with her via any of the contacts below:

www.kendalltalbot.com
Email: kendall@universe.com.au

Or you can find her on any of the following channels:

Amazon
Bookbub
Goodreads

Books by Kendall Talbot

Maximum Exposure Series:

(These books are stand-alone and can be read in any order):

Extreme Limit

Deadly Twist (Finalist: Wilbur Smith Adventure Writing Prize 2021)

Zero Escape

Other Stand-Alone books:

Jagged Edge

Lost in Kakadu (Winner: Romantic Book of the year 2014)

Double Take

Waves of Fate Series

First Fate

Feral Fate

Final Fate

Treasure Hunter Series:

Treasured Secrets

Treasured Lies

Treasured Dreams

Treasured Whispers

Treasured Hopes

Treasured Tears

If you sign up to my newsletter you can help with fun things like naming characters and giving characters quirky traits and interesting jobs. You'll also get my book, Breathless Encounters which is exclusive to my newsletter followers only, for free.

Here's my newsletter signup link if you're interested:

http://www.kendalltalbot.com.au/newsletter.html

DEADLY TWIST

Book Two in the Maximum Exposure Series

KENDALL TALBOT

Published 2020 Kendall Talbot

Deadly Twist

Book Two in the Maximum Exposure Series

© 2020 by Kendall Talbot

ISBN: 9798637918553

v.2021.10

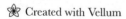 Created with Vellum

Chapter One

Lily Bennett reached into the satchel at her side and placed her hand on the leather-bound journal that had triggered her traveling more than three thousand miles out of her comfort zone.

She'd already memorized everything inside its weathered pages. Especially her late father's sketch of the unusual temple, which she'd been shocked to see on CNN six weeks ago. According to the news report, the newly discovered, three-thousand-year-old Agulinta Temple had been hidden for centuries—literally consumed by the Mexican jungle.

Yet, somehow her father knew it existed.

The temptation to open the journal again was impossible to ignore.

She pulled it from her satchel and flicked over the yellowed pages, stopping on his drawing of a hollowed-out circular statue, like a giant donut. Around the face of the structure, pictographs appeared to tell a story.

CNN had shown footage of a statue at Agulinta Temple like this.

Exactly like this.

A branch with enormous elephant-ear-sized leaves swiped the

side of the taxi, brushing her elbow as she leaned out the window. It was hard to know what was worse—the hot air seeping through the car vents or the humid air blowing in from outside. Shifting on the cracked vinyl seat, she tugged her cotton dress over her knees, hoping for a slight breeze up her skirt, but it was pointless.

She cleared her throat. "How much farther?"

The taxi driver looked at her in the mirror and smiled, showing off his chipped front tooth. "Not long."

That's what he'd said an hour ago.

Her mind drifted back to the horror written on her mother's face when they'd opened the beat-up old suitcase they'd discovered in her father's shed after he'd passed away. Lily thought she'd known her father well, until that moment.

Alongside the leather-bound journal, they'd also found a collection of black-and-white photos. The implications behind the pictures further shattered her mother's already broken heart. His sudden death meant their future was forever changed. However, the mysterious items they'd found in that case, changed their past too.

For nearly a year, she'd watched her mother's slide into a grieving darkness, dragging Lily and her brothers along with her. Lily had feared the secrets her father had taken to his grave were destined to remain unsolved.

Until CNN revealed Agulinta Temple to the world.

From the moment she'd seen that news report and heard the archaeologist's declaration that the unusual shape of the ancient statue was one of a kind, she'd made it her mission to travel to Mexico and see Agulinta for herself. She needed answers, as did her mother. It'd been a whirlwind couple of weeks, and she still couldn't believe she was here.

Lily took a tissue from her satchel and dabbed it across her neck and chest before using it to soak up the sweat under her armpits. The driver snuck a glance at her but, when she met his gaze, he quickly looked away.

She was used to that. With six older brothers, and overprotective parents, she'd always felt the eyes of someone watching her. It was like living in a snow globe, and when things tipped upside-down, they'd all be looking to see how she'd handle it.

That wasn't how she'd ended up here, though. Traveling to the middle of the Mexican jungle had been her decision. She'd listened to everyone's objections, fielding calls from every member of her family and her girlfriends.

Her boss had put his foot down, proclaiming the trip too dangerous for a woman like her, which made her even more determined. Taking her new position with '*More to Explore*' was a stepping-stone for her career. It had also relocated her from Montana, where she'd grown up under the wings of her protective family, and into her own dinky little apartment in Seattle.

Defying them all, she'd taken unpaid leave to make this journey from Seattle to the jungles of Mexico. Once she'd proved her decision was final, her boss, being the dirtbag he was, had added a caveat: If she did write a story, and *if* it was any good, the magazine would publish it.

Everybody thought she was crazy.

Maybe she was.

But this was something she had to do, for her mother's sake, and for her own. People had been controlling her all her life. It was time to show everyone that Lily had grown up.

Without slowing, the taxi crashed through a pothole that must've been the size of a trash can and Lily's head rammed into the smoke-stained vinyl roof. "Shit."

The driver squinted at her through the mirror. "Sorry." The grin on his face contradicted his apology.

It wasn't the first time she'd hit the roof, and based on the number of potholes pockmarking the road, it wouldn't be the last.

For more than twenty-two hours, she'd been traveling. She just hoped when she finally arrived at the one and only hotel in Corozal that they had hot running water, good pillows, and a decent restaurant.

The taxi skidded to a stop, launching her forward. "What's wrong?"

"Sorry lady, big snake."

"What? Where?"

"There." He pointed out the front windshield.

The mottled brown and green snake spanned the width of the dirt road. Both its head and the end of its body were out of sight. It was as thick as her bicep and slithered out in the open, as if it had all the time in the world. A snake that big probably did.

"We let it pass." The driver grinned at her via the mirror. "Don't want it caught in my engine."

She shook her head. "No. No, you don't."

Lily wiped the back of her hand across her forehead and caught the trickle of sweat that'd dribbled down her temple. Waiting in the oppressive heat brought out all manner of smells, most of them unpleasant.

The driver himself was a cloying combination of body odor, stale cigarettes, and garlic.

She put the journal away, leaned her head out the window, and inhaled the fresh jungle air, hoping to remove his scent from her nostrils.

The snake's tail finally appeared and she watched, fascinated, as it glided over the gravel and disappeared into the vegetation. She'd seen her share of snakes, having grown up on a dairy farm in Montana, but she couldn't recall ever seeing one that big.

The driver stomped on the pedal again and she slipped back on the seat. For twenty more minutes, they barreled along the jungle track carved through the dense forest, until, suddenly they were in the open. Out her window, and a long way below, was a river. The driver didn't slow, weaving along the narrow cliff way too fast for her liking and her breath caught at each turn.

Below, the thundering river spouted white water at every rock it tumbled over. She leaned out the window, eager to appreciate the whole spectacle. A few minutes later, the river became a waterfall, tumbling twenty or so feet into a large green pool.

She fished her iPhone from her satchel. There'd be no signal; she'd already checked a dozen times since she'd climbed into the taxi. She flicked it on and snapped several photos, hoping she did the pristine ravine the justice that its beauty deserved. Lily was

4

known for her terrible photography, and when she flicked through the blurry shots, she groaned. Her reputation would remain intact. It'd become a running joke with her family and friends.

Seconds later, they were back in the jungle. Trees as thick as her oldest brother's chest lined the track, and vines wove up and around them in a dense tapestry.

Movement high in the tree caught her eye, and she thought she saw a monkey swinging from branch to branch. "Are there monkeys here?"

"*Sí*, everywhere. But they bad. Don't touch."

"Bad? What do you mean bad?"

"Crazy. *Loco*." He spun his finger around his ear. "If you get bit . . ." He made a weird cackling noise, and it took Lily a moment to realize he was laughing. "You will be *loco* too."

"Oh, okay. That's good advice. Thanks."

He grinned at her through the mirror. "Why you come to Mexico?"

She hesitated, unsure whether to tell this complete stranger her plans but, other than his erratic driving, he seemed harmless. "I'm here to report on the new Mayan temple that's been discovered."

"Ahhh. Agulinta. Yes, we get many visitors now. Are you a TV reporter?"

"No, I'm a journalist for a magazine." Although it was true, she still felt like a fraud saying it. So far, the only articles she'd been permitted to write were on the latest lipstick shade or a new shoe trend, topics that bored her, topics that were a world apart from where her heart lay. Her new position at *More to Explore* promised to fix that. However, she hadn't written a single article for the travel magazine yet.

She reached into her satchel for her Dictaphone. "May I ask you a few questions?"

His eyes lit up. "Me?"

She refrained from pointing out that he was the only other person in the vehicle. Instead, she just nodded and returned his smile.

"*Sí, sí*. Will I be in your paper?"

"Maybe. What's your name again?"

"I'm Otomi Gonzales-Jose."

The faded identification card on the dashboard was impossible to read, so she asked him to spell out his name for her records.

"Do you live around here?"

"*Sí*. I live in Corozal my whole life. My parents are here, my brothers, my sisters, my wife, my kids, nieces and nephews. Nobody leaves. We love it." Although his strong accent veiled his English, he was still understandable.

"How many people live in Corozal?"

"Oh, about three hundred. Half of them are family." He laughed again, flashing his yellowed teeth.

"What do you know about Agulinta Temple?"

His already dark eyes darkened even further. "We were shocked like rest of world when they found it. I've been crawling through jungle since I was a *bebé* and I never knew it was there. The jungle swallow it up."

This was consistent with what Lily already knew. Nine weeks ago, a team of *National Geographic* archaeologists from Italy, who were doing further research on the ancient Mayan temple of Yaxchilan, had detected an anomaly in the vegetation whilst flying over in a helicopter. When they went in for a closer look, they discovered a temple so overgrown with vegetation that barely two percent was visible. They noted its position, and a fortnight later arrived at Agulinta Temple on foot.

After crashing through another massive pothole, the car plunged into broad daylight. The first sign of civilization for three hours was a welcome sight that was short-lived. Corozal looked more like the set of a bad Western movie. Annoyed that she hadn't thought to interview the driver earlier, she clicked off her Dictaphone and shoved it away.

The town consisted of one main street, with wooden, two-story buildings lining either side. Each building had a front veranda, and nearly every one had a couple of gray-haired men seated out front. Abundant wrinkles, lining their faces, deepened as they followed her taxi's slow cruise through the center of town.

They passed a general store, a saddlery, a barber, a clothing store, a few buildings without any signage, and two saloons. Otomi pulled the car to a stop outside Hotel Corozal. The sign, dangling lopsided from a chain attached to just one corner, had two letters missing, so it read Hot Corozal.

It was a bad sign. Literally.

Chapter Two

O tomi came around and opened the taxi door for Lily. She peeled her sweat-soaked legs off the vinyl seat, climbed out, and curled her head from side to side in an attempt to loosen up cramped muscles. Otomi removed her brand-new hiking pack from the trunk, and she followed him up the three small steps, through the front door, and over to the counter.

"*Renata, dónde estás, tienes un invitado.*"

Lily wished she knew what Otomi had said.

A large woman, with rosy-red cheeks and a colorful flowing dress, stepped out of a doorway and walked toward them, wiping her hands on a frilly apron. She was the picture of homely bliss, and Lily's initial grim opinion of the hotel quickly changed for the better.

"This is my sister, Renata. She will look after you."

The woman grabbed Lily's shoulders and planted a kiss on each cheek. "Welcome. Welcome."

Lily chuckled at the woman's friendliness. "Hello, I'm Liliana Bennett."

"Yes. Yes, I know who you are. Come, your room is ready." The woman grabbed Lily's pack off Otomi and waddled away.

"I just need to pay for--"

"It okay. You pay me tomorrow." Otomi cocked his head at Renata. "You better go, she no like to wait."

"Oh, are you sure?" Letting someone else take her bag was bad enough, but her research about Mexico had led her to expect her taxi driver to ask for payment up front. She thought they would haggle back and forth, come up with a mutually acceptable arrangement, and only then part ways.

Her mind raced. Something wasn't right. She just didn't know what.

Otomi tipped his imaginary hat at Lily and walked away, leaving her no choice but to follow the abundant derrière making its way up the corridor.

Renata's hips bounced off either side of the walls as she led Lily up a very narrow set of stairs. At the top, Renata walked along a corridor and paused to use a large, old-fashioned skeleton key to open the third door along.

Lily followed her into a very small room, furnished with a single bed, a small round table, and two chairs. The wardrobe was a free-standing white cupboard painted with little pink butterflies and looked old enough to be a family heirloom.

Renata hefted Lily's pack onto the bed and the springs twanged in protest, then she turned to Lily. "Your room is good, *sí?*"

"Yes, thank you." Lily frowned, looking around. "But where's my bathroom?"

"Ahhh, come, come." Lily followed her farther along the corridor to another doorway. "Here is bathroom."

A bath, skirted with a blue plastic curtain adorned with more pink butterflies, dominated the room, and Lily counted seven toothbrushes in a chipped coffee mug on the corner of the sink.

She cleared her throat. "My travel agent said I'd have my own bathroom."

"*Sí.*" Renata grinned, but failed to elaborate or apologize.

Clearly it was a pointless argument, but the number of toothbrushes concerned her. This little room could become very busy in the morning. "How many guests are in your hotel?"

"Two." She beamed. "Very busy since they discover Agulinta. Is good, *sí?*"

"Yes. *Sí.*" This was a timely reminder of why she was here. It didn't matter what her accommodation was like. Visiting the mysterious ancient temple, meticulously detailed in her father's journal, was the only thing that mattered.

Lily desperately wanted a shower, but her hunger pangs were more dominating. "Renata, is there a restaurant near here?"

The Mexican woman's eyes widened, showing off the yellowish tinge around her black irises. "*Sí*, Zanbrero, is cantina down street. The chicken burritos is good, but if Gonzales in kitchen, just have salad." She scrunched up her face. "*Sí?*"

"Oh, okay." Lily cringed, wondering how she'd ascertain who the suspect chef would be. "Is it far?"

Renata chuckled. "Nothing is far in Corozal."

Lily believed her. From the drive in, it looked like the entire town consisted of just one street.

Renata handed Lily the giant brass key. "I make you beautiful breakfast at seven o'clock tomorrow, *sí?*"

"Yes, thank you." Renata's suggested time was late enough to allow Lily to get ready for her guide, who was due at eight o'clock in the morning.

After Renata waddled away, Lily returned to the bathroom to wash her hands and face. In her bedroom, she unpacked only the couple of items she'd need for the night, then she grabbed her satchel containing her most important possessions, locked her door behind her and headed downstairs.

She stepped down the front stairs of Hotel Corozal and strolled in the opposite direction from which she'd arrived. Other than two pairs of elderly men, who still sat on the porches, the street was deserted. She smelled forest leaves and spicy food. Four small black pigs ran out from beneath a building and barreled right at her. Lily dodged to the side at the last second, and the pigs continued squealing up the street like a wolf was on their tail.

The high-pitched cackle of children laughing somewhere in the distance was welcome relief as the words *ghost town* tumbled across her brain. Lily was once again reminded of Western movies as she climbed the four rickety wooden steps to the cantina, and stepped in through the swinging saloon doors.

Several men seated upon bar stools turned to her, and a line of unease crept up her spine. Although their sneers indicated her presence wasn't welcome, her hunger couldn't be ignored any longer. Lily had what her mother called a bottomless stomach.

Defying the impulse to walk right back out the door, she strode to one of the booths near an open window, sat down, and reached for a menu. Grumbling, she tossed it aside; it was written entirely in Spanish.

A man with a solid three-day growth walked toward her, wiping his hands on his grime-smudged T-shirt. "*Qué puedo conseguirte?*"

"Do you speak English?" She offered him her most becoming smile.

"*Sí*, little." He held his finger and thumb an inch apart.

"Oh good. Are you the chef here?" She pretended to toss a salad, trying to emulate what she was saying.

He palmed his chest. "*Sí*."

Grinning, she offered her hand. "I'm Lily. I've just arrived in your lovely little town. What's your name?"

"You want food?" He scowled, clearly uninterested in chitchat.

Stewing over what to do, she scanned the room, trying to see other diners' meals, but nobody appeared to be eating.

If she only had a salad, her grumbling stomach would wake her in the middle of the night, yet she didn't want to risk the chicken disaster Renata had hinted at. An idea hit her. "Do you have bean burritos?"

He nodded. "*Sí*."

Her stomach grumbled as if relieved. "Can I have three bean burritos and a beer, please?"

The chef nodded and left Lily to contend with the creepy stares from all the other men in the room. She couldn't decide if women weren't supposed to come to this cantina or if the locals didn't like strangers in their little town. The discovery of Agulinta would've brought more visitors to this area than they'd probably seen in an entire decade. Not everyone liked change.

Ignoring the leering eyes of the men at the bar, she scanned the room, looking for any hints her late father may've once been here. It was a crazy notion really. Her father had never mentioned to anyone that he'd been to Mexico.

Yet, the photos they'd found after they'd buried him and his drawings in the journal, indicated he had, though exactly where was unclear.

In an attempt to make sense of it all, Lily had spent hundreds of hours researching and memorizing her father's notes.

This expedition was a mission to try to decipher his drawings and ramblings. The father she'd known was a dairy farmer who adored his animals almost as much as he adored his family. They thought they knew everything there was to know about him, especially Lily's mother, who'd been with her father for more than thirty years.

They were wrong.

Out the window, the sun offered its last gasp, piercing long beams through the trees to create mottled light and dark shadows down the main street.

The bulbs in the cantina flickered to life, and Lily turned her attention to the décor. The restaurant was in desperate need of renovation. Colorful paint on the walls was peeling and faded, and the eclectic collection of hanging trinkets was plastered in dust. A multicolored rug hanging on the wall was decorated in Mayan symbols, and she recognized some from her recent research.

As she contemplated how long the rug had been hanging there, the chef returned to her table with her beer, meal, and a knife and fork wrapped in a yellow serviette.

"*Espero que os guste el burrito de frijoles, la amiga.*"

"*Gracias.*" Other than the word *burrito*, she had no idea what he'd said. If she'd had more time to prepare for this visit, Lily would've invested hours into learning basic Spanish. But in the six weeks from when she'd made up her mind she was going, to when she stepped on the plane in Seattle, her life had been a crazy whirlwind of phone calls from her concerned family and friends, making difficult travel arrangements, and studying her father's notes over and over again. Learning Spanish was allocated little priority.

Lily twisted the plate to examine the burritos nestled within a mound of brown rice and topped with lush red sauce. If it tasted even a fraction as good as it smelled, then this promised to be good.

She started with the León beer, a brand she'd never heard of. She took a tentative sip and the bubbles soothed her parched throat. The beer was cold, slightly sweet, and tasty. Satisfied, she took another mouthful, and this time she savored the semi-dark ale.

It was lucky Lily enjoyed a bit of spice because the delicious burrito, while abundant with flavor, was loaded with jalapeños and cayenne. She tempered the spicy flush crawling up her neck by alternating mouthfuls of food with swigs of the cold beer.

Halfway through her meal, a man walked into the cantina who looked as much out of place as she felt. Unlike everyone she'd seen since she hit Mexico, he was blond with fair skin. Lily hadn't seen fair hair since she'd left the American border. His full beard concealed most of his face, and his shoulder-length hair was a tangle of soft curls. She couldn't decide if the lighter strands near his temple were gray or sun bleached.

With a broad smile, the man swaggered up to the bar, as if it was something he did every day. He tugged one of the wooden stools out from beneath the counter and ordered a beer.

Going by his accent, Lily was confident he wasn't from Mexico. He wasn't American either. Based on some of the celebrities she'd heard on TV, Australian was her best guess.

He attempted small talk with the locals, who clearly weren't interested. Concentrating on her meal, she tried not to listen to the one-sided conversation. Once she'd eaten everything, she stood and left enough Mexican pesos on the table to cover her bill and a generous tip.

With her stomach now full, it was her weary body that was demanding attention. The sooner she hit the pillow, the better. Her intention was to sneak out while the newcomer was attempting to engage the disinterested men. But her plan was obliterated when he spun on his bar stool toward her. His eyes were an interesting blend of green and bronze and his smile accentuated the creases lining their sides.

"*Hola, señorita.*" Shifting his gaze from her eyes to her mouth, he flicked a wayward curl off his forehead.

"Hello." She offered a quick, carefree smile.

His eyebrows jumped up to his wavy bangs. "American?"

She nodded and, determined to get away before he asked any more questions, she adjusted her shoulder strap and headed out the door. Stepping over the threshold, she heard the men laughing and wondered if she was the focus of their joke.

It wouldn't have surprised her; the white cotton dress she'd put on that morning had been chosen for comfort and coolness for the long journey, not sitting in a dirty little cantina in the middle of a Mexican jungle. *I should've changed before leaving the hotel.*

The main street didn't have any lighting, except what filtered from the buildings flanking either side. Clutching her satchel strap, she hustled toward the single dangling bulb lighting up her hotel's front porch in the distance. She picked up her pace, peering into the darkness between each building she passed. Halfway along the street, the silence engulfed her.

A nervous tingle raced up her spine.

She spun to a crunching sound behind her. Her instincts kicked in and she ducked, but it was pointless. Her feet were tackled from beneath her. She fell to her knees and screamed, more for attention than pain. Her heart exploded when her attacker grabbed her satchel.

She clawed at the leather. Blind terror drove her desperation.

Her most precious items were in that bag and she was not letting it go.

Her attacker was barely visible; his dark skin, dark hair, and dark clothing blended into the blackness around him, but she knew he stood above her. She swung her right leg, connected with his knees, and tackled him to the ground.

Jumping to her feet, she dropped, elbow first, into his solar plexus.

The wind punched out of him with a wounded howl.

Acid churned her stomach as she scrambled upright again. The thief kicked the backs of her legs. She lurched forward, her hands slicing on the gravel, and she screamed her fury.

He grabbed her satchel.

She did too.

He heaved it and she used the momentum to haul herself upright.

A light came on in a nearby building, highlighting his face. She paused at his youthfulness, but only briefly. Taking aim, she rammed her closed fist into his nose. Bone and gristle shattered beneath the punch. She clutched the satchel to her chest, and, as he hit the ground in a full body slam, she turned and ran.

Her feet pounded beneath her. Her breaths shot in and out in short, sharp gasps.

She tasted blood, barely noticing she'd bitten her lip and with every stride, she braced for attack.

She bounded up the hotel's front steps, slammed open the front door, and it hit the wall as loud as a gunshot. Stumbling forward, she clutched the railing. Her mind told her to get up the stairs, but her legs wouldn't obey. Her heart thumped in her ears. Stars dazzled her eyes.

Renata appeared in the hall, eyes wide, mouth ajar. "What's wrong? What happened? Oh, my Lord, look at you. You're a mess."

"Someone tried to steal my bag." With trembling fingers, she gripped her satchel. Her legs weakened with relief that it was still there. She had thought it'd be safer to keep her prized possessions on her at all times—it may've been the wrong decision. "I'm okay."

"You're not okay. Look at your clothes."

Her cotton dress was ruined, stained with both blood and dirt. Blood oozed from her knees, and it was only now that she felt her stinging flesh.

Renata fussed over her, straightening her dress, dusting dirt off her back and hip. All Lily wanted to do was get to her room and shut the door.

She gripped the railing, ready to climb the stairs, but waning adrenaline had turned her bones to jelly. "I didn't see him very well, but I think he was just a kid. I'm okay, really. But he might not be. I may've broken his nose."

Renata gasped and covered her mouth. "You broke his nose?"

"I think so."

Renata blinked at her, and for a moment appeared to be more horrified by what Lily had done to her attacker than the other way around.

"I just need a shower and a good sleep. I'm fine. I'll see you in the morning."

Renata backed away. "*Sí, sí*, okay. Good night."

Lily's muscles protested at every step. By the time she reached her bedroom, a lump had formed in her throat. By the time she pushed into her room, she could barely breathe. She shut the door, locked it, and a sob burst from her lips.

Bile rose to her tongue as she crumbled onto the bed. Flicking away tears, she examined her injuries through blurry eyes. Her palms were a mess, blood and grit mingled together. Her knees were the same. As she touched one sore after another, she tried to come to terms with what happened. She could almost hear her family's reaction. They'd tell her to forget her stupid quest and return home. But she wouldn't do that. Couldn't.

This was not going to beat her. It was just some stupid kid, desperate for cash. Nothing more.

Drying her eyes, she grabbed her toiletries bag and a towel and pulled open her door. She stepped into the hallway and nearly smacked straight into a man. Her heart leapt to her throat until she realized who it was.

"Holy shit. What happened to you?" The blond-haired man from the cantina eyed her up and down.

She straightened her shoulders but avoided his gaze. "Nothing. What're you doing here?"

"I'm staying here too. Are you okay?"

"Yes. I'm fine."

"You don't look it. What'd you do? Fall over or something?"

"Yeah . . . something like that. Nothing a hot shower and good sleep won't fix." She forced conviction into her voice.

"Right then. Some of those cuts may need dressing. Want some help?"

Lily resisted the temptation to look at her bloody hands. "No, I'm fine. Good night—"

"Carter," he prompted.

"I'm Lily."

"Nice to meet you, Lily. Hope you feel better tomorrow."

She left him in the hall, entered the bathroom, and locked the door. Determined not to cry anymore, she reexamined her legs. Both kneecaps had lost skin, guaranteeing nasty scabs in a couple of days, and a red rash covered her right shin.

After undressing, she stepped into the shower and allowed the warm water to massage her weary body. Her wounds stung, but pushing through the pain, she ensured all the dirt was gone. She would've stayed in there for hours if the hot water hadn't abruptly shuddered off.

She dried herself, wrapped her towel around her body, then tiptoed down the hallway and arriving at her room uninterrupted, she closed and locked the door behind her. Lily pulled out the little first-aid kit she'd brought with her and winced as she rubbed antiseptic into her wounds, and bandaged both her hands and knees.

By the time she crawled onto the lumpy mattress and tugged the sheet up under her chin, she was beyond exhausted. Every part of her body ached.

Her friends and family told her not to do this.

But damned if I'm going to give up this quickly.

It's only four days.

Closing her eyes, she repeated the mantra, *I can do this*, until sleep silenced her overactive brain.

Chapter Three

Carter woke just before the sun spread its light across the sky. It was a habit that'd been with him most of his life and had proven impossible to break. He couldn't remember ever needing an alarm to wake up, which was a gift, given that he'd traveled a vast majority of the world. It didn't matter what time zone he was in, his body always knew when daybreak was about to hit.

He reached for his camera and hoisted up his bedroom window to investigate the view. He adjusted the focus and explored different parts of the little Mexican town below, searching for the perfect scene to take his first photo of the day.

For more than two decades, this ritual had been crucial to his waking routine. His Morning World collection of photos had not only landed him a job as a freelance photographer with *National Geographic*, but they'd also won sufficient awards to have his collection displayed in several countries. That little bonus provided him with enough cash to keep traveling, doing what he loved.

An elderly man was walking up the street aided by a wooden cane. A plume of smoke tumbled from his mouth and vanished into obscurity around him. Carter adjusted the lens to take in every crease of the old man's face. He clicked off a few shots, focusing on the wrinkles that deepened when the man drew in on a pipe that drooped from his lips to his chin.

Carter took a series of photos capturing the first rays of sun that speared over the jungle treetops and onto the old man. The light aged him further, adding years to his already ancient frame.

Thirty or so shots later, Carter put his camera aside, threw his towel over his shoulder, and left his room for the bathroom. The bathroom door was shut and, for some reason, he hoped the person he heard showering in there was the woman from last night.

Covered in dirt and blood like she was, she'd seemed almost fragile, yet he'd seen fortitude simmering in her eyes as well. Although, one glance was enough to know she was cruising well outside her comfort zone. He hoped like hell she wasn't planning on going to Agulinta, 'cause it'd be no picnic.

Propping one foot on the wall, he leaned back, and waited for the door to open.

He didn't have to wait long, and his first glance at her made him glad he'd waited. Dark, wet hair tumbled around her face, accentuating her stunning, dark-rimmed blue eyes. Her skin, perfectly toned in a mellow tan, was a striking contrast to the white towel wrapped around her body. "Morning." He couldn't stop the smile curling on his lips.

"Hello." She squeezed the towel around her breasts. "Excuse me."

"What's the magic word?"

She cocked her head, seemingly unamused. "Please."

Grinning, he dropped his foot to the floor.

She scurried to her room, and glanced over her shoulder at him once, before she disappeared from view.

Carter stepped into the bathroom and felt the ridiculous need to splash water on his face to cool down. He hadn't felt even a hint of desire for a woman in years—hell, more like decades—but this woman had some kind of magic potion, stirring up his dormant libido.

The reaction was as unwanted as it was ridiculous.

After a quick shower, he returned to his room and packed his things into his rucksack. He usually preferred a little R & R between jobs, but Agulinta was an opportunity too good to miss. It was like he was destined to score this one. He was the closest *National Geographic* photographer within spitting distance of the temple, and he had the time and the money to do it. With a bit of luck, he'd beat every other bastard there and get to see it before the masses trampled it to death.

He checked his camera was on charge and headed downstairs for breakfast. Lily had beaten him there, and the sun streaming in from the open window cast her in a golden glow. His heart skipped a beat at her appearance. She oozed youthfulness, innocence, and a leave-me-alone attitude that had him dragging his eyes away. He sat at the only other table in the room.

Renata waltzed in moments later, with a large coffeepot and a just-as-impressive smile.

"*Hola, señor*, coffee for you?"

"Absolutely."

She filled his coffee mug, and left the room.

Lily had a notepad open on her table, and she alternated her glances from out the window to her dancing pen. Carter couldn't take his eyes off her. He had to resist raising his camera and taking a couple of photos. Everything from the intense focus on her face to the dust particles drifting about in the morning sunshine made the scene perfect.

She spun to him. "You know that's rude, don't you?"

"What?" He frowned at her.

"Staring." Her lips drew in a thin line.

"Oh, sorry. It's just . . . sorry."

Renata's timely return saved him. She carried two plates of steaming food and, as if on cue, his stomach rumbled. Huevos rancheros filled his plate. He'd have no hope of eating it all. Renata offered salt and pepper, before striking up a catchy tune as she left Carter and Lily to their breakfast.

The two of them ate in silence, and he was halfway through the meal when he was tempted to undo the button on his shorts. Lily, however, was still going, delicately loading her fork and eating each mouthful like she was analyzing the flavors. He was mesmerized over how she kept at it until she'd consumed everything on her plate.

The second she finished, she checked the clock on the wall, folded up her notebook, pushed back from the table, nodded in his direction, and left the room.

But one glance at the clock was enough to know the day ahead wasn't going to go quite as planned. . . for either of them.

Chapter Four

At reception. Lily adjusted her satchel strap while she waited for Renata. She was ten minutes ahead of schedule—exactly how she liked to be.

Several photos adorned the walls behind the counter. Each one was of a smiling Renata surrounded by an abundance of happy children. One portrait had Renata seated, holding a baby in her arms, a stately looking man at her side, and seven children positioned around them. Lily's mother had a similar photo above their sofa at home. All six of her brothers had been positioned behind her parents, and Lily was the baby in her mother's arms.

She found herself staring at another photo; the familiarity of it rose the hairs on the back of her neck. The picture was of three people, a family it seemed: mother, father, and a little girl. The parallels between it and a picture they'd found in her father's suitcase were startling. She leaned over the counter, attempting to get closer. Even the dress the little girl wore was strikingly similar, right down to the little flowers decorating the bottom hem.

"Oh, sorry, Miss Lily. I didn't know you were there."

Lily jumped at Renata's voice and turned to watch her waddle up the hallway, wiping her hands on an apron.

"It's okay." Lily cleared her throat and stepped back from the desk. "I was just admiring your photos."

"*Sí sí*, my family." Her broad grin emphasized her pride.

Lily pointed at the picture that had caught her eye among the dozen or so others. "Who's in that photo?"

Renata glanced at the picture and turned back to Lily. "That's my *madre*, *padre*, and me, of course." Her grin was photo worthy.

"Oh." For a split second, Lily resonated disappointment. That quickly shifted to annoyance. She mentally slapped herself at the acknowledgment that her self-inflicted pressure to find answers was already clouding her judgment. Shoving the admission aside, she glided her room key over the counter. "Can I pay with American Express, please?"

"*Sí. Sí.*" Renata took Lily's credit card and swiped it through a machine.

Lily studied the photos again and, recalling the collection of toothbrushes in the bathroom, wondered if this hotel was actually Renata's family home. Otomi's comment yesterday about his extended family living here flashed into her mind, and she remembered she'd yet to pay him. "Oh, Renata, I haven't paid Otomi for the taxi yesterday."

"It okay, he be here soon."

"Oh, good."

Right on cue, a horn beeped outside.

Renata showed Lily where to sign the paperwork and, once the account was finalized, Lily adjusted her satchel on her shoulder and swung her pack onto her back. "Thank you, Renata. Have a great day."

"*Sí, gracias,* you too."

Lily stepped through the front door into the humidity and blazing sunshine. Wishing she had her sunglasses on, she navigated the stairs and walked to Otomi's waiting taxi.

He stepped out of the car, smiling. "*Hola te pierdas*, Lily." He leaned into his taxi and popped open the trunk.

"Hello, Otomi." Lily dropped her pack and as she reached into her satchel for the money she'd discreetly hidden in an inner pocket, Otomi picked up her luggage.

"Excuse me." Lily lunged at her bag. "What're you doing?"

"We go in my car. I'm your guide."

"You are?" She released the strap and squinted against the blazing sunshine. "But the email said my guide's name was Miguel."

"Yes, it was. But he . . . had accident. I take you now."

"Oh . . . so you know how to get to Agulinta Temple?"

"Of course. I go there three times now. I know good shortcut too." His lopsided grin didn't instill any confidence, but she was far too invested to cancel. Her mother depended on her.

Backing down was not an option.

Otomi opened the car door with a weird grin that wasn't exactly welcoming.

Lily climbed into the back seat and jumped. "Jesus, Carter! What're you doing here?"

"This time it's you following me." He grinned.

"Pardon?" She plonked her satchel next to his pack on the seat between them.

"Otomi told me your guide was hurt last night. So, he asked if you could come with us instead."

Lily's mind flashed to her attacker. *Was he my intended guide? But he looked so young.* In an attempt to calm her swirling thoughts, she opened the side zipper of her satchel and fished out her sunglasses.

"Or you can wait until your guide is available." Carter's Australian accent seemed stronger this morning.

"No . . . I, um, I can't." She sighed and put her glasses on. "Thank you."

He nodded. "You're welcome."

Otomi opened the driver's-side door and tossed a large chicken onto the front passenger seat. The bird shook its plump body, casting rust-colored feathers about the taxi.

"What the hell?" Lily scowled.

"Sorry." Otomi's grin said he wasn't sorry at all. "My wife make me take Pompa. But don't worry, he be good."

Carter's huge smile confirmed he was enjoying her reaction.

She swallowed back her objection and returned his smile. "Of course, bring the chicken."

Otomi jumped into the driver's seat and shut his door. "Not chicken. Rooster."

The car kicked into gear and they sped through town as if mobsters were behind them. At each building along the way, the pairs of elderly men sitting on the balconies followed the car's progress.

Where the main street ended, the dense vegetation began. Dark shadows and earthy jungle scents enveloped the car, and a kaleidoscope of green hues was displayed in every direction.

Sensing Carter's eyes on her, she spun to him. If he was embarrassed to be caught staring, he didn't show it.

"I guess we're going to be travel companions for a couple of days." She couldn't decide if that was good or bad.

Carter picked at his fingernail. "Guess we are. Have you been to Agulinta yet?"

"No, first time. You?"

"First time too." He huffed. "We're both Agulinta virgins."

She wrinkled her nose. "That's one way to put it. Where're you from?"

"Australia. Have you heard of Byron Bay?"

"No." The car lurched over a bump and Lily slammed forward. She winced and edged her knees back from the rough vinyl of the driver's seat. Cringing, she raised the cuff of her cargo pants. Fresh blood dribbled down her right leg. Earlier, she'd debated over reapplying her bandages, but had decided against it. It hadn't taken long to regret that decision.

Carter groaned. "Oh shit! That looks bad."

She plucked a packet of tissues from her satchel. "It's fine."

"It's not fine. I've got the perfect thing to stop the bleeding."

"No. No, it's okay, really."

"If you don't stop the bleeding, it'll be covered in flies before you can blink an eye."

"Oh." A rotten visual had her rethinking. Her bandages were in her backpack in the trunk. "What do you have?"

"Plastic skin. Hurts like hell, but covers the wound, and it'll stop the bleeding."

He reached into his canvas rucksack, tugged out a blue lunchbox and lifted the lid. He removed a small spray can and shook it. "Okay, put your foot up here." He tapped his thighs.

"I'm not putting my foot on your lap."

"Do you have to argue about everything?"

"I don't believe I've argued with you about anything."

"That's twice in two seconds."

Her jaw dropped. "Is this the way it's going to be for the whole trip?"

"Depends on you, honey."

"Don't call me that." Her new boss called her honey, and despite voicing her distaste over the term, he'd carried on using it.

"Look, do you want this or not?" Carter shook the can and viewed her with indifference.

Lily conceded she didn't really have a choice. She brought her new hiking boot up onto the seat between them. Bending her knee was excruciating, but she had no intention of placing her foot onto a stranger's thigh.

"It'll hurt."

She met his eyes. "Just do it."

"Okay. One, two—" He blasted her knee and she gasped.

The torture was worse than the initial injury. Clenching her jaw, she forced back the scream in her throat. It wasn't until she was breathing again that she lowered her foot back down.

"Show me your hands." Carter reached out.

"They're fine."

He cocked his head. "Your hands, now."

Reluctantly, she held out her palms and without warning he sprayed them too.

Tears stung her eyes and as she tried to shake out the pain, the car bounced over a bump, launching Lily forward again. She squealed, the rooster crowed, and before she knew it, she was wedged sideways between her seat and Otomi's. Embarrassed, she sat there, staring at her wounded palms.

Carter burst out laughing, and she glared at him. "It's not funny."

"Come on . . . it's funny. You'd laugh if it were me."

His laughter was infectious and despite herself, she giggled too. She tried to haul herself out, but it was impossible. Accepting defeat, she sighed. "Can you help me, please?"

Carter leaned forward, wrapped his hands around her biceps, and lifted her onto the seat.

She flicked her ponytail over her shoulder with the back of her hand and adjusted her sunglasses. "Thanks."

"You're welcome."

Studying her wounds, she was impressed that the stinging in both her knee and palms had stopped.

"Better?" He nodded at her wounds.

"Nearly." She turned to her travel companion, taking in his scruffy hair and equally unkempt beard. "So, what brings you to Agulinta?"

"I'm a photographer, looking for my next big *National Geographic* prize winner. How about you?"

Since she'd taken up her career, every man she'd met felt compelled to boast about himself. It seemed Carter was no different. "I'm a journalist . . . looking for my next Pulitzer Prize." She ensured there was sufficient sarcasm in her voice.

She'd always known her chosen profession would be cutthroat, but that hit a whole new level when she'd started her new job at the male-dominated magazine. It was just another reason why she was determined to make this trek a success.

Carter huffed and turned his attention out the window.

She did too, just in time to see a monkey swinging through the trees. It wasn't the first time she'd wished she was good at photography.

The car bumped and jerked along the track for hours, yet the scenery from the window didn't change. Trees, trees, and more trees. It really was a jungle out there.

Otomi whistled along to the crackling radio. The rooster alternated from standing and pooping on the passenger seat to roosting on the floor. And Carter continued to silently brood and stare out the window.

Lily concentrated on the scenery around her, taking it all in, ready for the article she hoped her boss would approve when she returned home. She removed her notebook from her satchel and jotted random notes about their journey: the visuals, the smells, and the sounds. She'd learned a long time ago that little details were what gave life to a story.

The road changed from shabby bitumen to a dirt track, riddled with even more potholes that had her already full bladder close to bursting. If they didn't stop soon, she'd have another embarrassing moment on her hands. She didn't want to ask Otomi to pull over though; the last thing she wanted was to look weak.

"We stop soon." Otomi eyeballed her in the mirror. Maybe he'd seen a pained grimace on her face.

"Okay. Thank you."

"Thank God." Carter huffed. "I'm busting." They were the first words he'd said in hours, and Lily felt compelled to answer.

"I thought we'd never stop."

Otomi slowed down and turned onto yet another dirt track. There was nothing to indicate the road was even there, and it was a miracle they hadn't whizzed right past.

The winding path skirted enormous trees and, several minutes later, opened up to a clearing. Beyond that was a large building with a substantial balcony that appeared to wrap right around it. If it wasn't for the six groups of tables and chairs set up on the side veranda, she'd assume this was somebody's home. Behind the building was a vast river that had to be at least a hundred and fifty feet wide.

It was the Usumacinta River that divided Mexico from Guatemala. The brown expanse of water looked to be flowing slowly. Lily's research told her that this river was the reason the

Mayans had built their temples in this area. These days, though, the river was the lifeblood for locals, businesses . . . and ruthless pirates.

Otomi pulled the car to a stop in the shade of trees and jumped out to open Lily's door. Her aching knees made the exit painful, and her spine groaned as she stood. Carter rubbed his lower back and grimaced as he too slowly rolled upright.

Otomi wrestled his squealing rooster from the car and, as he carried him in the crook of his elbow toward the building, Lily prayed the bird wasn't intended for the menu. She followed their driver up a set of weathered stairs, and Carter's heavy footfalls sounded behind her.

Warm breezes drifted from the water and crossed the broad expanse of the veranda. In the distance, a boat motored away, and she shuddered at the thought of being on that muddy water.

Otomi led them to one of the tables already set with plates and cutlery and indicated for them to take a seat.

"May I wash my hands first?" Lily asked.

"*Sí*, sorry, *retrete* around corner."

She turned to Carter. "Do you want to go?"

"Ladies first."

Graciously accepting his offer, she strode away. To her relief, the restroom was clean and stocked with ample toilet paper. Able to breathe again, she washed her hands twice and headed back to the table. Carter had a camera with a large lens set up on a tripod and was gazing through it, across the water.

"You don't waste any time." Lily shielded her hand against the sun, in an effort to see what he was focused on.

"Have to be quick to catch these kinds of shots."

"What're you looking at?"

"Crocodiles." He clicked off a few photos.

"What? Really?"

"Yep." He stepped back. "Check it out?"

"Oh, thanks." She peered through the lens. On the opposite side of the river in a small muddy patch where there was no greenery, she counted seven crocodiles basking in the sunshine. The largest one at the front had its mouth wide open, as if panting.

"Wow. They're enormous."

"Nah, they're about average. I've seen much bigger."

"Really? Where?" She stepped back from the camera.

"Australia. Africa. Help yourself." He indicated to the lens again. "My turn in the bathroom."

Through the lens, she stared across the river at the enormous beasts and was only distracted when delicious aromas had her stomach twisting into angry knots. Otomi appeared from a doorway and placed several plates on the table. "I hope you like my sister's cooking."

Lily chose a chair to sit. Just looking at the meal had her salivating but she resisted the food *and* the beer, waiting for Carter's return.

"Will you be joining us, Otomi?" She smiled up at him.

"No. No. My sister, she kill me." His rotund belly nearly wobbled out of his belted pants with his laughter.

"What've we got, Otomi?" Carter strolled toward them, rubbing his hands together as he took a seat.

Otomi pointed at the whole fish on a silver plate. "Pescado frito. Leticia's own recipe."

The fish had four diagonal slits across the body, and it'd been heavily seasoned with herbs and spices before being fried to a crisp.

Otomi pointed at each dish, naming them. "Tamale Pie. Maíz en la mazorca. Buñuelos de queso, pollo chimichangas. Okay, I leave now. Enjoy." He waddled away.

Lily eyed the food. "This looks so good."

"Sure does. Dig in."

She reached for a corncob, took a bite, and it was everything it promised to be—sweet, juicy, and spicy.

Carter placed a chicken chimichanga on his plate. "Have you been to Mexico before?"

"No, first time."

"Have you done much traveling?"

Lily wiped a trickle of sweat from her temple. "First time outside America."

His eyebrows shot up. "And you chose the middle of the Mexican jungle. You're keen."

"When I saw Agulinta on the news, I just had to see it."

He huffed. "I can relate to that."

She felt the need to elaborate, but had no intention of mentioning her father's journal. It was hard enough for *her* to comprehend, let alone explaining it to a complete stranger. Using work as the motivation seemed the perfect answer. "My boss wasn't keen, though."

He took a bite of his chicken. "Why's that?"

Lily could still hear her boss's cackle when she'd pitched her concept for an article on Agulinta Temple. "My usual reports involve the latest lipstick trends." She cringed at the embarrassing admission.

Carter's laugh was deep and hearty. "Who do you work for?"

"I worked for *Curve* magazine in Seattle for three years, but two months ago I started a new job with the magazine *More to Explore*. Have you heard of it?"

"No." He licked his fingers and reached for his beer. "So you wanted to show them what you've got."

"Something like that."

"Why wasn't your boss keen?"

She shrugged. "Because I'm new there. Because I've never done anything like this before." She cocked her head. "Because I'm a woman."

"Ahhh, he underestimated you, hey?"

"When I told him I'd take leave without pay, he looked like his kidneys had been ripped out."

Carter laughed, and when he wiped his hands on a napkin, she noticed he wasn't wearing a wedding ring. "So, what's your story?"

He sliced a large chunk off the fish's backbone. "Would you like some?"

"Yes, please."

He placed a slab of white flesh on her plate and claimed a portion for himself. "Like I said, I'm a photographer. I travel the world looking for the next best shot."

"By yourself."

"Usually."

Carter was older than her; based on the lines around his eyes, she guessed he was at least forty. "Ever had any photos published?"

He shrugged. "A few."

The fish was delicious, delicately spiced and finished with a hint of citrus. "Are you freelance or employed?"

"I'm freelance."

"So where do you live?"

"Hey, hold off a bit. I feel like I'm being interrogated."

She huffed. "Just making conversation."

Carter sat back, patted his stomach, and reached for his beer. "Well, we don't want to run out of things to talk about. We've got four whole days together."

Lily copied him with her own beer. It was bitter, cold, and refreshing.

He raised an eyebrow at her. "Are you normally a beer drinker?"

"Yeah. Other than Mom, I grew up with seven men, so there wasn't much choice."

"Seven men?"

"Six older brothers and my dad."

He whistled. "Where'd you grow up?"

"Now I'm the one being interrogated."

He held his palms up. "Just small talk."

Lily leaned forward and reached for another chicken chimichanga. "I grew up just outside Montana, on a dairy farm."

"Ha. You don't look like a farm girl."

"Really? What do I look like?"

He swigged his beer, maybe stalling his response. "I don't know . . . you just seem more like a city chick."

She was happy with that answer. Even though she'd grown up on a farm, she much preferred living in the city. Farming was hard work, and while she wasn't against getting dirty, she much preferred using her head than her hands.

She finished the chimichanga, and as she hadn't tried the beans yet, she spooned some onto her plate.

"Hungry, hey?" Carter said.

"Always." The beans had a distinct smoky flavor, and like everything else on the table, they were spicy. "Yum. You should try these."

He rattled his lips together. "No thanks. I'm full."

Otomi returned to the table, grinning. "Our boat is ready."

Lily choked on her beans. "Boat! What boat?"

Chapter Five

Carter lugged his backpack down to the water's edge. The boat Otomi had referred to was a ten-foot wooden craft painted in uneven green and red stripes. A small cover, made of grass thatch and hemmed in with black plastic, offered some protection from the sun.

As much as Otomi grinned at their new form of transport, Lily scowled. She stood on the riverbank, hands on hips. "Nobody mentioned a boat."

"Only way to get there," Otomi said.

"Well, nobody told me."

"It okay. We do this many time."

"But we saw those crocodiles, and what about pirates?"

Otomi chuckled. "No worry about pirates. They down near Esperanza—not here."

"And the crocodiles?"

"They no worry in boat." Otomi reached for her pack, but Lily clutched its handle as though it were a lifesaving device.

"What if we fall out?" She spoke through clenched teeth, and Carter saw past her initial anger over not knowing about the boat. Now, he saw her fear.

He walked to her side. "You don't want your boss to win, do you?"

Her blue eyes blazed at him. "No, I don't want him to win." She brushed her bangs off her forehead. "But we must be able to get there some other way."

She turned to Otomi, and the guide shook his head. "This only way."

Lily sat on the ground and hugged her knees to her chest.

Carter squatted in front of her. "What's wrong with taking a boat?"

Her shoulders sagged. "Would you give me a minute, please?"

"Okay." He stood and stepped back. "We'll get the rest of our gear from the car."

Otomi and Carter left Lily to her brooding and made their way back up to the hut and out to the car.

"How bad are the pirates along this stretch of river, Otomi?"

"Here, not bad. We protected by the curve in the river. If they attack here, they be caught and killed. Very safe." He was casual enough; he could have been talking about beer choices.

They plucked the gear from the trunk and Carter hesitated when he reached for Lily's pack. Whatever was driving her fear appeared to be deep-seated, and he wondered whether she'd carry on with the journey.

For decades, he'd done his traveling alone, but for some reason he hoped Lily would continue. He picked up her pack and was surprised at how light it was. He'd never met a woman who traveled this light before.

Between the two of them, he and Otomi managed to transport the rest of their luggage and the camping gear down to the waiting boat in one trip. But Lily wasn't there, and Carter assumed she'd gone to the bathroom again.

Otomi disappeared into the building and returned seconds later carrying the rooster in a metal cage.

Carter frowned. "You're taking the bird."

"Of course."

"Can't you leave it here?"

"No." Otomi's eyes bulged. "My sister will eat it . . . then my wife kill me."

Otomi loaded the rooster cage onto the boat and positioned it at the bow. Carter helped Otomi distribute the gear evenly, and soon the only item left on shore was Lily's backpack.

When Lily finally appeared, she'd transformed dramatically from the woman who'd sat on the riverbank just five minutes ago. Her smile was broad, her step was lively, and her approach to the boat was without hesitation.

"Okay, time for a boat ride." She picked up her pack and tossed it so hard at Carter he grappled to remain upright. Lily climbed aboard, looking the happiest he'd seen her, and he decided she was either putting on a brave front or she'd popped a happy pill. He hoped like hell it wasn't the latter, because he wouldn't put up with that shit.

Otomi pushed off the shore with an oar and started the engine. Black smoke spewed from the noisy contraption. It chugged once, then roared to life, spearing them across the murky water with ease.

The sun-baking crocodiles on the other side maintained their stance as the boat cruised right by them. For Lily's sake, Carter was grateful the river was wide enough to keep them at a distance.

He reached into the pack at his feet and removed his Canon EOS 1D Mark IV camera. It was both his prized possession and his most expensive purchase yet. However, despite the initial eight-thousand-dollar dent in his bank account, the asset had already paid for itself ten times over.

Otomi navigated the plethora of rocks protruding from the water, and after a slight bend in the river he accelerated away, elevating the bow out of the water. Pompa wrapped his claws around the rungs on the bottom of the cage and spread his wings to the breeze, like he was flying. Carter had a feeling the bird had done it many times before.

Lily rubbed suntan lotion over her long, tanned legs and, determined to ignore her flash of skin, Carter tested his camera's settings and adjusted it according to the boat's speed. The Canon was designed for rapid shooting, which made it suitable for wildlife or sport. His passions were animals, nature, and history. He'd yet to find a sport that was more interesting.

They carved up the water in their noisy craft, and the river and dense vegetation lining the banks whizzed by in a blur. Carter fired off a series of shots, taking in the muddy water, the lush vegetation lining the banks, the intense indigo sky, and Pompa, the crazy orange-and-black rooster that was *flying* in its cage.

Conversation over the engine noise seemed impossible. Even so, once Lily finished with the lotion, he joined her under the canopy with the intention of doing exactly that. However, after a few fruit-less attempts he drew his hat down over his face and succumbed to a quick nap.

The shift in the engine noise woke him, and lifting his hat, he pushed upright. Otomi was guiding the boat toward a levy tucked in amongst the foliage.

Carter turned to Lily. "What're we doing?"

She shrugged.

Otomi cut the engine and, as they drifted to the riverbank, he moved from the back of the boat to the front. Like a true expert, just before they crunched into the bank, he jumped off and eased the boat into shore. Lily climbed out first and Carter followed her to the grassy clearing.

Otomi grinned at them like they should applaud. "Our camp-site." He spread his arms, showing off the tiny area.

"What? Here on the edge of the river?" Lily's dropped jaw high-lighted her horror.

Carter studied her fright-filled eyes and once again wondered why this trip was so important to her. She was clearly out of her comfort zone. "It's okay, the crocodiles only live on the Guatemalan side." He struggled to keep a straight face.

At first, he thought she'd believed him, then she reared back. "Very fun—"

An ear-piercing screech erupted from the jungle behind them.

"What the hell was that?" She edged toward the boat, easing in behind Carter.

"Monkeys," Otomi said. "But it okay, we stay here." He reached for the rope at the front of the boat and tied it to the nearest tree.

Otomi moved with fast efficiency despite his rotund belly, and between them, in a very short time, three one-man tents were set up and a campfire was blazing. Lily held her own with the setting up, and Carter was impressed by the way she wielded the hammer. Once the campsite was complete, Lily claimed her tent and vanished inside with her things.

Otomi carried Pompa to his tent and let the rooster free inside. The bird crowed at its release and the monkeys set off again like they were protesting. Their ferocious roar had Carter wondering if the rooster's presence was a good idea.

Contemplating that thought, Carter chucked his things into his tent and set up his tripod in the hope of catching the monkeys on film before nightfall.

Otomi carried a large pot down to the river, and Carter was grateful Lily didn't see him fill it with the muddy water. The pot went onto the flames and Otomi added a few more ingredients, then squatted by the fire and began singing to himself as he stirred with a large metal spoon.

Carter peered through his lens at the tree canopy, determined to find something photo-worthy. But, the moment Lily reappeared, he lost all focus on the jungle. If he didn't know better, he would've assumed she'd had a shower in that tent. Unlike how Carter felt, Lily looked refreshed and clean.

"Something smells good." Lily ambled toward the fire, scooping her long hair up into a high ponytail.

"Tomato, rice, and beans." Otomi showed off yellowed teeth with his cheesy grin.

"Fabulous. I'm starving."

Otomi scooped the meal into three bowls and handed one to each of them. Lily sat on a towel she'd placed near the fire and Carter sat cross-legged on the grass. The second Carter took his first mouthful, the monkeys belted out a cacophony of screeches that made the hairs on his neck stand on edge.

"It is sun going down. Not my cooking." Otomi laughed and pointed at the darkening sky.

"So they'll settle once the sun sets?" A frown corrugated Lily's forehead.

"Sometimes, yes. Sometimes, no."

Her shoulders sagged, and Carter had to bite his tongue before he offered to share his tent. His body was reacting to her presence in all the wrong ways.

The sooner I finish this assignment and get going again, the better.

Chapter Six

Lily crawled out of her tent before daybreak, and using the flashlight that her brother had given her, she moved to the edge of the bushes to relieve herself. Before she finished, another tent zipper opening confirmed someone else was awake. She flicked off her light and tried to hurry up. Footsteps crunched in her direction. "Can you wait a minute, please?"

"Oh, sorry. Didn't know you were there." Carter cleared his throat. "You're up early."

She would've preferred him to walk away, but instead she replied, "Always."

"Are you a morning person too? It's the best part of the day, isn't it?"

"Yes, it is." Lily finished, pulled up her pants, and scurried from the spot before she turned the flashlight back on and headed toward his light.

"How'd you sleep?" He wore dark shorts . . . *only* dark shorts, and her light illuminated finely toned muscles lining his stomach. She decided he was younger than she'd originally thought.

"Great." It was the truth. Lily could sleep anywhere, no matter what the noise or situation; it was one of her talents. "How about you?"

"It was okay, but the damn monkeys woke me a few times."

"Huh, I didn't hear them."

"You're lucky. At one point I thought they were fighting right outside our tents." He screwed up his face. "Excuse me, need to use the bushes."

He walked toward the trees and Lily turned her attention to the fire. She squatted down and prodded the ashes. Small red embers still burned beneath a lump of charred wood, and she soon had flames licking up through a stack of twigs. She was placing progressively larger sticks onto the blazing fire when Carter returned.

"Wow! You did that quick."

"My brothers and I did a lot of camping. We used to fight over who lit the fire."

"Ha. There's nothing like staring into dancing flames."

She blinked at him, surprised by his poetic words.

The sun was only just illuminating the horizon when Otomi's tent zipper rolled up and he stepped out, rubbing his eyes. "You up early. I thought you sleep more." The rooster crowed from inside the tent.

"We've discovered we're both morning people." Carter scratched his fingers through a small patch of chest hair. "You can go back to sleep if you want."

"No, it okay. I get food ready."

"Yes, please," Lily said. "I'm always hungry, but don't go to any trouble."

"It not take long." Yawning, Otomi headed into the bushes.

Carter stood and disappeared into his tent. Moments later, he emerged carrying his camera. He walked down to the boat, and with his camera aimed toward the golden horizon, he sat perfectly still. Lily heard a series of clicks as he photographed the first rays of sunshine over the distant jungle.

With the sun's arrival came a slight breeze that coaxed away the morning mist that'd hovered over the river like fluffy balls of cotton. Otomi brought the rooster out, and as the bird ruffled its feathers and pecked away at the grass, Otomi filled the cooking pot with river water and then placed it on the fire.

"You're not using that water, are you?" Lily's stomach squirmed.

"Si." Otomi blinked at her. "Cook rice."

She watched Otomi's cooking with skepticism. He tossed in dried spices that he'd secured in a little Ziplock bag, and twenty minutes later their rice with tomatoes and black beans was served. After a few tentative bites, she decided it was acceptable and devoured the entire plateful.

After breakfast, they packed their camping gear back into the boat, pushed off from shore and scooted upstream, cutting through the final threads of the remaining mist. Their cruise to the next stop was uneventful and, within six hours, Otomi pulled into another levy along the Mexican side of the river. This one was a replica of the last, except for a series of stone steps that led up into the bush and disappeared among the thick vegetation.

She turned to Otomi. "Are we nearly there?"

"We hike up to Yaxchilan." He pointed to the steep stairway. "We stay there tonight. Tomorrow we go to Agulinta."

Otomi lashed the boat to the shore, and Lily and Carter jumped out. Their guide then handed over all the necessary equipment and they placed it on the shore.

Carter cocked his eyebrow at her. "You know we have to carry this stuff up that hill."

"I know." She thrust her chin at him.

"It's a steep climb."

"So I've heard." Her internet research had provided plenty of information regarding the grueling hike to Yaxchilan. It was the trek from Yaxchilan to Agulinta that had lacked any details.

Otomi handed a tent to Carter, and he passed it her way with a cocky grin. "We could save on weight by sharing a tent."

She rolled her eyes. "Hmmm, no thanks."

"I hope you don't regret that decision."

"I won't." She took the weight of the rolled-up canvas, and comprehending she'd be carrying it as well as her own pack, hoped he wasn't right.

They divided up the cooking equipment, food, and water, and by the time she loaded up everything, and shoved her father's journal and her leather satchel into her pack, Lily estimated she was carrying an extra twenty to twenty-five pounds.

She turned her attention to the steep steps cutting through the thick vegetation only to vanish high above them. Each stone block had a slight depression in the top, the result of centuries of use.

"It's not too late to change your mind on the tent." Carter's smug grin suggested he doubted her ability.

"No need." She flashed a confident smile. "I'll be fine."

Otomi picked up the rooster cage and turned to them. "Who wants to go first?"

"I will." Carter headed to the base of the steps like a man on a mission. With each stride the heavy-looking camera hooked around his neck hung swung back and forth on his hip.

Otomi indicated for Lily to go next. She placed her foot on the first step, put her head down, and climbed. Unlike normal steps, the risers were very tall and the higher they went, the mossier the uneven stones became, adding slipperiness to the equation.

Before long, sweat trickled down her lower back and under her arms, her thighs and knees burned, and her breathing grew labored. Yet, the steps continued. Without breaking stride, she applied insect repellant and deodorant, doubtful that either would work for long.

A monkey released its terrifying screech, and she used the distraction as an excuse to stop. It sounded very close, and looking up, she hoped to spot it amongst the foliage. The patchwork of green and brown above her was so dense she couldn't even see the sky, which was a blessing, because without the shade it would be unbearable.

Otomi reached her and paused, wiping his forehead.

"What type of monkey was that?"

"Howler monkey."

Lily understood how it got its name. She gulped two refreshing mouthfuls of water from the bottle at her hip, then adjusted her backpack and started up the hill again.

44

It seemed like hours before the steps stopped and an upward sloping path took over. Her legs appreciated the change of terrain.

A dull roar echoed from the trees around her, and at first she thought it was an animal, but the sound remained consistent. With each turn in the path, it became louder, and when a fine mist blanketed the air, she realized they were approaching a waterfall. Based on how loud it was, it had to be a big one.

Just the thought of a refreshing splash on her face put energy back into her pace. The path widened ahead, revealing an enormous cascading waterfall through the trees

"'Bout time you got here," Carter called out.

Lily searched for the source of the voice, found his gear at the water's edge, and then spotted Carter sitting on a rock beneath the tumbling waterfall.

The scene was heavenly, and the stream called to her like it had its own voice. Although she had no intention of swimming, she wanted to get in that water. Grateful that she'd worn matching black bra and underpants, rather than a G-string like usual, she stripped down to her underwear and strode waist-deep into the water.

"Come on, it's wonderful." Carter stood on a rock and held his arms out like the statue of Christ the Redeemer. The tumbling water bounced off his head, shoulders, and biceps, almost swallowing him in the cascade.

Carter dived off the rock into the pool of water, and her breath caught in her throat. She counted the seconds until he resurfaced. Seven seconds later he did, with a big cheesy grin that he directed at her.

"Come in. The water's beautiful."

She waved him away. "No thanks, I'll be fine."

"Come on."

"No, this is good enough for me."

"Your loss." He lay on his back, floating, and used his hands to paddle himself around in lazy circles, then rolled onto his stomach, breast-stroked across the pond, and stepped out. "How good was that?"

She followed him onto the grass. "It's magic. I was so ready for a shower."

"Yeah, me too." He touched his nose and she knew exactly what he meant.

Otomi appeared from the bushes carrying three plates of food.

"Oh, excellent, thank you." She accepted the meal, placing it on a rock at her side. Once again, the meal consisted of beans, tomatoes, and rice, topped with a thick slice of what looked like corn bread.

Her first thought was *Where's the meat?* Her second was *This isn't enough.*

She tried to take her time, savoring every mouthful, but she was so famished that she finished before both men. Lily was close to asking for seconds when Otomi offered extra slices of corn bread to each of them, which she gratefully accepted.

Once finished, they washed the dishes, filled their water bottles, loaded up their gear again, and set off in single file along a different path that Lily hadn't noticed. Carter led the way again, and disappeared up and over the slope before she'd even found her rhythm.

Buzzing insects had her removing her triple-strength insect repellant from the Velcro pocket in her cargo pants and rolling it onto her exposed skin. It didn't take long to get sweaty and disgusting again, and she no longer felt the invigoration she'd enjoyed after the swim.

The overgrown vegetation was a repeat of the landscape they'd trekked through all morning except the path was slightly wider, which meant the sun occasionally shone through gaps in the canopy like laser beams, momentarily blinding her.

A monkey hung down from a nearby branch, reaching for a bunch of black berries, and with sweat dribbling from every part of her body, Lily paused to admire the cute little thing for a couple of moments.

She moved on, and with each turn in the path, the jungle heat intensified.

Finally, they reached a section of stairs where, based on the amount of sunshine at the top, looked like they might've arrived.

She unhooked her thumbs from the straps on her pack and stormed up the incline.

At the top, the last ounce of her breath evaporated as she scanned the magical scene. Two enormous trees served as gate-keepers to the ancient ruins beyond them. Where the jungle stopped, the buildings started. She walked between the trees and entered a magnificent archaeological site.

Dozens of buildings were scattered around, all in different states of decay. The ruins spread wide and high, extending much farther than she'd anticipated. This initial sighting already made the arduous hike worth it. An iguana, the size of her forearm, basked on a giant flat rock adorning the well-worn path toward the first temple. The lizard was a rust color and sat so still that she wondered if it was real.

A large central grassy area was surrounded by several stone ruins. Some were just sets of stairs topped with piles of rubble, whilst others were buildings that stood several stories high.

The trees dotted throughout the ancient city were enormous, and she half expected Indiana Jones to come swinging into action at any second. Otomi led the way, explaining the ruins with an obvious passion that surprised her. So far, she'd had the impression that their guide was there by default, but based on his seemingly extensive knowledge, he'd been there many times. As they traipsed from one ancient building to the next, she truly felt as if she'd entered a lost city that'd been miraculously recovered from the relentless creep of the vegetation.

Otomi explained how the site itself was perched atop a high bluff overlooking a horseshoe-shaped section of the Usumacinta River. The location was perfect for defending against attack on all sides, except for one narrow strip of land on the southern approach. The success of the position had allowed the Mayan city to thrive by controlling trade, and of course, taxing goods being transported along the river.

After the guided tour, Otomi offered to sit with their gear whilst Carter and Lily explored the ruins. She plonked her pack on the ground, took out her satchel and when Carter went one way, Lily went the other.

She headed to a temple that Otomi had called the Labyrinth. The main building was a series of steps upon steps situated to the left of the central acropolis. The front façade was made up of four doorways and three niches that were framed in the same way as the doorways.

Lily touched the emerald-green moss that'd made nearly every structure its home. The moss consisted of thousands of tiny leaves, making it as soft as marshmallow. It was a refreshing contrast to the rustic stone surrounds.

She entered the temple through the middle doorway and was surprised to find a headless statue adorning the entrance. The stone figure reached her shoulders and was intricately carved, much like the pictures she'd seen of the terracotta warriors in China.

It was amazing no one had stolen the whole thing.

Although, given the effort it took to reach the site, if it was as heavy as it looked, it'd be impossible to get the rest of the statue down that hill without some serious planning.

Lily sat on the stone platform beside the headless statue, pulled her notebook and pen from her satchel, and began to sketch her surroundings. A light breeze filtered through the narrow hallway that ran left and right of her, and she smelled a combination of old stone and fresh jungle. The monkeys set off in a menacing chorus of howls and screeches, and she described how their call of the wild drove shivers up her spine.

"What do you write in that thing?"

She jumped at Carter's voice and snapped her notebook shut. "I write about what I see."

He touched his camera. "That's what this baby's for."

"Yes, but you're so busy looking through that lens that I wonder if you see the big picture."

His eyes drilled into her. "I see you."

"Really?" She cocked her head. "And what do you see?"

"I see a woman who's determined to prove herself . . . no matter how far she's out of her comfort zone."

It scared her how well he'd described her feelings, yet she thrust her chin at him. "Is that so bad?"

"I didn't say it was bad. I'm just saying what I see."

She shoved her notebook under her elbow and stood. "I'm going to explore a few more buildings."

"See ya, then." Carter said it as if he didn't have a care in the world.

Maybe he didn't. With no wedding band on his finger, she wondered if he had anyone to be accountable to. He looked like a drifter. Unkempt hair, long beard, baggy and disheveled clothing, dirt under his fingernails . . . he appeared as well-worn as his rucksack. The only thing he seemed to care about was the camera that barely left his side.

As she made her way to a structure in the central acropolis, the rooster crowed, setting the monkeys into a frenzy. So far, the monkeys' howls had sounded distant—now, though, they seemed both close and angry. The horrid screeching noise grew louder, and she looked to the giant trees.

Several monkeys swung through the branches in a synchronized display of agility and strength, and one by one the monkeys congregated in the enormous tree nearest to Otomi and Pompa. When they'd lined the top half of the tree, they jumped up and down, screeching a terrible affront at the rooster, or so she assumed.

Otomi had let the bird out of its cage and it pecked at the ground, seemingly oblivious to what was going on above it. Lily wasn't sure if letting Pompa out was such a good idea. She flipped open her notebook and described the spectacle, aware that she might never experience such a raw, energetic display of nature again.

Just as quickly as the monkeys had gathered, they dispersed, swinging through the trees until they disappeared into the dense canopy.

Lily finished her notes and climbed the steps of the temple that Otomi had said was built in around 756 AD by Bird Jaguar IV. The structure was perfectly positioned to take in the view over both the plaza and the river. Again, this temple had three doorways, the difference being that above each of the entrances was an intricately designed lintel carved into the stone.

Otomi had explained that the lintels were a series of three panels that Bird Jaguar IV had commissioned. The middle lintel detailed one of the Mayan king's wives during a bloodletting rite. While the king held a flaming torch over his wife's head, she threaded barbed wire through her tongue.

Lily shuddered at the ghastly carving.

She progressed farther into the building to a room with a surprisingly well-preserved roof and an intricate frieze that stretched the length of the wall. She sat cross-legged in the middle and absorbed the history around her.

It was hard to believe these magnificent structures had survived the persistent vegetation that, for centuries, had made nearly every single stone its home. Whilst this site was impressive, she was looking forward to seeing Agulinta and experiencing a Mayan temple that had only recently been found.

She reached into her pack, removed her father's leather-bound journal, and flicked to the circular statue drawing. According to the archaeologists on CNN, nothing like it had ever been found before.

Yet, her father somehow knew it existed, about thirty years before they did.

Chapter Seven

As the sun reduced to a sliver of white over the towering treetops, Carter took his final shots of the day. Satisfied with today's photo session, he clicked out the SD card, and ensuring neither Lily nor Otomi were looking, he unzipped his cargo pants and slipped the card into a secret waterproof pouch he had hidden in his underpants.

The pouch was a cheap purchase from a roadside seller in Peru. Inside it, he kept a little slip of handmade paper with a couple of gold flakes that an old Japanese woman he'd met in Narita had given him for good luck. It was also where he kept his SD cards until he could upload the pictures to his Dropbox.

As the sun vanished and darkness seeped into the surroundings, he clipped a fresh SD card into his camera, hooked the heavy equipment around his neck, and headed toward Lily and Otomi. Their guide was busy shoving the bird back into his cage while the rooster crowed its apparent dislike at the situation.

"We go now," Otomi announced, when Carter reached him. "Must set up camp before sunset."

"Oh, I thought we'd camp here." Lily frowned.

"No. No. Illegal. We go higher."

"Higher?" Her shoulders slumped.

"Not far." Otomi picked up the caged rooster and set off again. Carter let Lily walk in front of him, and they set off in single file with Otomi in the lead. Before they exited the clearing, Carter looked up the hillside. Even with the fading light, the hilltop loomed above them, giving him a sinking feeling the stairs they'd climbed earlier that morning were going to be a breeze in comparison to what lay ahead.

They circumnavigated the temple complex and, at the far edge of the clearing, at its highest point, they stepped onto a narrow path that looked to be nothing more than a goat's track that wove through the thick vegetation.

Agulinta was a new discovery, and as far as Carter knew, only archaeologists and a few adventurous reporters had made it to the site. That meant there was every probability the track to it would be a grueling one.

The century-old steps were nearly completely consumed by snaking tree roots and a carpet of dead leaves. Every step had to be carefully assessed, and with the weight on his back, his creaking knees, and the fading light, he had to resort to brute determination. At each turn in the path, he expected Lily to stop and call it quits, but she trudged on, relentless. Some of the steps were as high as her kneecaps, yet she climbed them with nimble tenacity.

For a man who always traveled alone, he was suddenly enjoying the company. It was a strange acknowledgment.

The path grew even narrower, and with it came a new challenge. Thorn-laden vines lined the track and caught on clothing and skin with equal brutality. Soon, his arms were laced with fine gashes that oozed blood in jagged lines across his skin. He hugged his chest, trying to make his body smaller so that only his elbows suffered the attack.

Despite this new onslaught, Lily maintained her steady pace. He was impressed. She was on a mission, and after seeing her already fight her demons by the river, he would bet on her making it.

They reached a pinnacle, and the final steps launched them onto a large, open bluff. Above the jungle, the sinking sun was a fiery streak that reflected off the clouds in a grand display of orange and purple. He squinted against the glare. When his eyes adjusted, he took in the magnificent panorama. The Usumacinta River glinted in the sunshine, weaving its way through the jungle like a giant golden anaconda.

He turned to Lily. "This makes the climb so worth it."

Her face was tomato red, her fringe was glued to her temples, and her chest heaved up and down with every breath. Yet, despite her obvious exhaustion, she smiled a glorious smile. "Sure does."

"I set up tents." Otomi wasn't even out of breath, and set about erecting tents and starting the campfire. The man was a machine.

Carter held his water bottle toward Lily. "Cheers." They clunked their bottles together and with every warm gulp, he wished it were icy cold.

Lily flopped back on the grass and looked up at the sky. When Carter copied her, he groaned at his protesting muscles. Stars magically appeared above them, and soon the sky turned to a velvet black dotted with millions of twinkling lights.

"Oh, look." Lily pointed to her right. "A falling star."

"Make a wish."

"I am."

He wanted to ask Lily what a beautiful, intelligent woman like her could possibly wish for, but resisted.

A pleasant memory drifted into his thoughts. He had parked his beat-up old station wagon on a bluff that was famous for being Australia's easternmost point, and he and his daughter were lying on the hood, stargazing. Despite being just nine years old, she'd pointed at the stars and named every constellation correctly.

Those were special times. His daughter had never declared her falling-star wishes, but he'd like to think all of them had come true.

Carter had seen this star-bedazzled spectacle many, many times in his travels. . . Peru, Egypt, middle of Australia, and Iceland, where the northern lights spun colors like fine woven silks. Tonight's show might've topped the list. And sharing the spectacle with a stunning woman made it even better.

He mentally slapped himself. *What am I thinking?* Lily was half his age, and had the whole world at her feet. *She doesn't need an old man like me drooling over her.*

He dragged himself upright. "I'm going to help Otomi get dinner ready."

"Great," Lily said. "I'm starving."

DINNER WAS A REPEAT OF LUNCH, AND CARTER HAD A SINKING feeling that the next two days' meals were destined to be a duplication. His stomach grumbled at that thought. After today's workout, a huge T-bone steak would've been a more satisfying feed.

Otomi had placed a blanket on the dense grass. Carter sat beside Lily and they stared at the dancing flames as they ate their bean-and-rice stew. Otomi, however, remained standing on the other side of the fire to eat his meal.

"So, Miss Journalist, what would your report say about where we are right now?"

A small smile curled on Lily's lips, and as the flickering fire danced in her eyes, her chest rose and fell with a deep breath. "I'd write about the smell of the jungle being fresh and alive." She closed her eyes. "I'd describe the crackling fire and the embers that drifted up into the black sky only to vanish moments later. I'd write about stepping back in time and the vastness of the jungle around us, and the billion stars that dot the velvet sky."

Her description perfectly matched their surroundings, and when she paused and opened her eyes, he didn't want her to stop.

She turned to him and crinkled her nose. "Sorry, I get carried away."

"No, no, don't stop. I'm impressed."

"Thank you. This's what I was trying to tell you earlier. Your profession only focuses on one of the senses, and these days photos are manipulated so much that you can't guarantee what you're seeing is actually what it looks like."

He cocked his head. "So, journalists don't sensationalize, elaborate, or manipulate the truth. Is that your argument?"

"Not the true professionals."

"Are you a true professional?"

"Yes, I am."

He huffed. "Go on, then. Tell me about your favorite piece."

Lily screwed up her face, cleared her throat, and when she ate her final spoonful of food, he thought she was stalling.

"You're changing the subject. We were talking about how photographers these days can manipulate photos. Believe me, I'm grateful that software can fix most photos, because my photography is appalling."

"So, what you're trying to tell me is that your job is more important than mine."

"What?" Her eyes drilled into him. "No, I wasn't!"

"Not in so many words, but you did."

"No. I said what I do is important."

"And what I do isn't."

"I didn't say that." She wiggled her head. "Don't worry, you wouldn't understand." She stood. "Would you like some help cleaning up, Otomi?"

"No, no, I do it."

"Thank you, that was delicious." She handed her empty plate to him. "I'm going to freshen up."

Carter watched her until she disappeared into her tent, and wondered what it was that he didn't understand. The rooster came near and ruffled his feathers, puffing himself to twice his size.

The irony wasn't lost on Carter. Somehow, he'd ruffled Lily's feathers, and he had no idea why.

He lay back on the blanket, and as he stared at the Milky Way and listened to the crackling fire, but the wonderful sense of contentment he'd felt when Lily was at his side had drifted away.

Chapter Eight

Archer woke to an aching back and a bursting bladder. He unzipped his tent and was shocked to see Lily sitting on the blanket by the fire. The sun was barely a glow on the horizon. He meandered toward her.

"Wow. You really are an early riser."

She shrugged. "An old habit from my dairy-farm days. What's your excuse?"

"I don't really have one. But, for as long as I can remember, I've always woken before sunrise. Excuse me for a sec." He walked around the back of the tent and relieved himself in the bushes. Before he returned to Lily, he ducked into his tent to grab his trusty camera.

Returning to her, he switched it on and the camera did its usual series of whirs and checks. "May I?" He indicated toward the blanket.

She shuffled over and Carter groaned as he eased onto it. "Man, my back's sore. How about you?"

"I'm fine."

"What? Not even a little bit sore?"

"No. All good."

Resisting a debate that was hot on his tongue, he removed the cap on his camera and looked through the lens at the skyline. Above the distant treetops, the sun developed into a bright orange fireball that shot laser beams into the scattering of low-lying clouds. He clicked off a few shots, capturing the intense yellow outline of one particular cloud.

Movement caught his eye, and he adjusted the lens to focus on a thick-branched tree, high on their ridge. Four monkeys, with orange chests and black faces, stared right at him. As he clicked off a few shots, a baby monkey appeared over the shoulder of one of the bigger monkeys. The cute little thing had big black eyes that peered out from his flesh-colored face which was covered in a thick white beard. His face, neck, and chest were scattered with long white hairs that jutted out at random and wafted in the breeze.

In the space of about a minute, he'd clicked off roughly fifty shots. The sun pierced through the monkey tree, and Carter caught its rays silhouetting the baby monkey. It was the shot of the day, something he aimed for each and every morning, no matter where he was.

"Looks like you found something interesting."

He blinked at Lily. He'd been so engrossed in the moment that he'd forgotten he wasn't alone. "Want to see?"

"Love to."

He turned on the camera display and found the photo he liked best. He held the camera toward her and her jaw dropped.

"Oh, Carter, that's magnificent." Her eyes dazzled in the dawn sunshine and she ran her tongue over her lips, bringing out their rosy color. As she continued to study the photo, he studied her, taking in every line of her beauty. His groin stirred, and his arousal was so swift it caught him by surprise. "Sorry, nature calls."

Jumping to his feet, he dashed toward the bushes again. He drove his fingers through his hair; one snagged on his curls, and he tugged it free. "What're you doing?" he mumbled to himself, pacing back and forth until his libido simmered down.

The rooster crowed, and peering through the bushes he watched Otomi and the noisy bird emerge from their tent. Satisfied that his unreliable body part had settled down, Carter joined Lily and Otomi at the fire.

"You wake early again?" Otomi asked Lily.

"Unfortunately. It's a habit I'm yet to break." She held the camera toward Carter and he looped the strap over his neck. "I hope you don't mind me starting the fire?"

"No. Is good." He let the rooster out of the tent and, as it ruffled its feathers, Carter snapped a few photos of the bird puffing out his chest and crowing its morning welcome.

"Pompa seems to like it up here," Lily said.

"Sí. That is why I bring him."

She cocked her head. "How many times have you brought him?"

"*Seis*." Otomi held up six fingers. "My wife, she say happy Pompa make happy chickens, and happy chickens lay more eggs. We feed whole Corozal with eggs. No eggs make people mad."

Carter chuckled, and Otomi turned to him.

"It true. My wife very superstitious. First time I brought Pompa was because he got out of cage and ate my wife vegetable patch. He in big trouble. Nearly lost his head." He ran his finger across his neck. "I save him by taking him up here. But, when he came back, we have many eggs. So now, when chickens stop laying, I take Pompa, and when we get back . . . happy chickens."

Lily laughed and Otomi's grin showed off his chipped front tooth. Carter snapped a couple of photos with particular focus on the contrast between the weathered lines around their guide's eyes and the polished skin on Lily's face.

It may also have been the shot of the day.

"I get food." Otomi trotted off to his tent.

"The simple life, hey?" Carter raised his eyebrows at Lily.

"Doesn't sound that simple. Carrying that bird all this way each time is hard work."

"True." Carter collected a stick and poked the fire. "Think we'll have something different for breakfast?"

"I bet we have beans, rice, and tomato, with a side of cornbread."

"No bet. I think you're right."

Sure enough, breakfast was a repeat of the last couple of meals, but it was filling, and Carter had certainly had worse in his travels. He recalled a similar photo opportunity at a Mayan temple in the northern regions of Mexico when he'd suffered serious dysentery. It'd taken him nearly a week to recover from that one. Carter was quite happy to take his chances with rice and beans.

When the sun was a huge fireball hovering over the distant tree line, they set off again. His gear seemed notably heavier today, and he groaned as he loaded it onto his back. They kept the same formation as the prior afternoon, with Otomi taking the lead and heading into the trees.

If Otomi was actually following a path, Carter couldn't see it. Occasionally, they came across a series of rocks that may've been carefully laid centuries ago to form a step or two, but these were the only indication that people had ever walked this way. Carter liked to think he was going where no man had ever been before. Of course, that wasn't true, but only a handful of people had been to Agulinta, so that still made it special.

Otomi trudged on, unerringly following an invisible trail toward the world's latest ancient ruin discovery. Today's hike wasn't anywhere near as steep as yesterdays, and the air was cooler in the dense foliage, making the journey quite enjoyable, especially as his view included the bulge and flex of Lily's long calf muscles as she made her way up the hill in front of him.

Lily pointed out one thing or another, and Otomi answered all her questions like a professional guide. He knew every single plant. Either that, or he was a very good liar.

"Holy cow! Look at the size of that spider." She pointed beside her right foot.

Carter followed her outstretched finger.

"Ahhh." Otomi grinned. "That not spider. It is tailless whip scorpion." He beamed as if he were presenting a gold nugget. "See? Only six legs."

Carter peered through his lens, zooming in on the creature that was easily bigger than his palm. The sandstone-colored rock the scorpion was on, provided the perfect backdrop for the photo. At the head of the scorpion were two long, narrow claws, and Carter counted eight eyes. The creature had crept right out of an alien movie. He zoomed in closer and noticed little green bugs clinging to its back. "What are those green things?"

"Oh, they her babies."

Carter stepped back. Spiders were creepy enough, but this thing with its eight eyes and crawling babies had just moved to the top of his nightmare list.

"Don't worry, they no hurt you. Besides, this one only baby— they grow this big." Otomi held his hands about two feet apart and Carter shuddered.

Lily clapped him on the back. "You don't like spiders, huh?" Her grin showed she was enjoying his discomfort.

"Nope. Nor this thing."

Lily seemed unperturbed.

The rooster's crow signified it was time to keep moving, and Carter slung his camera to his side and strode away. About twenty minutes later, a dull roar emanating from the jungle raised his excitement. The noise could only be that of a waterfall, and the thought of a refreshing swim revitalized him. Seeing Lily in her underwear again would be nice too. He quickly slapped that visual from his brain, before his body reacted to it.

"Is that a waterfall?" Lily asked, reading his mind.

"Yes. Nearly there," Otomi answered.

Across the path was an enormous tree that, based on its state of deterioration, had most likely fallen decades ago. The width of the trunk reached Carter's chest. He looked for a way around it, but the tangled vines and virgin jungle that it'd fallen into would take too long to navigate. The only choice was to go over it.

Otomi put the rooster's cage down. "We work together." He pointed at Carter. "You first." He cupped his hand for Carter's foot.

Carter stepped up and Otomi hoisted him onto the giant log with ease.

"Okay, I give you gear." Otomi passed up the pieces of equipment, one by one, and Carter stacked them along the log.

"Your turn." Otomi repeated his move, and Lily placed her foot in his palm and reached for Carter to take her hand. She had no trouble and beamed when she stood at the top.

Otomi handed up the caged rooster, and then offered his hand for Carter to help him up. Otomi rolled onto his stomach and slid down the other side. Carter and Lily handed Otomi the equipment, then they copied his move to get down.

"That was cool." Lily dusted bits of powdered bark off her torso, and once again Carter was caught off guard by her spunk. On one hand, she gave the impression she'd rather be sipping cocktails at a fancy rooftop bar—on the other, she looked right at home traipsing through the Mexican jungle.

Mysterious . . . that's the word he'd use to describe her.

They shouldered their gear again, and set off in the direction of the thundering waterfall. It was only a couple of minutes before an enormous chasm opened before them. Water tumbled from a powerful deluge at their left and poured into a deep gorge in a frenzy of white foam that roared past them.

Branches from the giant tree they'd climbed over stuck out over the void like a hand with long, knobby, outstretched fingers. Their path skirted the edge of the gorge on a narrow ledge that was barely two feet wide. Lily didn't seem to have any fear as she walked ahead of him with confident steps.

Vines as thick as Carter's arm crept out from the jungle floor and tumbled toward the water at regular intervals. His foot kicked out from beneath him, and Carter clawed at a tree branch, just in time. His heart pounded at just how close he'd come to tumbling into the barreling water.

Sucking in huge breaths to calm his nerves, he couldn't believe neither Lily nor Otomi had even noticed. He could've vanished from sight and they'd have had no idea where he'd gone. Shaking his head, he took another tentative step.

After a couple more paces, he saw how they were going to cross the gorge. A rope bridge.

The recent discovery of this ancient site meant this bridge was new. It must've been put up with haste, and based on many Mexican constructions he'd encountered in his travels, it probably would've been built with minimal safety checks.

"Look at that." Lily pointed forward.

From behind, Carter couldn't tell if she was processing the same concerns as he was.

They arrived at the bridge and offloaded their gear.

"This's magnificent." Lily turned to him, beaming.

Nope, she was not apprehensive at all.

He wished he'd had his camera ready to capture her enthusiasm. At that thought, he unhooked it from his hip and peered through his lens. The scene was straight out of the *Avatar* movie. Carter had stepped into another world—a glorious ancient world that, other than the rope bridge, hadn't been ruined by civilization.

He lived for these moments.

The bridge consisted of two thick ropes the size of Carter's wrist, which were tied between trees on either side of the gorge. These ropes were drawn as tight as wire. From them hung thinner ropes that were strung from one thick rope to the other, in a series of loops that ran underneath long planks of wood. The planks were simply sitting on the thinner ropes, not even tied down. The theory seemed to be they walk along the planks and hold on to the tight ropes to traverse the gorge.

The biggest issue Carter could see, besides one of the ropes snapping, was if the person crossing should wobble it too much, the planks might slip out.

"I go first." Otomi picked up the rooster cage and held it in front of him as he stepped onto the first plank. The crazy guide didn't hold on to any ropes as he crossed, and as he obviously couldn't see his footing, on account of the cage he was carrying. He inched along by shuffling his feet.

One wrong step would plunge Otomi and the silly bird to a certain watery death.

Otomi was a brave man.

Or completely stupid.

Chapter Nine

Lily barely blinked as she watched Otomi traverse the thundering gorge with the rooster cage. It was about eighty feet to the other side, and their guide seemed to take forever. Lily let out the breath she'd been holding when he finally stepped onto solid land.

"He made it."

"Made it look easy too." Carter sounded skeptical.

Otomi put the bird down, and cupped his hands around his mouth. "Your turn." His words drifted across the water.

Lily looked to Carter.

"Ladies first."

She nodded, expecting as much.

"Be careful."

She loaded up her gear and turned her attention to the bridge. Reaching for the rope, she wrapped her fingers around it and was surprised at how tight it was, just like the high-tensile wire they used back home on the dairy farm fencing. With both hands clutching the ropes at shoulder height, she stepped onto the wood. With each step, the plank wobbled more from side to side. Fifteen feet along, it got out of control.

She clutched the ropes and stopped, desperate for the wobble to stop too.

After several calming breaths, she glided her fingers along again. The ropes in her hands didn't move, but the ropes holding the planks beneath her feet certainly did. Each step forward increased the sway from side to side. Halfway across, she stopped again.

The sheer volume tumbling down the waterfall was extraordinary. It fell from a height of about one hundred feet and pummeled blackened rocks at its base in an explosion of white water.

"You okay, Lily?" Carter's voice reached her over the roar of the water.

"I'm fine. Just taking in the scenery." She hoped he didn't notice the quiver in her voice.

Continuing on, she quickly closed the distance to the other side. As she stepped onto safe ground, Otomi reached for her forearm and guided her away from the edge.

Her legs still wobbled, her heart still raced, yet she smiled a triumphant grin. "That was incredible."

Otomi turned back to the bridge and waved Carter across, and he arrived on their side of the gorge without incident. "That was awesome. Where to now, boss?" Carter nodded at Otomi.

"This way." Otomi pointed to his right, then picked up the birdcage again.

Otomi set off and was instantly swallowed up by the jungle, and was only just visible through the vegetation, even though he was only about four feet in front. With each step, the plants attacked from all sides, adding more scratches to their limbs.

Despite the harsh environment, the scenery was also enchanting. Towering trees stood like giant sentries, driving upward in their search for sunlight. And hundreds of vines, some as thick as her forearm, weaved among them in a random tapestry.

Otomi stopped ahead of Lily, and when she reached his side, her jaw dropped at what she saw. A set of stairs, completely covered in dense moss, rose up from the jungle floor and hugged a rock wall that had come out of nowhere.

"Holy shit! Will you look at that?" Carter whipped the camera off his hip and clicked a series of photos. "I was beginning to think we were lost."

Other than the bridge, they hadn't seen any signs of human presence since they'd left Yaxchilan yesterday, yet, somehow, Otomi knew the way.

The dense moss had made the rock wall its home, covering nearly every inch in its green blanket. Lily trailed her hand up the rocks as she climbed. The top of the stairs revealed more overgrown jungle. Hopes of being near Agulinta were crushed as Otomi set off yet again into the sea of green.

After what seemed like hours, they reached another set of steps. These, however, were in a much worse state of decay than those prior.

Lily had a feeling they'd arrived. If she was right, at the top of these stairs was an ancient construction that only a handful of people had witnessed first-hand in thousands of years.

When she finally reached the top, a bolt of light pierced the tree canopy and caught her eyes, forcing her to squint against the glare.

Otomi tugged back a few enormous leaves, and when her eyes adjusted, she saw the sculpture depicted in her father's journal. Her chest squeezed as an overwhelming sense of emotion gripped her. Despite the carved stone nearly losing its battle against the robust vines threatening to consume it, its unusual shape was still discernable.

Fighting tears until they stung her eyes, she stepped the short distance to the circular gateway and placed her hand on the statue. Its warmth gave her a weird sense that it was a living, breathing thing. "We're here." The lump in her throat made it difficult to speak.

"We made it." Carter placed his hand on her shoulder.

She nodded and blinked back tears, hoping he wouldn't notice.

"You okay?"

"Just a bit emotional. You go on ahead."

He touched her arm, surprising her with his tenderness. "You sure?"

She nodded a second time, unable to speak.

"Okay." With one last glance her way, he stepped over the center of the circular statue and traipsed through the thick plantation toward the ruins, about a hundred feet away.

The donut-shaped structure was so high she couldn't reach the apex. She tugged away a few of the creepers to view the carvings in the stone. Centuries of weather had taken their toll. However, some of the intricate carvings were still visible. Lily dropped her heavy pack and sat on a large rectangular block at the base of the statue. With her emotions subsiding, she opened her pack and freed her father's journal from within.

She turned the pages to the drawing that had caught her attention nearly a year ago and held the sketch up so she could compare it to the actual sculpture.

Over the centuries, robust vines had made the stone their host, which meant the statue itself was almost completely concealed. Only random scatterings of the original stone were still visible.

She stood, put the journal down, and tugged the vines away from a section at eye level, on the left-hand curve of the circle. Reaching into her backpack, she removed the pocketknife her oldest brother had insisted she take with her. Flicking out one of the blades with her thumbnail, she cut away a portion of the stranglers to reveal one whole lintel.

The ancient sandstone was stained olive and black, and numerous small chunks had crumbled away, but the fine craftwork was still evident. The carving showed a person—it was hard to tell if it was a woman or a man—dressed in an elaborate robe, and kneeling down. Weaving up the left-hand side of the lintel was a giant serpent. Its head was poised above the person, and its mouth was wide open, ready to swallow the human whole.

Her father's drawing of the lintel, and the entire structure itself, were exactly the same. She had no doubt he'd drawn it from seeing the real thing—which was confirmation that her dad had been here before he'd met her mom thirty years ago.

"What were you doing here, Dad?" Dozens of questions whizzed through her mind, but she had answers for none of them.

She flicked her gaze from the drawing to the statue, in a desperate search for resolution.

Finally, she conceded she was no closer to getting answers, and frustration set in.

The grueling hike up here was all for nothing.

Lily grabbed a stick and pegged it at the statue. It glanced off the stone and disappeared into the bush beside it.

Inhaling deep breaths to simmer her anger, she tried to think outside the box. Was her father an explorer? She nearly chuckled aloud at that thought. He'd often got lost in shopping center parking lots.

Was he a treasure hunter? That too seemed ludicrous. He'd placed no value on objects.

Was it cursed? That thought did make her laugh. Her dad had been a salt-of-the-earth kind of guy. He'd always laughed at her mom's obsessive superstitions, like spilled salt and walking under ladders. Lily couldn't imagine any talk of ancient curses scaring her father into silence.

She tried to imagine what would make *her* keep something like this hidden. The only answer that made any sense would be if someone's life was in danger, should it be revealed. But even that didn't help.

The sound of footsteps had her shoving the journal into her pack, just before Carter emerged from the bushes.

"Hey, are you okay? You seemed pretty emotional when we arrived. Want to talk about it?"

Carter's concern was unexpected, and she felt she owed him some explanation. "It's just. . . I never thought I'd actually get here. So many people tried to talk me out of it."

A smile lit up his face and he raised his camera. "Well, how about we show all those negative bastards exactly how good you are?" He clicked off a few photos. "Move closer to the statue." He stepped back and adjusted the lens.

Lily pointed at the section of the statue where she'd removed the vines. "Can you zoom in on this, please?"

"Sure." He walked back a foot or two, turned, and snapped several shots.

"You ready to see the rest? It's amazing."

"Yes, love to." She hoisted her pack onto her shoulders, stepped across the heart of the large stone structure, and followed Carter through the dense vegetation.

After a few minutes battling through the shrubbery, she arrived at the base of the ruins. The ancient construction was small in comparison to the ones they'd seen at Yaxchilan. This one was pyramid shaped, with a series of steps that rose up from the jungle floor at an approximate forty-five-degree angle and reached about sixty feet high. Only the very tip of the structure, an area that looked to be about two feet square, was exposed to the sky. Almost every inch of the ancient building was covered in green. The jungle camouflage was extremely effective.

Without Otomi's guidance, it would have been easy to miss.

"It's a miracle it was ever discovered," Carter said.

Halfway up, a dark arch in the center of the front façade looked to be a doorway. She pointed to it. "Did you go inside?"

Carter beamed. "Sure did. Come on, I'll show you." He plucked a flashlight from his pack, hiked up the dozen or so steps to the opening, and Lily followed him up the giant blocks. She had to duck her head to enter, and followed their light beams down the narrow stone passage.

The flat blocks were motley shades of green and sandstone, and the walkway had a steeple roofline, rather like the architecture of a simple church. The passageway opened into a surprisingly large hexagonal room. Light streamed in from dozens of openings dotted around the sides and roof.

"Oh, wow! This is magnificent." Lily eased up to one of the walls where stone lintels were carved in intricate detail. The pictures were in a row that traversed all six walls of the room.

Carter clicked away with his camera, and Lily opened her note-book to write about her first impressions of the breathtaking site. Using her flashlight to examine the carvings more closely, she quickly noticed a common theme to the pictures. They featured a man with a heavily decorated robe, and Lily assumed he was the king. Glancing from one intricate carving to the next, she sighed.

I still don't have the answers to dad's mysterious drawings.

"How lucky are we?" Carter approached her side and the sun pierced through the roof, raining sunlight over him and capturing the bronze flecks in his green eyes.

Dragging her gaze away, she turned her attention back to the wall and ran her finger over one of the stone carvings. "I want to pinch myself; make sure I'm not dreaming."

"It's a bit like that. I've seen a few Mayan temples, but people had been traipsing all over them for decades. This . . . this is special."

"Oh, where else have you been?"

"Chichen Itza, Uxmal, Lamanai, Palenque, Ek Balam, and now Yaxchilan and Agulinta." He rattled off the names of the ancient ruins like they were items in a pantry.

"Wow . . . how long have you been in Mexico?"

He shrugged. "Hmm . . . about eight months."

"Really? So, where do you live?"

He turned to her and his eyebrows knotted together. "I don't really live anywhere."

"What do you mean?"

"I've been traveling the world."

"Huh. When were you last home?"

He looked upward as if trying to work it out. "About four years ago."

"Four years? What about family?"

"I check in whenever I can." He peered through his camera lens.

Lily stared at him, trying to comprehend a lifestyle like that.

"You know that's rude, don't you?" He grinned.

She snapped her eyes away. "I'm sorry. I just. . . I can't imagine not seeing my family. If I didn't go home a couple of times a year, my brothers would come get me."

"How many brothers do you have again?"

"Six."

"Shit. That's a big family."

"That's only the beginning. They're all married with kids."

"Not you?"

She wriggled her unadorned left hand. "Except me. What about you? Not married either?"

"No." The way he said it, gave her the weird feeling he was lying.

"Food ready." Otomi's voice echoed down the passage.

"Oh, marvellous, I'm starving." Carter strode from the room.

She followed behind, wondering what would prompt him to lie.

Chapter Ten

Their lunch, as expected, consisted of rice and beans. Carter would happily pay a hundred bucks for a steak right now.

He couldn't deny that he was worried about Lily. Not that he didn't think she was capable, but more that she wouldn't admit when she wasn't. He'd learned from experience that denial could be hazardous. Watching her chat with Otomi, her energy was electric. And her beauty breathtaking. So much so, that as he'd already discovered, just one glance her way could arouse his libido.

Lily was dangerous. And the sooner he got off this mountain, the better.

After lunch, Carter spent the rest of the afternoon photographing every aspect of the Agulinta ruins. He caught Lily sneaking glances at him several times, and was fairly certain she'd picked up on his lie. But the last thing he wanted to do was explain his marriage situation, especially when, in two days' time, they'd go their own ways and never see each other again.

By late afternoon, after he'd taken an abundance of photos, he found a shady spot under a tree and lay down to stretch his back muscles. His eyes snapped open at a different noise and he searched overhead for its origin. A toucan. The bird's large beak was a rainbow of red, blue, and green. He reached for his camera, careful not to scare the bird. Zooming in, he focused on its black eye, nestled within a bed of tiny green feathers. Carter took about fifty photos as the bird tipped its head from side to side, like it was dancing to imaginary music.

"Hey, what're you doing?"

Carter jumped at Lily's voice. He glanced from her to the tree, but the bird had gone. "I *was* taking photos of a toucan. Here, take a look."

"Wow. It's magnificent. Wish I'd seen it."

"Well, if you hadn't romped in like a herd of goats, you would've." He chuckled at his own joke.

She turned on her heel, and sashayed off.

"Lily, come back . . . I'm joking." He watched her long legs stride away.

Good. Keeping her at a distance is a good idea.

After a brief check in the branches, where he didn't find anything else of interest, he put the lens cap back on his camera, climbed to his feet, and went in search of Otomi.

Their guide sat on the ground with his back against the ruins. Smoke from Otomi's cigarette trailed from his nostrils and drifted over the three-thousand-year-old blocks. At his feet, Pompa pecked at the ground. Carter paused to take a few photos, feeling Otomi's sense of contentment. For the umpteenth time, Carter contemplated how the simple things in life could provide the most pleasure.

"Hey, Otomi, this's been excellent. Thanks for bringing us here, mate. Do we camp here tonight?"

"No, we still have few hours 'til sunset. We go other place where is flat ground."

"Okay, perfect. I'll go see where Lily is."

Using his flashlight, Carter entered the temple again. She was in the hexagonal room. His feet crunched over the dirt, and she snapped shut her leather-bound journal, on his approach.

That was the second time she'd done that, and he wondered

what she could possibly be hiding. "We're going soon. Are you finished?"

"I could be here a month and not be close to finishing."

"Sorry, we don't have enough food for that."

Lily huffed. "I could eat a horse."

Carter burst out laughing. "I bet you could."

She climbed to her feet and dusted off her legs. "Oh, and you couldn't?"

"Hell yeah. The horse and its rider."

"Ewww, that's gross."

He cocked his eyebrow. "And . . . eating a horse isn't?"

Carter led the way out and they made their way toward Otomi.

Their guide had everything packed up ready to go, and Pompa was back in his cage. "You ready, Miss Lily?"

"How far is it to the next campsite?" Lily tugged her water bottle from her hip.

"Not far." Otomi hoisted his pack onto his back. "We take shortcut back to boat."

"Shortcut?" Carter wondered why they hadn't taken that route up here.

"Yes, no need to go Yaxchilan. We go straight down to river and find boat. It okay, I know the way."

"Why didn't we come up that way?" Carter had to know.

"It too steep to climb up. But down is okay."

Lily glanced at Carter, and he thought he saw concern in her eyes. He shrugged. So far, Otomi hadn't missed a beat with his directions.

Otomi handed each of them what looked like a strip of dried meat. "Eat."

"What is it?" Lily sniffed the leathery-looking morsel.

"Beef *cecina*. It good. Give you energy. We go now. Must make camp before sunset."

They set off again with Otomi in the lead, and Carter took his position at the back of the line. Just like the hike to Agulinta, there appeared to be no obvious trail. How Otomi knew which way to go was a mystery to Carter, yet the Mexican continued on unerringly. The terrain was relatively flat, maybe with a slight incline, but was dense with vegetation. Every step involved shoving one plant or another out of the way.

It was an hour or so before there was any change in the terrain, but when it did change, it wasn't subtle. One minute they were walking on relatively flat ground, the next minute they tramped down a very steep decline. The pressure on Carter's knees had him wincing at every step, and, not for the first time in his life, he cursed his old rugby-playing days

The sun struggled to cut through the dense canopy, but the change in temperature had Carter sensing sunset wasn't too long away. He hadn't worn a watch in five years, and hadn't felt the desire for another one since. It'd been liberating—the last thing he needed was to see the countdown on his life.

A scream shattered his reverie.

Carter jumped and cast his focus down to Otomi, who'd fallen over face-first. The screaming man rolled onto his side and clutched his leg above his knee. *Shit! Otomi must've broken his leg.* He scurried down the embankment, but the second he saw Otomi, his brain lurched. It was a hell of a lot worse.

Midway down Otomi's calf were two bite marks.

"Oh, Jesus!" Carter knelt beside him. "Is that a snake bite?"

Otomi's face twisted with pain. "Snake. Snake. Very bad." He clenched his teeth in obvious agony.

"Shit!" The blood drained from Lily's face. "What do we do?" Her eyes darted from Otomi to the surrounding bush, probably looking for the snake.

Carter flipped his pack off and tugged Otomi's pack away.

"Lie down." Carter tried to push him back to the dirt, but Otomi's writhing and rigid clutches on his leg made his attempts useless.

Carter reached into his pack and, despite knowing there'd be no signal, checked his phone anyway. *None.* He glanced at Lily.

Her terrified eyes matched his own thoughts.

"Help me keep him still. He must stay calm."

Carter yanked his first-aid kit from his bag and flicked to the index in the emergency handbook. Blocking out Otomi's sickening howls, he searched for the right page.

Carter found the snakebite page and skimmed the instructions. "Take off his shoe," he demanded.

"Okay." Lily shuffled to Otomi's feet and untied his shoelaces.

Carter plucked two bandages from his first-aid kit, and kneeling at Otomi's side, squeezed his shoulder. "Listen to me."

Red spider veins riddled Otomi's eyes.

"You need to keep still. Very still. Understand?"

The guide released his grip above his knee and leaned back. Because of the angle of the hill, it was impossible for him to lie flat, which was a good thing, as he needed to keep the bite below his heart to slow the poison flow.

Grabbing his water bottle, Carter poured a generous amount onto the bite mark and blood flowed in rivulets down Otomi's calf. Carter tugged a shirt from his pack and dabbed at the area around the wound to dry it. Working as quickly as possible, he fought against Otomi's jerky movements and wrapped a bandage across the fang marks several times.

Otomi's howls echoed about the trees.

His body jolted in painful spasms.

He glanced at Lily. "Hold him still."

Trying to ignore his trembling fingers, he secured the end of the bandage in place with a couple of butterfly closures. Using the second bandage, Carter wrapped the rest of Otomi's leg to his ankle and foot.

"Otomi, please keep still. Keep still, buddy. Deep breaths in and out. In and out. Understand?"

Otomi sucked in a shaky breath. "Yes. Okay. But it hurt."

"I know, buddy." Carter turned to Lily. "Show him what to do. Deep breaths in and out. He needs to stay still and calm."

She nodded and placed her hand on the guide's forearm.

Carter stood. "We can't stay here. We need to find flat ground."

Carter set off down the hill. The decline was extreme, testing his already aching knees. With continual glances over his shoulder to make sure he didn't lose sight of Lily, he made his way downward, scouring the area for a level patch. Ideally, the spot would be big enough to put up at least one tent.

Sheer desperation had Carter choose a giant stone that jutted out from the cliff face. It was relatively flat, but barely big enough to pitch one tent, let alone two. Carter tore off his shirt, tied it to a branch of a nearby tree, and then charged right back up the hill.

By the time he returned to Lily, Otomi's screams had reduced to agonized moans. He had deteriorated dramatically. Sweat poured from his forehead, his flesh was ghastly gray, and his eyes flickered beneath his closed eyelids, fighting the horrific nightmare.

He knelt at Lily's side. "Have you tried your phone for a signal?"

"Yes. Nothing!" Her voice was shrill. "What do we do?"

Carter touched Otomi's forehead and recoiled at the furnace beneath his pallid skin. "Let's get him to flat ground for starters. I'll have to carry him."

"What can I do?"

"Just help me out. Bring a pack and tie something to a tree so we can find the rest later."

"Okay." Lily tugged a white T-shirt from her bag and tied it to a branch.

Carter readied to pick up Otomi, who was a big man, maybe two hundred pounds. Gritting his teeth, he lifted.

Otomi screamed, and his eyes snapped open.

Carter gasped at the bloodshot pools.

But he blocked out the sight and took his first step downward, but Carter's knee crumbled beneath him and he howled as he fell backwards. Otomi landed across his lap, but the guide barely whimpered.

Lily sprang to Carter's side. "Are you okay?"

"My bloody knee gave way. That's all. I'm fine." He glanced downhill and was horrified at the distance he still had to cover, but put one foot in front of the other and aimed for his shirt hanging limply dozens of feet below.

Finally, at the rock, Carter groaned as he placed Otomi down.

"Help me sit him up a little. Put your pack behind him. We need to keep his leg lower than his heart."

Lily rushed to kneel at his side and wedged her pack behind Otomi.

Carter crumbled to the ground and touched Otomi's forehead. Fire burned beneath his flesh.

"His lips are blue." Tears pooled in Lily's eyes.

"I think it's just shock. Blue lips are a sign, *and* profuse sweating."

"But how do you know it's not the poison?"

"I don't." Carter placed his hand on Otomi's arm. "Hey, buddy, can you hear me?"

Otomi moaned and opened his eyes.

"You're going to be okay." He turned to Lily. Her skin was ghostly pale. "Keep talking to him. I'm going to get our stuff."

Carter headed back up the grueling incline. He arrived at their abandoned gear, fell to the ground, and sucked in deep breaths, fighting back severe dizziness. Glancing around, he grew acutely aware of the darkness creeping over the jungle. The sun was setting.

He shoved his first-aid kit into his pack and hoisted it onto his back, then put Otomi's pack over his right shoulder and, picked up the rooster cage.

He was barely able to breathe when he finally returned to them. "How is he?"

"Not good." Lily's eyes pleaded. "Do you have any medicine?"

Carter shook his head. "The guidebook said not to give him anything, not even water."

She sucked in a shaky breath. "What're we going to do?"

"I'll set up the tent. Can you get a fire going?"

"Yeah, sure."

Carter unhooked a tent from the pack and zipped it out of the flimsy bag.

Once Lily had a small fire going, she helped Carter with the tent poles. The woman who'd oozed vitality over the last couple of days looked completely shattered, and the temptation to wrap his arms around her and tell her everything would be okay was powerful.

But he couldn't. Everything was far from okay.

When the tent was finished, she blinked at him, as if awaiting instruction. She was relying on him to have a plan. He wished he did.

"Do you want to get some rice on?"

"Okay." She turned, her shoulders slumped, and every step she took toward the packs looked like a chore.

Carter checked on Otomi. "Hey, buddy." He put his hand on Otomi's forehead and although he couldn't be certain, he thought his body temperature had dropped at bit. "You're going to be okay."

Otomi mumbled something. His voice was a croaky whisper.

Carter leaned in. "Hey, mate, what'd you say?"

"Rattlesnake." Otomi's eyes opened. They looked like they were bleeding. "It was rattlesnake. I am going to die."

Carter's blood turned to ice. "No. No, you're not. We'll get you out of here."

Otomi slowly shook his head. "Too far. I won't make it."

"That's enough of that talk. We'll get you home."

Lily knelt at Otomi's side. "Hey, you're awake." She dabbed a damp cloth to his forehead.

Otomi blinked slowly and turned to her. "I am dying."

Otomi turned his gaze from Lily to Carter. "Please take Pompa back to my wife and tell her and my children I love them."

Carter's heart stung at the resignation in Otomi's words. "That's enough of this talk." He patted Otomi's chest. "Let's get you inside the tent."

Once he was inside, they sat him up, then Lily ducked out of the tent and returned a moment later with a sleeping bag and towel that she placed under Otomi's torso and head to elevate him. "There you go. Have a sleep."

When they laid him back, Otomi groaned and reached out to clutch her wrist. The whites of his knuckles bulged. Carter swallowed, waiting for Otomi to speak, yet also dreading what their guide would say. "Please come back for me. I want to be buried with my father."

Lily's chin dimpled, a tear spilled over her cheek and she sucked in a sob. "We're not leaving you."

Otomi released his grip on her wrist and closed his eyes.

Lily met Carter's gaze and he shook his head, fighting his own tears.

He didn't want to say it, but he feared they might have just heard Otomi's last words.

Chapter Eleven

The sun set at lightning speed, bringing with it plagues of insects and bloodcurdling howls from the monkeys. Darkness consumed them in a flash.

Lily had a decent fire blazing between the tent and the rotting jungle floor, and though its heat wasn't welcome, the light and protection it provided were. From where Lily sat, she heard every ragged breath rattling from Otomi's throat. While he lay in an apparent state of unconsciousness, Carter rummaged through Otomi's backpack, looking for a satellite phone, or at the very least a map.

Lily didn't put much hope on either miracle. Her mind flitted to her father's final moments of life.

Her dad had been out on one of the back paddocks when he'd had his heart attack. Three of her brothers had been with him when it had happened. Two had stayed at his side, alternating turns at CPR, while Danny had raced the four-wheeler back to the farm to call an ambulance.

Lily, her mother, and her three other brothers had made it back to her father's side in time to be with him when he passed away. The ambulance had arrived more than an hour later to announce what they already knew.

His death had somehow seemed peaceful. His final moments were on a lush patch of green grass that he'd tended with his own hands. His fat milking cows had circled around them, curious about the attention. And her father had been surrounded by his wife and all seven of his children, when he drew his last breath.

Her father was sixty-six years old when he died. His days had been filled with working on the land, and she'd always thought he was as fit as his sons were.

Apparently not.

Once Carter finished tugging everything out of Otomi's pack, he splayed his legs out before him and let out a big sigh. "I know it was a big ask for a satellite phone, but at least a map would've been helpful."

She'd heard what he said, but her mind was a black fog, unable to comprehend the enormity of his statement. Her eyes drifted to Otomi and she stared at his chest, desperate to see it rise and fall.

"I have a compass, but it's only really helpful if we knew which direction we were heading. Here's what we do know." Carter drew her attention away from Otomi's near lifeless body. "Otomi said he was taking us on a shortcut. I figure if we keep heading downwards, then surely we'll hit the river. All we have to do then is find the boat."

The firelight gave her a very small viewing area. The rooster caught her eye. It pecked away at something in the bottom of its cage, oblivious to its owner's life-or-death battle. "Shouldn't we go the way we know? Back up to Agulinta and then to Yaxchilan?"

Carter blinked a few times, then frowned. "But that took two days. We don't have enough food for another two days."

"We'll ration it." Lily wiped sweat from her forehead, feeling grit and dirt beneath her fingertips.

He was silent for a few heartbeats. "Do you think we'll find the way? I haven't seen any tracks so far."

"It's better to go where we've been than try to figure out where we haven't."

"I guess so."

"What about Otomi?"

Carter nodded, as if he'd expected her question. "We'll make some kind of stretcher and carry him up with us."

She nodded, and the shadow that clouded her heart lifted a fraction. "Okay. We can do that."

"Of course we can. But you need to eat first." Carter held her plate toward her. "Please eat, you need your energy."

She spooned a small portion of rice into her mouth.

The monkeys struck up a howling frenzy, blasting out a deafening noise that made it impossible to continue their conversation. It went on for several minutes, and Lily assumed the final gasp of the sun had vanished from the horizon. As suddenly as the cacophony had started, it abruptly stopped, plunging them into eerie silence.

Carter stood and let Pompa out of the cage. As the fat bird spread its wings and ruffled his feathers, casting fluff into the air, Carter strolled to their packs, and began plucking items from them. "I figure it'll take at least two more days before we reach the river again." He looked to her, possibly for confirmation.

She shrugged. "At least. We've had two overnight camps since we left the boat, and we took our time at each temple. But we'll be slower carrying Otomi."

"And we don't know where we're going."

"Right." She nodded. Whether they went up or down, they were in trouble.

"Between us we have three half bottles of water and one full one, but we'll need to be conservative, because we won't run into fresh water again until we get back to Yaxchilan."

That wonderful experience already seemed like a week ago. "What about food?"

He pointed at the diminished sack of rice. "I'd say we have enough rice for at least four more meals, and there's one tin of corn and two tins of beans. So we're fine."

She thought his comment was a gross understatement. Lily finished the last mouthful of her rice and had a small sip of water.

"Remember, this is worst-case scenario. Chances are, we'll run into other people along the way."

"I hope so." However, she doubted it.

Otomi moaned, and both Carter and Lily raced to his side. Carter touched his shoulder. "Hey, buddy, we're here."

Lily placed her hand on his chest. Otomi's eyes flickered open and he turned to Lily, but stared straight through her. She shuddered at the sight. His breathing was erratic, just inhaling seemed to be a challenge.

"Can we give him water?" Lily looked to Carter.

"The book said no."

Otomi jerked and spluttered as a coughing fit wracked him violently. Carter rolled him onto his side and patted his back.

When he settled again, Otomi whimpered, and a tear rolled down his cheek. His breathing slowed, and Lily assumed he'd fallen asleep. Carter nodded at her, and they crawled out of the tent. Pompa pecked at the ground and somewhere in the blackness, a bird squawked out a mournful call.

Carter reached for a stick near him and used it to poke the flames. Sparks floated upward, caught in the slight breeze, drifted over his shoulder, and were swallowed by the dark void around them.

Lily felt him watching her, and locked eyes. "He's going to die, isn't he?"

Carter tossed his stick aside and crawled to her. He put his arm around her shoulders, tugging her body to his, and she couldn't hold back anymore. The tears flowed and she sobbed into his chest, crying for a man she'd known for just four days. The fact that Carter hadn't answered her question confirmed it.

Otomi was going to die.

The shocking consequence of his death suddenly hit her. She pulled back from Carter's chest. "Are *we* going to die?"

"No." His hazel eyes pierced her. "We are *not* going to die."

"But we're lost in the middle of the jungle."

He removed his arm from her shoulder and tugged on his beard. "We're not lost, yet.

We're in Mexico, in the Yucatan. And we know enough to get us out of here. We know that above us are two ancient temples. All we have to do is find our way back to them."

She studied him. The soft glow from the fire highlighted a deep scar over his right eyebrow that she hadn't noticed before. "You make it sound easy."

He nodded with conviction. "Because it will be. We'll need to carry Otomi somehow. Want to help me build a stretcher?"

"Sure." She nodded, grateful to have something to do.

Walking side by side, they headed away from the camp and into the dense jungle. Carter suggested they'd need about six sticks, and they stepped farther and farther from the campsite.

Lily suddenly stopped. "Oh shit!" The jungle floor had literally dropped away. She stood on the edge of the world.

"Jesus." Carter dropped the branches and eased up beside her.

Their flashlights highlighted nothing but blackness.

Other than the moon and stars, there were no other lights. No big cities shimmering in the distance. No floodlit roads cutting through the landscape. Not even a plane in the sky. The isolation was shocking.

"We're in the middle of nowhere."

"Welcome to the Yucatan jungle." He actually seemed chirpy.

They stood for a long time, silently staring into the blackness, and she wondered if he was gripped with the same sense of foreboding she was.

Carter bent down to collect the branches again. "Come on, we've got work to do."

Eventually, they meandered back toward the flames, and while Carter fiddled with the branches, she went into the tent.

Each breath Otomi inhaled looked torturous, and his leg had swollen so much that the bandages strangled his calf. "Carter!"

He was there in a flash. "Look." Otomi's foot was dark purple and had ballooned to at least twice its original size.

"Shit! Shit!" Carter scrubbed dirt off his hands. "That's not good. The guidebook said to bandage the appendage up but I think we need to take it off."

"What about the poison?"

"It's too tight. He'll lose circulation."

Acid burned her stomach at the thought of touching Otomi, but as Carter moved to their guide's feet, she had no choice.

"I'll lift his foot and you undo the bandage." Carter placed his hand under Otomi's ankle, and Lily flipped the bandage around and around, gradually revealing red and purple-mottled skin. The higher she went, the worse the smell became.

The two puncture marks were no longer tiny pinpricks; they were great, festering abscesses.

Oh god. Otomi won't make it through the night.

With nothing else to do, they retreated back outside. She sucked sweet forest air into her lungs, crumbled to the ground and wrapped her arms around her legs.

"Lily, we have a very big decision to make. What to do with his body."

"What do you mean?"

"Well . . . we could try to take him with us." He paused, as if letting her finish his train of thought. "Or we leave him here."

Both Carter's options were hideous. The thought of carrying a dead man for miles made her stomach turn, but the other option was appalling too. To leave him here, all alone, was wrong on so many counts. "This is so messed up. Everyone told me this was dangerous. You know what my boss said? He said a girl like me wouldn't survive out here."

"Well, he's wrong. You will survive. *We* will survive." He tossed the branches they'd so carefully gathered for Otomi's stretcher into the fire. Then he came around to her. "You and I *are* going to walk out of here and tell the world all about what happened."

She nodded, wanting to believe every word he'd said. He put his arm around her shoulders for a quick squeeze. "Help me catch that silly bird, then we'll get our beds organized."

Pompa wasn't as hard to catch as Lily had thought; the bird was obviously used to being handled. Once he was safely in his cage, she turned to Carter. "Tell me we're taking the rooster with us."

He didn't respond.

"Carter, I'm not going without the bird. You heard what Otomi said. Pompa is important to their family. To their income." She paused, letting it sink in. "It was Otomi's dying wish. Are you going to deny that?"

Twinkling flames reflected in his eyes, making them impossible to read. "Are you going to carry him?"

"Of course."

"Okay then." He turned toward the packs. "Let's get our beds sorted."

Because of lack of space, they had to settle for the second tent folded up as something to lie on instead. They reached for their sleeping bags for extra cushioning.

"Which side do you want?" Carter asked.

"The one closest to the fire, please." Lily tugged out a few pieces of clothing, and shoved them inside a T-shirt to create a makeshift pillow, and crawled into the slot between Carter and the fire. "Carter?"

"Yes."

"Promise me we'll return Otomi's body like he asked."

He placed his hand on her shoulder. "I promise."

With the enormity of that decision made, she sighed. "Thank you."

"Good night, Lily. Try to get some sleep."

Another log tumbled into the fire, and the flames flickered in protest. "Good night."

Lily stared into the fire, listening to Carter's breathing grow deeper.

What would my brothers do if I never came home?

Chapter Twelve

Carter woke to the darkness, and it took a couple of heartbeats to orient himself.

Lily was crouched by the glowing coals and a golden hue illuminated her face. The strong, confident woman he'd witnessed during the last couple of days was gone. Instead, he saw a crumbling shell. He pushed up from his elbow. "Hey . . . you okay?"

She shook her head but didn't lift her eyes.

He reached for the flashlight he'd placed at his side before he fell asleep, turned it on, and went to the tent. The second he unzipped it, the smell and heat hit him with equal intensity. Swallowing back the bile in his throat, he checked for a pulse. He'd needn't have bothered though; Otomi's tongue, purple and swollen, spilled from his mouth, and his eyes stared at nothing.

Their guide was dead.

Carter closed Otomi's eyes, crawled out of the tent, and sucked in cleansing breaths.

The sun was yet to rise, and other than his flashlight, their only light was from the glowing embers. He strolled to Lily and sat beside her.

"Did you sleep at all?

She nodded. "Some."

"Okay, that's good."

"I can't believe how quickly he died."

Carter sighed. "I know. Me neither. He said it was a rattlesnake."

"No one ever said to watch out for snakes. They were more worried about me being mugged, and lucky me, I ticked that off on day one."

He frowned at her. "What do you mean?"

She huffed. "My knees and hands . . . someone tried to steal my satchel on my way back from the cantina that night."

"Shit, Lily. Why didn't you say something?"

"It didn't matter." She curled a loose hair behind her ear. "Nothing was stolen."

"That's not the point. You could've been seriously injured."

"I'm fine. The guy wasn't, though. I think I broke his nose. Heard it crack. I don't think he'll pick on a woman again."

Carter huffed. "I'd like to have seen that."

She shrugged. "I grew up with six older brothers."

"Right then. Mental note . . . don't wrestle with Lily." He chuckled and Lily scrunched her nose at him. She was fast becoming one of the most fascinating people he'd ever met. Though the jury was out on whether that was a good or bad thing.

"Let's get something to eat. We're in for a big day." He stood and hauled Lily to her feet. They were down to four half-bottles of water. Their next source of water was at Yaxchilan, but how long it'd take to get there was anyone's guess.

Eating only black beans was an option, but a crappy one.

They needed energy to get back up that damn hill. With the decision made, he poured half a bottle of water into the rice and carried the pot to Lily, who already had the fire at full blaze.

As the rice cooked, Carter reached for his camera, turned it on, and as he waited for the darkness to dissipate, he tugged back the flap on Otomi's tent, tied it open, then he took a few paces up the hill and turned to observe their campsite.

As the miracle of daybreak unfolded, he peered through his

lens, waiting for the perfect shot. Just off-center, to the right of the scene was the tent. Inside, the bottom half of Otomi's body was clearly visible. His swollen leg and foot were as ghastly from that distance as they were up close. To the left of the tent, Lily crouched by the fire, stirring the pot. As smoke drifted across the tent and the rooster fluffed up its feathers and opened its mouth to announce the arrival of a new day, Carter clicked off a dozen or so photos.

That shot of the day was likely to be one of his most powerful and thought-provoking yet.

With each second, the darkness drifted away and Carter was able to see more and more of their surroundings. He stood and went in search of the cliff they'd discovered last night.

He found it quicker than expected, and, as he stood on the edge of yet another giant boulder, he glanced out over the jungle below. The vastness highlighted their isolation. Nothing, not a single thing, showed him the way.

He returned to Lily as she poured a can of black beans into the cooked rice. His instant reaction was to stop her, but it was too late, she'd already opened the can, and they had no means to store it. Rationing food was critical. As was nearly every other decision they'd make from now on.

He'd been in dire situations before.

The worst one still haunted him. The gun-wielding bandits who'd taken him and nine other journalists' hostage in Somalia were soft-spoken, but the blasts of their battle-hardened weapons forever scarred his memory.

The hangover from that terrifying two-week ordeal was that loud noises often had him ducking for cover. He'd had six years to analyze why he'd lived when others hadn't. It was a pointless reflection. That experience had taught him one thing though . . . remaining positive was just as important as food and water.

Forcing an upbeat attitude to the forefront, he rubbed his hands together. "What yummy creation have you whipped up?"

"Ha ha. Beans and rice. Again."

As they ate breakfast, Carter took mental stock of their belongings. Between the two of them, it would be impossible to carry everything.

Lily paused with a forkful of rice at her lips. "What do we do now?"

"First, we'll need to go through our gear and pack the absolute bare minimum. Everything else we'll leave here for when we come back for Otomi."

Lily nodded again and placed her half-empty plate to the side.

"We're not starting, though, 'til you finish that."

She wiped the back of her hand across her mouth. "I'm full."

"No, you're not!" He didn't mean to sound as forceful as he did.

Her jaw clenched.

"Sorry, but you need all the sustenance you can get. The other day I saw you devour more food than me at that lunch. Look, we won't eat for hours and we can't store the food, so we're not going to waste it."

"You're right. It's just . . . I feel sick over what happened to Otomi."

"I know. Me too. But we can't think about him now. We need to think about us and how we're going to get through this, like eating when we can."

Carter left her to finish her food, and set about rolling up their sleeping bags.

Going through his gear and Otomi's, he separated the belongings into what they'd take and what they'd leave behind. Obviously, they'd take all the food and water. One tent and two sleeping bags were necessary; as was the saucepan, first-aid kit, socks, hat, sunscreen, insect repellant, compass, and one change of clothes.

Lily placed her empty plate aside, grabbed her pack, and tipped the contents onto the rock. It surprised him how light she traveled. In the end, everything but one pair of sandals, a leather satchel, and a few clothes were in one pile. The items she planned to take included her notebook and well-worn leather-bound journal.

Carter pointed at them. "Do you really need those?"

"Yes!"

The fight in her voice surprised him. "Lily, be practical."

"I see you're taking your camera."

"Yes. We need to document where we've been so we can find our way back."

"I'm not leaving these behind, so you can forget it." Her clenched jaw indicated the end of the conversation.

He huffed. "Okay, then." If she wanted to carry it, then it was her problem.

Carter dropped the subject, and while he set about distributing the equipment between their two packs, Lily caught Pompa and put him back in the cage.

The sun speared the lush canopy with equal intensity of light and heat and it wasn't long before sweat trickled down his lower back. "Hey Lily, I noticed you have a pocket knife. Can you help me cut this into strips?" Carter tugged Otomi's thin blanket toward her.

"What for?"

"We'll use them to mark our route and it'll help us relocate Otomi, later."

She flicked out the blade on her pocketknife, sat cross-legged on the rock, and began slicing the blanket into two-inch strips.

When she finished, Carter bundled the strips and wrapped one around it to tie them together. He finished the packing, zipped up the bags, and turned to Lily. She stood by the drifting smoke with her hands across her chest, hugging herself.

"Ready to load up?"

"I'll just say goodbye." She stepped into the tent, knelt down at Otomi's side, and placed her hand on his shoulder. "We'll come back for you, Otomi. I promise." Carter left her to say her goodbyes, and walked to their gear. When Lily emerged moments later, Carter was surprised she was dry-eyed.

He took his turn and tried not to gag as he stepped into the tent. "Hey, buddy." He knelt on one knee and placed his hand on Otomi's chest. "I promise you'll be buried next to your father, soon."

Carter backed out, untied the flap and zipped the tent closed for the last time.

Silently, they loaded their gear onto their backs. Lily gathered the rooster cage into her arms and together they walked away from the tent and back into the dense jungle.

Carter glanced up the hill, identified the direction on his compass as south, south west, then he hooked it to the shoulder strap of his pack and took the lead. The instant he left their rocky precipice, his knees protested at the severe incline.

Steps were often impossible without clutching onto a tree or branch to help haul his ass up. He had no idea how Lily was doing it *and* holding the rooster's cage.

Every fifty or so paces, Carter stopped to tie a marker in a tree. Glancing back down the way they'd come, though, he realized the fabric strips might be pointless. He could only see a handful of them. Every damn tree looked the same.

He took photos often, seeking something different through his lens each time, but it was futile. At the rate he was going, he'd have a hundred photos that meant nothing at all.

The monkeys swung through the trees above them as if following their progress.

When the sun did penetrate through the canopy, it speared straight down like a laser beam, indicating it had to be close to midday, but he struggled to believe they'd been walking that long.

When he couldn't take one more step, he tore his pack off and tossed it down. He crumbled to the base of a mammoth tree and tugged his water bottle from his hip.

Lily lowered Pompa's cage, sat on it, and reached for her bottle too. She unscrewed the lid and paused. "Have you recognized anything so far?"

"Nope. It all looks the bloody same."

"Mmmm, me neither. Do you think we're doing the right thing?" She wiped sweat from her forehead.

"What do you mean?"

"I've been wondering if we should've gone down instead and tried to find our way to the river."

The distress in her eyes cut deep. He stewed over her statement before he answered. "I reckon we'll be wallowing in the shade of Agulinta's ancient walls before lunchtime."

She tilted her head, and he was certain she saw through his lie.

Before she could question his resolve, he screwed his bottle cap into place and rolled onto his knees to stand. "Ready?" It took all his might not to groan, as he hoisted the equipment back onto his body.

She huffed. "I can't wait to get this hill out of the way."

"Me neither. My bloody knees are killing me. My old rugby days play havoc on them, occasionally."

Lily grumbled as she lifted Pompa's cage.

"Here, let me carry the stupid bird for a while."

"He's not a stupid bird."

"Actually, you're right; he's the smart one. We're the idiots for lugging him around." Carter hooked his fingers into the cage, lifted it to his chest, and took the lead again. The cage blocked his view of his feet, so he just gazed ahead and concentrated on putting one foot in front of the other. The extra effort with the cage had him marvelling over how Lily had done it.

Although he could barely talk, he needed a distraction from his creaking bones. "Tell me about your brothers. You have six, right?"

"Yeah. Bobby, Andy, Billy, Danny, Harry, Barry and then there's me, Lily."

Carter laughed. "Bloody hell, you sound like the seven dwarfs."

"I guess so. Our real names are Robert, Andrew, William, Daniel, Harrison, Barry, and I'm Liliana."

He paused to tie a ribbon to a tree. "Liliana . . . I like that."

"I was named after my mom's grandmother, but I prefer Lily."

"So, your parents kept trying until they had a girl?"

"Maybe. They never said."

"What do your brothers do?"

She cleared her throat. "Bobby, Andy, Billy, and Barry all still work on the farm. Danny's a vet and Harry's a mechanic."

Carter missed his footing and realized the elevation had changed. "Hey, it's not so steep. We might be at the top."

"Thank God."

Sure enough, within a few paces, the steep angle leveled out and walking became easier. The vegetation was still as thick as ever and Carter failed to see anything that indicated they'd come this way before. Now that they were on flatter ground, it was easier to look where he was going, but it didn't matter where he turned—everything seemed the same. Every tree, every shrub, every minuscule patch of sky. The monotony drove him crazy.

"How long have we been walking?" Lily asked.

"Feels like ten hours."

"Pfft, I hear you."

"I reckon about four or so. I don't know, I don't wear a watch," he said.

"Me neither. My dad gave me a watch for my twenty-first birthday. But . . ." She paused and he resisted glancing at her again. "By coincidence, my watch died a couple of days after my father passed away. I never had the heart to replace it." Sadness tainted her voice.

"I can understand that."

"So why don't you wear a watch?"

"Simple, don't like seeing my life ticking away. I still have so much more to do. For starters, I've had a goal for a few years to see all Seven Wonders of the World."

"Oh? How many have you seen?"

"Well, there's actually eight; the pyramids of Giza have an honorary mention because they're the only remaining ancient wonder. Anyway, I've seen six of those eight."

"That's magnificent. Which ones haven't you seen?"

"I haven't seen Petra in Jordan or the Taj Mahal. I'll get there, though."

"Sounds like you have an amazing life."

She didn't sound exactly convinced, and he had a terrible feeling she was about to ask again if he was married. He needed a change of subject. "I'm starving."

"Me too."

"You ready to eat the horse and rider yet?"

"Yes." She laughed; the first genuine laugh he'd heard from her all day.

Carter saw something through the vegetation. "Look, another toucan." He put the cage down and reached for his camera.

"Where?"

He pointed high in a tree to their right, raised his camera, and searched for it through his lens. "Here, take a look. It's magnificent." He handed the camera to her and directed her toward the bird.

"Oh, I see it. It's beautiful."

Her whole face lit up and the transformation from frowning to grinning was glorious.

He was tempted to check the photos, but his rumbling stomach convinced him to keep moving. "Come on. Let's see if we can find this damn temple before nightfall."

"Oh God, don't say that. We must be getting close now."

"I hope so."

The sun cut through a break in the canopy, unleashing its power upon him, yet despite its appearance, it was still impossible to work out the time of day. The only thing he *was* positive about was that the more frequent flashes of sunlight and leveler ground meant they had to be near the top. At least that's what he was hoping for.

His spirits lifted at the thought and he trudged on, pushing through the agony in his back and knees. The monkeys struck up a frenzied howl and Carter silently prayed it didn't mean the sun was setting. *We haven't walked the whole day.*

Have we?

He resorted to counting the steps: nine, ten, eleven . . . thirty-five . . . ninety. He stopped at a hundred, annoyed that he'd even got to that number. The giant trees, the brutal vegetation, the heavy gear, the blazing sun—all of them were constant. With each pace, his hopes sank, and when he couldn't take another step, he plonked the birdcage down and slumped to the ground. "I'm done." He fell back onto the mulched leaves and gazed up to the towering trees that swirled overhead as if made of rubber.

"Me too." Lily fell at his side, and he listened to their ragged breaths.

"Why didn't you say something?"

She wiped sweat from her nose and cheeks. "I'm fine."

"Lily, it's okay to say when you're tired."

They lay in silence, staring up at the trees and panting out the exhaustion that wracked their bodies.

"I thought we'd be there by now." Lily huffed. "You don't think we've passed it, do you?"

"I don't know."

"I feel like we've walked farther than we did yesterday."

"Me too. But then again, it was uphill today, and we're exhausted."

She nodded. "That's true."

"How about I leave this stuff here with you and I scout about for a bit?"

"You're not going anywhere without me."

He frowned. "I won't leave you behind, Liliana."

"I told you I prefer Lily." She glared at him. "Are you always this annoying?"

"No one's ever complained before."

"That's because you usually travel alone."

"Touché." He rolled his head from side to side. "Before we get moving, let's have something to eat."

Her eyes lit up. "Great idea. I'm starving."

"Okay. You want to start the fire, Liliana?"

Grumbling, she stood, and started gathering sticks.

Carter let the rooster out of the cage and reached for his camera, hoping to glimpse the elusive Agulinta through the vegetation, but, as if possessed, his aim went toward Lily. The contours of her tanned skin were highlighted by a light sheen of moisture. Her cheeks were flushed just the right amount of red, and every time she licked her lips, he captured it with the click of a button.

Shit! What the hell are you doing?

Shoving the camera away he stood and fished around in their packs for the food and equipment.

Lily had the fire going, and as Carter rested the pot onto the flames, he tried to remember the last time he'd eaten meat. It seemed like months

When the water boiled, he tipped in their ration of rice.

Lily turned to him while stirring and a dark cloud crossed her eyes. "Are we going to starve?"

"No, of course not. We'll be sitting back at that crappy cantina in Corozal before you know it." He hoped he wasn't lying.

They ate their miniscule meal in silence. Once finished, Carter was in no hurry to get going again. He plucked the pocketknife from the side of Lily's backpack and tugged out the remainder of Otomi's blanket. He had a horrible feeling they were going to need many more fabric markers. Lily watched with apparent disinterest as he sliced through the patterned wool.

The squawk of the rooster had them both jumping to their feet. Feathers flew as Pompa flapped his wings and raced at them full speed. A giant lizard, about the size of Carter's calf, was up on its hind legs, tearing up the jungle floor as it dashed after the terrified bird.

Carter didn't even think. Clutching the knife, he dove forward, aiming at the back of the iguana's neck. It was a perfect attack. The lizard snapped around, teeth gnashing. Carter jerked his hand away and lifted it off the ground to remove its traction on the dirt.

It weighed a ton, and as its tail snapped back and forth like a wire whip, Carter's arms burned with the weight of the writhing beast. The lizard weakened and soon its head slumped downward. The only movement was its chest, which swelled and collapsed with each breath. "Grab the rooster," he yelled to Lily.

She spun on her heel and chased after the bird.

Carter lowered the lizard to the ground and when it stopped moving completely, he ran to a shrub and threw up what little content he had in his belly. Over and over he heaved, until he had nothing left. When he stood again, Lily was at his side, handing him a water bottle.

He wiped the back of his hand across his mouth and gulped a few refreshing mouthfuls to rid the bitterness from his mouth. "I can't believe I did that. I've never killed anything before."

"Really?" She blinked. "I have. Heaps of times."

Chapter Thirteen

L ily tried to ignore Carter's gaze as she scooped the dead
iguana off the dirt and set about making it into a meal. First
job was to remove the intestines; this would reduce the risk of infection. Lily worked quickly, applying the skills her father and brothers
had insisted she learn. Carter sat beyond the fire, his camera at his
side, but so far, he hadn't lifted it.

She liked that he looked horrified by what she was doing.

Pinning the lizard between her feet she peeled the skin off its
tail. It took all her strength to do it, but it eventually snapped off like
an undersized pressure sock. She turned to grin at Carter with the
lizard's tail skin dangling from her palm, but he was gone.

A moment later, he threw up in the bushes again.

The amusement she'd felt just moments ago evaporated, and she
was disappointed in herself for relishing in his discomfort.

She worked quickly to skewer the chopped-up iguana meat onto
a long stick before Carter returned. Once it was ready, she sat by the
fire and held the fresh shish kebab over the flames, ensuring it didn't
get too close to burn.

Lily turned the kebab over, and the glorious scent of dinner
wafted in her direction. Her stomach growled in anticipation. The

rooster crowed, and when she glanced at him in the cage, he looking her way as if he too could smell the food.

It was a long time before the crunch of Carter's feet announced his return.

She was shocked at his pale complexion. His shoulders slumped and he clutched at his stomach as if it were cramping.

"Are you okay?"

He shook his head. "Feel like crap." Carter crumbled to the dirt on the opposite side of the fire.

"You need food."

"How'd you learn to do that?"

"I told you. I'm a country girl."

He cocked his head. "I haven't met a country girl yet who could skin an iguana."

"Yeah, well I've never done *that* before."

"Jesus, you could've fooled me."

"I just treated it the same as a snake, or a rabbit."

"You've skinned snakes and rabbits?"

"Sure." She shrugged.

"Oh my God. Who are you? Lara Croft?"

"Who?"

He frowned. "You're kidding, right? You don't know who Lara Croft is?"

She shook her head.

"The movie. . . Tomb Raider. You must've seen that."

Again, she shook her head.

"Wow, I really am getting old. It doesn't matter."

She burst out laughing. "You must've seen food prepared like that in your travels."

"Well . . . yes. Hong Kong and China had some pretty interesting stuff." He wiped sweat off his brow. "I guess it was just that *I'd* killed that lizard."

"Well, I'm pleased you did. It's going to taste delicious."

He huffed. "I'm not sure about that."

"Trust me."

"Trust you? I just saw you gut a two-foot-long lizard with a pocket knife."

"Stop your whining, and come grab this." She held the end of the stick in his direction.

He pushed off the dirt and crawled toward her.

"Hold it above the flames." She showed him the height she wanted. "Don't get too close or you'll burn it. Or worse, you'll set the stick alight, and it'll fall off."

"Yes, boss." He followed her instructions perfectly.

While he was busy, Lily attended to the rest of the lizard's carcass. The last thing they needed was a ton of flies ruining their meal. She took the large metal spoon and dug a hole a fair distance from the fire. The spoon was bent out of shape by the time she tossed the lizard remains in refilled the hole.

She returned to the fire. "That smells so good."

"I reckon." The color had returned to Carter's cheeks.

"Let me see if it's ready."

He handed her one of the kebabs and she slid a cube of lizard meat off the end, blew on it to cool it down and bit it in half. The remainder looked perfectly cooked, and she nodded at Carter as she chewed the rubbery meat. "It's perfect." She bit another chunk off the stick and tried not to laugh at Carter's tentative bite.

The disgusted scowl on his face showed how horrified he was at their meal choice. Though, if he felt anything like Lily did, his hunger pangs would overcome the shock pretty soon.

Lily devoured her kebab long before Carter had even finished chewing his first bite. She waited until he swallowed. "See? I told you it was good."

He nodded and ate more.

She leaned back with her hands in the dirt and scanned her surroundings. Nothing but vegetation filled the 360-degree view. And none of it was familiar territory. "We're lost, aren't we?"

Carter tossed his empty skewer into the fire and dusted his hands. "For now. But we'll find Agulinta soon." He nodded with conviction.

Lily didn't feel the same confidence.

Packing up their gear again, she noticed they only had about two half-full bottles of water left. *We need to find that temple soon, or the river. Or we're in serious trouble.*

Carter took the lead, pushing through the bushes with a new level of gusto. Lily remained hot on his tail, which she had to admit was an excellent view. Carter may have a ragged appearance, but she'd already begun to wonder how handsome he was under all that unkempt hair.

Carter captivated her more than any man had in years, possibly ever. He was very private, yet not afraid to probe her life story. The fact that he hadn't been home in years was fascinating.

She had the distinct feeling there were very strong reasons for him leaving and never going back. If she had to guess, she'd say a woman was central to the decision.

For a short distance, the terrain was relatively flat, but it wasn't long before she noticed a change. They were going downhill. And that wasn't good. Agulinta was at the top of the hill . . . they'd obviously missed it.

She was stewing over how to voice her concern when Carter paused at a giant log that blocked their path. "I think we crossed over this log before."

Lily put the rooster down and stepped back to take in more of the toppled tree. The bark was graying and covered in a motley pattern of white powder and green moss. She didn't recognize it. "I don't think so."

"Yep." He slapped the log, dispersing white particles into the air. "I'm sure we've seen this one."

"When?" They'd climbed over at least a dozen fallen trees in the last couple of days, but she was adamant this wasn't one of them.

"When we went from Yaxchilan up to Agulinta, after the rope bridge."

Frowning, she studied the fallen tree again, searching for something that jogged her memory. "Really?"

He slapped a second time. "Yep. So that means we missed Agulinta. But"—he rubbed his hands together—"we've saved time because we're closer to the river."

She weighed up the pros and cons before she spoke. "How'd we miss Agulinta?"

"We must've skirted around it somehow and came in from the same side we went up yesterday."

"Do you think we'll reach the river if we keep going this way?"

"Absolutely."

Lily wanted to feel his positivity, especially with their limited water supply. In the end, she decided there was no reason to doubt him. "Okay then. Lead the way."

Carter wasted no time in climbing onto the log. Once over, she handed Pompa's cage up to him, then climbed over and they set off again along a path that simply wasn't there.

"Tell me about your family." Lily needed a distraction.

"Huh?" He glanced over his shoulder at her and quickly averted his eyes forward again.

"What do your folks do?"

"Oh right. They're both gone now."

"Oh no, Carter. I'm so sorry."

"No need to be. It happened a long time ago."

He didn't elaborate, so she didn't push it.

"What about your parents?" he asked.

"Mom still lives on the farm, but Dad died a year ago."

"He must've been young?"

"Sixty-six."

"Wow, that *is* young. What happened?"

"A heart attack."

"That's how my dad died too."

She groaned. "Sorry to hear that. Did you see him before he passed?"

"Nope." He said it so matter-of-factly, that Lily now wondered if his parents were the reason he'd left Australia.

As the heat of the day intensified, so did the density of the vegetation. Several times they had to backtrack and go a different way because they simply couldn't push through the jungle.

"Tell me," Carter said, "did you really catch and kill your own food on the farm?"

She huffed. "My brothers did most of that. According to my dad, women were meant for the kitchen."

"Ouch." Carter twisted toward her. "I bet that pissed you off."

"Just a little."

"A lot, I'd say. So how did you learn then?"

"Fortunately, my Mom insisted that I be treated equally to my brothers. So, four times a year, Dad would drive my brothers and I to the far edge of the farm and we'd have to make our way back. We took our own tents and camping gear, and Mom would pack enough food for the hike. But we also loved catching our own. My brothers made sure I did my share of the hunting. Much to dad's disgust."

"Sounds like a load of fun. How long would it take you to get back?"

"About five or six days, depending on where we were to start with."

"Six days? How big was this farm?"

"Just under a thousand acres."

Carter whistled. "Well, I have to tell you, Lily, I'm mighty grateful your dad and brothers did that. Because I'm telling you now, I would've had no idea what to do with that lizard once I caught it."

"You would've figured it out. Besides, you did the hard part."

Carter shoved a giant leaf aside and jumped back screaming. "Fuck! Fuck! Fuck!" A giant spider web stretched from him to the bushes.

She dropped the birdcage and raced to him.

In a frenzy he plucked the sticky lace from his face.

"Where's the spider?" He slapped at his shoulders and chest.

"I don't see one." She checked his body and pack, and certain there were no creepy-crawlies on him, she tried to stifle a laugh, but it was impossible.

"It's not funny," he snapped.

"You're right. It's not. I'm sorry." But despite clamped teeth, she snorted a giggle.

"All right, Lara Croft, you can go first from now on."

She shrugged, then picked up the birdcage and handed it to him. "Your turn with the cage then." She pushed the large leaf aside again and, careful not to get the rest of the spider web on her, strode ahead. "You know, walking into a spider's web is supposed to be good luck."

"Yeah! Well, I'm ready for good luck any time now."

Lily hooked her thumbs into the straps of her pack and set the pace. Nearly every step required a plant of some sort to be shoved aside, and it was painfully obvious nobody had passed this way recently. Possibly ever.

They trudged on for what seemed like hours and her only judge of time was her rumbling stomach. Although she'd only seen glimpses of the sun, its presence was constant in the humidity trapped within the vegetation. The closeness was like a blanket, hot and heavy and bordering on unbearable. Pure determination drove her progress, but as time dragged on and the jungle darkened, even *that* began to wane.

"Do you hear that?" Carter's voice was loaded with excitement.

She turned to him as he put the birdcage down. "What?" All she heard was their ragged breathing.

He punched the air. "Yes. I knew it. That, Liliana, is a fucking waterfall." He picked her up and they spun around, laughing.

He lowered Lily to her feet, grabbed the cage and stepped ahead. "I can feel a skinny-dip coming on."

It was several more steps before she heard the dull roar. The glorious sound already had her feeling ten times better.

Despite the cobweb incident, Carter charged through the plants, a man on a mission. With every step, the rumble of the water increased. Finally, the jungle gave way and a giant gorge opened up before them.

They'd found the river, but the water tumbled a million miles an hour about twenty feet down.

Out of reach.

Chapter Fourteen

The river was a magnificent sight, one that normally would've taken Carter's breath away, but their inability to access it only pissed him off. He didn't even have the enthusiasm to take photos. To his left, water shot through an enormous spout ten feet above and smashed into rocks about twenty feet below them.

The fine mist thickening the air teased him, just enough to confirm it wasn't a hallucination, but inadequate to cool him down. He wondered if it was the same waterfall near the rope bridge they'd crossed the other day, but it only took one glance around to crush that hope. For starters, they were on the wrong side of the gorge. The formation of the rocks at the top and bottom were different, and the bridge was nowhere to be seen.

They were still lost.

He looked up, ready to scream to the heavens, but resisted by clenching his jaw instead.

Fluffy clouds, stained indigo and pink, dominated the dark blue sky, concealing the sun. After days in the dense jungle, the sight should've been welcome relief. It wasn't. Far from it. The frustration that hit him moments ago, hit a whole new level as he conceded the sun was setting. He couldn't believe they'd walked an entire day and not only did they bypass Agulinta, but they still didn't have fresh water. He clenched his fists until his nails dug in.

"Now what do we do?" Lily yelled over the thunder.

Carter pointed downstream. "We walk that way." With birdcage in hand, he took off and didn't look back to see if she followed.

His fingers strangled the bars of the cage as he negotiated the abundant obstacles . . . plants, rocks, giant trees . . . more bloody plants. The hurdles were endless. None of it easy. Traversing the edge of the gorge was hard enough, but just for a bit of fun, every-thing was slippery too. Clutching the damn birdcage didn't help, and he nearly tumbled several times. The temptation to toss the bird into the swirling water below increased with every step.

The bird spread its wings and crowed, clearly enjoying the expe-dition more than Carter and, seconds later, the monkeys belted out their hair-raising chorus. He was surprised he could even hear them over the tumbling water.

As much as he wanted to, he resisted looking skyward. Nothing good could come of it anyway. Darkness was fast descending upon them and the silent clock ticking in his head urged him to set up camp, ASAP.

Carter paused at a spot high above the river where a giant boulder blocked his nonexistent path. He had no choice but to veer away from the river and head into the jungle. After several minutes, a clearing opened up as if he was meant to find it. It was about twenty feet wide, relatively flat, and based on what he'd seen in the last twenty-four hours, a miracle.

He plonked the rooster down and turned to watch Lily stride over a small shrub with ease. "Found our campsite for the night."

"We're stopping?" Lily raised her eyebrows.

Carter was completely beat and refused to believe she'd have any stamina left either. "Yes, we're stopping." He made a show of tossing his pack to the ground.

"I thought we'd find somewhere along the river."

Carter rolled his shoulders, working out the stiffness, and glared at her. "Did you see a place to fit a tent?"

"Well, no. It's just—"

"Just what, Lily?"

"Don't take your frustration out on me." She balled her hands on her hips.

He sighed. "Sorry. That was uncalled-for."

After a pause she nodded. "Apology accepted."

"Are you okay if we camp here?"

She looked around as if assessing the site. "This will do fine." Lily slipped her pack off and sat down on the grass. The legs on her cargo pants drifted up, revealing the scabs on her knees. He'd forgotten all about them.

He sat by her side and gestured to her knees. "How are your wounds?"

She bent forward to look at them and frowned as if she too had forgotten. "Oh, they're fine."

"And your hands?"

"They're nearly healed. See." She flashed her palms at him. Red inflammation was still visible around the dark scabs.

Lily might look delicate and insecure, but that was deceiving. She was far from both those attributes.

She curled a loose hair out of her eye and glanced upward. "How long do you think before the sun sets?"

Carter glanced back the way they'd come and could only see a glimpse of sky. "Maybe thirty or forty minutes."

"Good. I have an idea for a way to get water." The confidence in her eyes dazzled as she tugged her pack toward herself, unzipped it, and pulled out another pair of cargo pants.

She pointed at his pack. "Can you get the saucepan, please? And I'll need a rope from the tent—a long one."

Intrigued, he fetched the items and watched as she tied knots into the legs of the khaki cargo pants. He handed her the pot and she manipulated it into the pants so the handle poked out through the zip and then zipped it up, securing the handle in place.

He admired her slender fingers as she wove the rope through the belt loops on the pants and tied it tight. She stood and turned to him with a huge grin. "Ready to go fishing?"

Caught up in her enthusiasm, he grinned with her and stood to follow.

They walked along the edge of the gorge with water tumbling dozens of feet below, trees towering dozens of feet above, and Lily traipsing over one obstacle after another and peeking over the edge, as if looking for something. After a few minutes, she lay face down on a level patch covered equally in rocks and grass. "Come on!" She patted her side. "Help me."

Curious, Carter lay down beside her.

"Okay. We'll do this together so we don't lose everything. I'm going to lower the pot over the side and we're aiming for that swirling eddy against the rocks there. See it?"

She pointed straight down, and Carter spied the mini whirlpool she referred to. "Yep."

"Okay. Both of us will hold the rope, because the last thing we want to do is lose the pot."

"Or your pants."

"Right."

His heart skipped a beat at the glorious smile she flashed at him.

Lily handed him the rope, and while he glided it through his fingers, she let out small lengths at a time, gradually lowering the contraption. The pot spun around as it caught in the breeze above the flowing water. "We have to time it so it's facing open to the current when it hits the water. Okay?"

"Yep."

The pot hovered inches above the flow and spun quite fast. "Ready?" Her voice was a pitch higher, loaded with hope. "I'll say when."

"Steady."

Anticipation hung in the air like an act in a magic show.

"Now!"

He let out a length of rope.

The instant it hit the water, they both strained against the dramatic change in weight.

"Pull," she yelled, and together they tugged the rope up. The pot was full as it eased out of the water. But as it spun, their precious cargo tumbled out. By the time they'd hauled it to the top, they'd lost half.

Carter chuckled at the success and it took all his might not to lean over and kiss her to celebrate.

"Shit." Lily settled the pot on the ground and huffed.

"What?"

"It's half empty."

"No, Lily, it's half full."

She turned to him. Her eyes seemed to truly pierce his and he slipped into those gorgeous blue pools like he was hypnotized. A beat passed between them. A hot, heady beat, and when she ran her tongue over her lovely lips, he fought the urge to lean in to kiss her. When her lips curled into a smile, the desire to kiss her moved from fleeting to unbearable. But he had to resist, for both their sakes.

Desperate to put distance between them, he pushed to stand. "I'll get the water bottles. We'll fill them up and do it again." As he walked back to their gear, he pictured her intense eyes. They were vibrant blue, like the shimmering shades he'd seen in the towering ice cliffs off Greenland. They were innocent eyes too, yet frequently flashed a touch of knowing.

In an instant, his groin bounced to life and he shoved the unwanted bulge down with the palm of his hand. "Stop it!" he hissed at himself and adjusted his shorts. He told himself his randy thoughts were the result of years of abstinence and his mind bounced to the last time he'd had sex.

It was in Myra, Turkey. He'd been there to photograph the rock-cut tombs of the ancient Lycian necropolis. The woman he'd met, Lynda, had shared a ride with him from the tombs to the sixth-century church of Saint Nicholas. She was Australian too, and also traveling alone. By the time they'd shared a meal together, he knew he'd be sleeping with her that night.

The sex was hot, needy—as if the two of them were thrashing out years of being in a coma. When he woke the next day, Lynda was gone, and he was grateful both for the sex and that he didn't have to have breakfast with her.

The feelings he was experiencing with Lily were completely

different. It wasn't just his need to feel her body—it was his unprecedented desire to know everything about her. Lily was young, gorgeous, and fascinating, and that made her dangerous. It made him dangerous too. He needed to keep his arousal in check or he was likely to start something he wasn't sure he could stop.

Carter plucked their water bottles from the packs, and at the sound of a spine-tingling howl he looked up to the trees. A group of monkeys, perched high on a branch, hovered above him like gargoyles. The biggest monkey with a fluffy gray beard reached out for something that looked like a green tomato hanging from a nearby branch. His fingers were humanlike as the primate plucked the fruit and fed it into his mouth whole.

Pompa crowed, and that set the monkeys into a frenzy. They howled and jumped up and down on their branches, beating out a war cry. The rooster carried on pecking at blades of grass it could reach through the bars of his cage, seemingly oblivious to the raucous company.

Carter dragged his eyes from the primal duel and returned to Lily. He knelt next to her and she reached for a bottle.

"You took a while. Everything okay?"

"Just Pompa entertaining the monkeys. He'll have to stay in his cage tonight."

"Poor rooster."

"Poor rooster? He's lucky we don't make him into roast chicken."

"Ha! Are *you* going to chop his head off?"

He cocked his head. "Maybe."

"You and I both know Pompa's safe." She smirked.

"For now. . . no promises when I'm starving though."

She rolled her eyes, clearly seeing his threat as idle. Which it probably was.

"I'll hold the bottle." She sat cross-legged. "You pour the water."

There was sufficient water in the pot to fill up two bottles and still have some left over. Lily took the sweatband off her wrist, dipped it in the pot, closed her eyes, and squeezed the liquid around her neck. Carter watched, mesmerized, as a droplet trickled down her chest and disappeared into the valley of her curves.

"You know that's rude, don't you?" The cheekiness in her voice confused him.

He snapped his eyes away and swallowed. For a brief moment, he considered that she'd been happy with him watching, but he quickly dismissed the thought as heatstroke stupidity.

"Come on." She slapped his thigh. "Let's get more. Maybe we'll have enough to actually have a wash this time."

Carter simply nodded, and quickly rolled onto his stomach to hide the bulge growing in his pants again.

They repeated the process twice more. The first time produced enough water to fill two more bottles, and the second time Lily glanced into the three-quarters-full pot and flashed a beautiful smile. "Here's our washtub for the night." She began to undo the buttons on her shirt, exposing her cleavage.

Carter jumped up, eager to get away before she showed any more flesh. "I'll leave you in peace and get the tent set up."

She carried on unbuttoning. "Okay."

Carter trotted away, forcing his brain onto setting up the tent and not the gorgeous woman who was stripping several feet away. He spent a couple of minutes clearing the area of vegetation, debris and rocks, then unrolled the tent, and unlike the previous night, had it up within a few minutes. He was hammering in the last peg, when Lily strolled toward him looking like she'd stepped out of a beauty salon.

Her hair was slicked back from her forehead, and her skin glowed fresh and clean. "Your turn." She'd tied her shirt in a knot at her waist and he didn't need to look hard to note that she'd left her bra off. "Do you want to get another pot of water?"

He cleared his throat and snapped his eyes away. "No, I'll use yours."

"Okay. I'll get a fire going, so we can sterilize water for our bottles."

"Good idea."

Carter dashed to his pack, grabbed his only fresh underwear, and fought the stirring in his groin as he returned to the ravine. He stripped naked, and using his dirty shirt, wiped days of sweat and grime from his body. The lick of the cool air over his wet skin was invigorating, and injected much needed oomph into his weary body.

The warm air and light breeze had him dry in minutes and he stepped into clean undies and shorts. By the time he walked back to the campsite, he felt like a new man.

His first sight of Lily had him ogling her again. She'd changed into a white tank top, and when she leaned over a stack of wood to blow onto it, his heart jumped to his throat at the view down her abundant cleavage.

He averted his eyes.

"I'll get our beds sorted." With clenched teeth, he walked to their packs and carried them into the tent.

Furious that his focus on Lily was intensifying, he gave himself a mental grilling as he rolled out the sleeping bags side by side. He copied what she'd done the night before and stuffed some of his clothes into a T-shirt to make a pillow.

"Do you want me to make your pillow up?" he called out to her.

"Yes, please."

He unzipped her pack and spied the leather-bound journal. The urge to pick it out and unwrap the leather thong to see what was inside was so strong that his mind launched into a mental devil-versus-angel debate.

He drove his fingers through his hair, furious that Lily affected him this way.

She was young, way too young for a man like him. Any advances he made toward her would be met with humiliation—of that, he was certain. Avoiding the journal, he plucked out her clothes and made her pillow too.

"Hey Carter, come check this out."

He tossed her makeshift pillow onto her sleeping bag, flipped back the tent flap, and crawled out. Night had fallen as swiftly as if a giant switch had been flicked. The blazing fire was the only light, illuminating their campground and casting flickering light onto the surrounding trees.

Lily was a goddess in the golden glow as she stood, hands on hips with her back to him. Her long, dark hair tumbled down her back to meet the belt around her tiny shorts, and for some reason her hiking boots made her long legs seem even longer.

She turned to look at him over her shoulder. "Come see this."

He walked to her side and followed the direction of her outstretched finger.

"See that fruit up there?"

"Oh yeah, the monkeys were eating them earlier."

"Good. I was wondering if they were edible."

He raised his eyebrows. "You don't plan on climbing that tree, do you?"

"Of course. How else are we going to get them?"

He scrutinized the tree. The glow from the fire only reached about twenty feet up. He guessed the tree to be at least three times that high. "They're a long way up."

"So?"

"Sooo . . ." He dragged the word out. "Lily, I don't know . . . It looks dangerous."

"I'll be fine. I've climbed much higher." She undid her shoes.

"What about the monkeys?"

"They're gone." She pulled her hair into a ponytail, using a band she plucked from her wrist. "Can you grab my pocketknife, please?"

Clearly, she'd made up her mind. He scowled, but conceding defeat, went to her pack in the tent again, and fished the knife from the side pocket. Outside, she was already on the first branch, straddling it like riding a horse. She grinned too, emphasizing her determination and perhaps daring him to defy her.

He handed the knife up and she tucked it into her shorts pocket. Then, without a moment's hesitation, she stood on the branch and reached for the next limb. Carter's heart was in his throat as he stepped back from the trunk and watched Lily's progress higher and higher.

The rooster crowed again and Carter was so worried about the monkeys returning that he was tempted to kick the stupid bird.

119

Lucky for Pompa, Carter didn't want to take his eyes off Lily. Each time she reached up on her toes for the next branch, his heart skipped a beat and a carousel of horrid thoughts whizzed through his brain.

He breathed a sigh of relief when she finally straddled the branch nearest the fruit. She seemed completely at ease as she leaned forward with the pocketknife.

"Ready?" she called down to him.

"Yep."

A green ball dropped from the tree. Carter made a perfect catch, but it splattered in his hands, covering them in a brown soggy mess. "Oh shit! I think it's rotten."

"Really? Rotten fruit usually falls from the tree."

"It looks like crap. Literally." He sniffed the brown sludge and was shocked by its distinct chocolate aroma.

"Taste it," Lily demanded.

Carter mumbled under his breath then took a small bite of the gooey slop. It was soft and slimy and, to his surprise, tasted like chocolate pudding.

"And?" Lily called down at him.

"I think it's okay. It tastes like chocolate."

"Fantastic. Here's another one."

She dropped the second fruit, and despite trying a cricket catch to soften the fall, it splattered in his hands too. He tugged a giant leaf off a nearby plant and pried the mess off his fingers.

Each time Lily tossed one down, the green ball split open when he caught it. By the time she'd finished, his hands and half his torso were covered in brown chocolate-smelling slop.

"I'm coming down now."

"Okay. Be careful."

He waited until she was on the lowest branch before he picked up the nine smashed fruits in the leaf and carried them toward the campfire. Lily was laughing by the time she arrived at his side. "You look like you had an accident in your pants."

"And rubbed it over my stomach?"

"Yeah." Now, she really laughed. "You need another bath."

"I guess so. I hope these are edible after all that."

"If the monkeys were eating them, then that's good enough for me."

She sat in the dirt next to the giant leaf plate and reached for one of the fruits. Carter sat at her side and scooped a portion too.

"It smells like chocolate." She scrunched up her nose.

"Yeah, I told you. Weird, hey?"

She bit into it. "Yum." Her eyes lit up and she licked her lips.

Carter shoveled more into his mouth. The consistency and taste of thick chocolate mousse made it a weird fruit but, despite its appearance, it was delicious.

She giggled. "It *is* chocolate pudding."

"I know. Crazy?"

"Have you seen these before?"

Carter shook his head as he scooped more off the leaf.

"But you've been in Mexico for eight months. You'd think these would be everywhere."

"Mmmm. Maybe they're not supposed to be eaten."

"Don't go saying things like that. I'm enjoying it."

"Well . . . just because it tastes good, doesn't mean it's edible."

"Now, who's being the pot-half-empty guy?" She cocked one of her perfectly formed eyebrows, and then took a giant bite.

By the time they'd devoured the fruit, they both needed another wash.

"Lucky we hadn't wasted time boiling that water, we're going to need it to clean up." She beamed.

The chocolate around her lips reminded him of a time he'd taken his daughter for gelato at In the Pink, a world-class ice creamery in Byron Bay. His daughter had taken so long to choose her flavor that the crowd behind her had grown restless. In the end, she'd chosen plain chocolate ice cream. It'd melted so quickly though, that she'd managed to wear nearly as much as she ate and ended up looking like Lily did now. Casting aside the wonderful memory, he rolled to his knees to stand.

"That was so good." She licked her lips and Carter had to fight the silly notion that she was deliberately trying to tease him.

He flicked the wet shirt he'd used earlier over his shoulder, grabbed a bottle of water, and crouched by the fire to clean himself.

With that done, they filled the pot again and back at the campsite, they put the pot over the coals to boil out the impurities. Carter settled by the fire and felt like every muscle in his body fought against him. Lily, however, looked like she could run a marathon.

"So . . ." She poked a stick at the glowing coals. "What's the most interesting place you've ever been to?"

He blinked at her and tugged on his beard. "Well, that depends on what you consider interesting."

She sucked her bottom lip and rolled her eyes upward as if considering his question. "Okay, start with the most remote."

"That's easy. Agulinta."

She rattled her lips. "Really? I'm surprised you say that. It didn't take that long to get here."

"No, but we had to walk most of the way. All the other remote places I've been to could be reached by vehicle, camel, or mule, or something like that."

"Huh, okay then. Which place did you stay at the longest?"

He poked at the fire too. "I think that was Pompeii."

"Oh wow. I'd love to go there."

"It was incredible. Both fascinating and macabre."

"What do you mean?" The glow from the fire intensified her frown.

"You know the story of Pompeii, right?"

She nodded. "Yes."

"Well, when the volcano exploded, it hit the town in a matter of minutes. Hardly anyone escaped."

"Mmmm, I can't imagine the horror."

"They reckon most victims didn't even see it coming. It's an incredible reminder of the power of nature."

"Mother Nature sure knows how to wield her fury."

The way she said it had Carter wondering if she'd experienced some kind of natural disaster. He let it slide for now. "Anyway, the lack of air and moisture created by the mountain of ash that fell on the city ensured the objects that lay beneath it were preserved in extraordinary condition. During excavation, archaeologists used plaster to fill in the empty spaces that once contained bodies. This meant they could recreate the exact positions the deceased were in when they died. They found men, women, children, babies, dogs, cats, monkeys." He shook his head. "Hundreds of creatures."

Lily shook her head. "Wow, that'd be spooky."

"Yep, that's what I meant by macabre and fascinating at the same time."

"I'd like to see that one day." She curled a loose hair around her ear and he admired how feminine her fingers were.

His mind drifted back to his photo collection from Pompeii. Prior to going to Pompeii, most of the photos he'd seen of the natural disaster focused on the horror that had struck the life forms. Carter centered his attention on the humans and their day to day lives, prior to the eruption. The photo that'd won him the most awards was of a plaster cast of a young woman's hands. He'd zoomed in on her delicate fingers and had imagined she'd been weaving an intricate cloth when the volcanic ash took her life.

His mind drifted to the photos he'd taken in the last four days and he wondered if any of them would win awards. If it was the one of Otomi in the tent after he'd died, it'd be a bittersweet moment. He cast the idle thought aside and rubbed his lower back, trying to work out the knot at the base of his spine.

Lily twisted from side to side. "My back's killing me too."

Carter was seconds away from offering to give her a massage when he caught himself. He replicated her movements instead, stretching out his lower spine until it cracked.

The water began boiling and Carter removed it from the coals and settled it on a nearby dirt patch to cool down.

They slipped into comfortable silence and the jungle noises around them seemed to come alive. The fire crackled and popped. Monkeys belted out their bloodcurdling howls in the distance. Other creatures. . . birds and mammals whose sounds he didn't recognize, added to the soulful chorus, and Pompa pecked at the ground with constant repetition.

Flames danced their reflection onto a nearby tree but, beyond the fire, the darkness around them was complete. He looked upward, but saw nothing but black. The dense canopy smothered any chance of seeing stars or the moon.

Lily yawned. "I think I'll sleep like a log tonight."

"Me too." He couldn't hold back the yawn that gripped him too.

"Do you think we'll find our way out tomorrow?" Golden flames danced across the pools of her eyes.

"I'm certain of it. The river's our ticket out of here."

"Good. I can't wait to eat a big juicy steak."

Carter burst out laughing.

"What?" She smiled at him.

"I just think it's funny that you put food over a hot shower."

"You can live without showers; you can't live without food."

And, in that moment, Carter was pretty sure he was falling for the mysterious, beautiful, and confident young woman at his side.

Chapter Fifteen

Lily woke to the sound of the tent zipper opening and, when she rolled toward the noise, Carter was on his way out. It was fairly dark. However, as she could make out the tent roof in the blackness, she realized it was already morning. She'd slept right through, and by the stiffness radiating from her neck, she assumed she'd barely moved all night.

She twisted from side to side, trying to manipulate muscles that stiffened in protest. The last time Lily had felt this physically drained was when she'd carted her furniture up to her fourth-story apartment almost all by herself.

If her neighbor hadn't conveniently appeared as she wrestled her double-bed mattress up the stairs, she would've left it in the stairwell and slept on the worn carpet on her bedroom floor instead.

That was three months ago, and although some days she hated that place, it was her own. That almost made up for the sleepless nights caused by the scurrying mice. *Almost.* Despite repeated requests to the apartment manager, very little had been done to eradicate the vermin that'd made Honeycut Apartments their home.

The freezing cold was another issue. No number of blankets could eliminate the cold that got right into her bones in the middle of the night. It was ironic that she slept better out here in the middle of the jungle than she did in her own bed.

She crawled out of the tent. It was indeed daybreak. Carter was returning from the nearby bushes when she stood and stretched her arms above her head. "Morning."

He turned to her. "Morning. Did I wake you?"

"I heard the zip. But that's okay, it's time to get up anyway."

He tried to run his fingers through his hair, but it must've snagged in the knots as he tugged his hands free. "Did you sleep okay?"

"Right through. How about you?"

"My grumbling stomach woke me a few times, but other than that, all good."

"Let's get that yummy rice and corn on the go then."

He chuckled and headed toward the pot near the now extinguished fire.

Between the two of them they had a good routine going. While Lily rekindled the fire and prepared breakfast, Carter packed up their campsite. When Pompa welcomed the morning with an excited crow, Carter grabbed his camera and walked a little way, before he squatted down among the bushes.

He looked through the lens, his lips pursed, his brows furrowed, and his hands steady. When the camera aimed at Lily, she poked her tongue out, but if he noticed, he didn't show it. He was frozen in the moment for several minutes, before he finally stood and strolled back toward her.

She pushed the cigarette lighter into her pants pocket, flipped the Velcro flap closed, and sitting with her legs tucked to her side, she picked up her bowl and began eating. "Do you always do that in the morning?"

"What?"

"Take photos before breakfast."

He tugged at his beard. "I've done it for as long as I can remember."

"What do you do with them all?"

"Try to get them published."

"Oh, that's right. *National Geographic*." It seemed like it'd been weeks since he told her who he worked for.

He nodded and she had a feeling he wanted to say more, but didn't. She was beginning to notice a pattern with his reluctant answers, so she pushed. "Tell me about your prize winner."

He blinked at her, loaded up his fork with rice, then turned his gaze to the fire. "I did a series of photos I titled Morning World. They spanned across a dozen or so countries. My concept was to take a photo of the first thing I saw each morning."

"Oh, that sounds wonderful. Did you sell them?"

"The collection has been exhibited in several countries, and I sell limited-edition copies. But the best part was it helped me score my dream job, freelancing for *National Geographic*."

The scruffy man in front of her had just become the most switched-on artist she'd ever met. Not that she'd met many. But it didn't matter, mysterious Carter just became even more intriguing. She tilted her head. "I'm impressed."

He palmed his chest. "Why, thank you, Tiger Lily."

"Tiger Lily? Really?"

"Yep, lethal, yet sweet and innocent." He laughed and she chuckled along with him, as she scooped a mouthful of food. She liked the nickname; with six older brothers she'd certainly been called worse.

Once finished, Carter packed up the rest of their gear, while she herded Pompa back into his cage.

"Ready?" Carter asked, lifting his pack onto his back with a groan.

"Ready enough."

They set off, just as the sun speared light beams through the foliage. Within a couple of minutes, they stood on the cliff above the raging river and Lily welcomed being in the open air again.

The giant boulder that blocked the path yesterday was their first obstacle, and they had to return to the jungle to circumnavigate it. The rock was about the height of a bus and probably just as long. It was hard work pushing through the lush plants and vines that'd flourished in the abundant, moist air.

By the time they returned to the cliff edge, the sun was in full view and radiated heat with such ferocity that the exposed skin on her arms and neck burned. She pulled up her collar and rolled down her sleeves, yet it made little difference. Her nose and lips suffered the full brunt of it and no amount of sunblock seemed to help.

The river, still flowing several feet below, remained a frustrating predicament. So close, and yet so far. Each time they turned away from the torrent to get around a fallen tree or giant boulder, she prayed that when they returned to the river, they'd be closer to the actual water.

So far, her silent prayers had gone unanswered.

She sipped on her bottle in the hope it'd settle the hunger that snapped at her stomach like starving piranhas. But it didn't. Eating the last of their rations earlier this morning now seemed like naïve foolishness.

A new sound caught her attention. It was a low hum, mixed with a repetitive beat. For a moment she wondered if her mind was playing tricks on her, but when Carter stopped, she knew he'd heard it too.

He spun to her; his eyes wide. "A motor! We're saved." He leaned over and their lips met, but then he snapped back as if she were a viper. "Sorry 'bout that." He looked horrified.

"It's okay. This's exciting." The kiss was brief, *way too brief*, and as far as she was concerned, it was fully justified.

He turned around and pushed on toward the noise.

With each step the sound increased, and she kept her gaze on the fast-flowing rapids, expecting to see their rescue boat at any time.

It wasn't long before the sound drowned out her own ragged breathing and it became apparent that it wasn't a boat making the noise. It was some kind of engine on the riverbank.

It was several more minutes before they arrived at the source of the noise. At the edge of the riverbank, high above the water, sat five water pumps lined up next to each other. They coughed black smoke and spewed water from cracked rigging as they sucked water from the river and pushed it into long black pipes that disappeared into the jungle.

Lily covered her palms over her ears to block out the sound, and when Carter turned to her, she saw the confusion on his face.

It wasn't exactly the welcome party she'd hoped for, but it was the first sign of civilization they'd seen in days. She'd thought he'd be happy, but his expression didn't convey that. Carter put Pompa down and tossed his pack onto the rocky ground. Lily dropped her bag too and used the water escaping from the pipe to wash her face and neck.

It was like a soothing balm.

Over Carter's shoulder, a tall, straight plant caught her eye and she squealed with delight. Corn. One glorious, healthy, overburdened corn plant was thriving at the edge of the jungle. She strode to it, plucked off a cornhusk, tossed it toward Carter, and grabbed one for herself.

Lily peeled back the large green leaf protecting the plump yellow kernels inside, and her whole body seemed to sigh with relief as she bit into the sweet juicy cob. She gnawed her way up and down and, once finished, plucked two more husks from the stalk.

Carter had yellow bits in his beard and teeth and they both grinned big, corn-filled smiles at each other as they devoured their second helping. When finished, Carter burped loud enough that she heard it over the motors. Chuckling, he rubbed his tummy, clearly satisfied.

Lily took a large swig of water from her bottle, and swilled it around to try to remove the bits from her teeth. She fed her cob remains into Pompa's cage, and he pecked at them with gusto. The poor bird was probably starving too.

Carter eased up beside her. "Ready to go again?" he yelled over the engine noise.

She nodded, returned to her pack, and reluctantly pulled it back on. Carter lifted Pompa, and they started following the snaking pipes back into the jungle. It wasn't long before the din of the motors was consumed by the thick vegetation again.

"I wonder if it's a farm up here?" she asked, once she thought Carter could hear her.

"I don't really care. Any humans would be good."

"I agree. Food, give me food."

Carter laughed. "Do you ever stop thinking about food?"

"Nope. My mom says I have a bottomless stomach."

"I believe her. Most women I meet are so worried about calories and fat or, salt content, that eating becomes a mathematical equation rather than enjoyment."

"Pfft. I'd hate to worry like that. I love my food."

"I've noticed."

"Oh really?" She said it with the sarcasm it deserved. "We've barely eaten anything out here."

"Lily, don't take it the wrong way. It's a delight to watch you eat. It's a refreshing change."

"Oh." She wiped sweat off her temple. "That's good, then."

The five pipes snaked under and over rocks and roots, and based on the plants growing around them, Lily assumed they'd been there a very long time. Back home on the farm, they were often changing irrigation pipes because they'd burst from heat, cold, or plant or animal damage. These, though, were so ingrained into the vegetation that they mustn't have been changed in years.

After about fifteen minutes, they stepped from the dense bush and into a corn plantation. The pipes disappeared into the stalks, and Carter and Lily had to barge their way through the hardy stalks to keep following them. If she'd thought virgin jungle was difficult to trek through, then this was downright torture.

Each plant she shoved aside bounced back and hit her arms, her face, her entire body. It was brutal, and the onslaught opened up the wounds on her palms and forearms that'd only just started to heal.

Mixed with the aroma of fresh corn was the stench of her own body odor, and she reflected that maybe Carter's suggestion of a shower before eating wasn't such a bad idea after all. Images of food kept her feet moving. But sheer exhaustion had Lily on the verge of tears, when the terrain changed again.

The corn stalks finished, and they entered a different plantation entirely. The stalks were much higher, bushier, and the star-shaped leaves were lush green. She was a couple of feet in, when Carter spun to her, eyes wide.

Fear riddled his features.

He wrapped her in a bear hug and tackled her to the ground. "Jesus Christ, Lily!" He whispered, "We're in a fucking marijuana plantation!"

"What?"

"Quick! We have to get out of here before someone sees us. But stay low."

Lily's heart was set to explode as she scrambled to her feet. Hunched over, she pushed through plants that were at least two feet taller than her.

Loud voices cut through the vegetation.

Carter pushed her shoulder. "Run!"

Chapter Sixteen

Running like crazy, Lily's legs threatened to buckle beneath her as the plants whipped at her face like torture devices.

"Go! Go! Go!" Carter's thumping footfalls were right behind her.

She raced into the cornfield and stumbled, slicing up her palms as she hit the rocky ground. Carter launched her upright and gripped her shoulder, his face two inches from hers.

"I'll go first, but you stay right behind me. Got it?" The fear in his eyes cut to the bone.

She nodded. "Okay."

More shouts reached them and she counted two men, maybe three. Then, she heard a whizzing sound.

"Fuck! They're shooting at us. For God's sake, Lily, run!"

He barreled through the corn, cutting a crude path. She gritted her teeth, clenched her hands to tight fists and kept right on his tail. Adrenaline drove her on. Fear drove her crazy. The yelling grew louder. The whizzing sounds became more frequent. And the corn plantation lasted forever.

Her heart pounded, her legs pounded, and her brain pounded

out what horrible things could happen if the men with the guns caught them.

It was an eternity before they escaped the cornfield and hit the dense jungle. Carter kept up his pace, and somehow Lily kept up with him. Fear was a powerful motivator.

"Drop your pack."

"What?"

"Drop your backpack." Carter tossed his pack aside, and that's when she noticed Pompa was gone too.

"I'm fine." She increased her pace to prove she could do it.

"Drop your fucking pack, Lily!"

"No!" She gritted her teeth.

Carter glared at her over his shoulder and she shook her head.

"Let it go!"

She hooked her thumbs into the shoulder straps, determined not to lose it.

A bullet whizzed over their heads and smacked into a branch above them.

"Fuck! Run!" Carter screamed.

Lily clenched her jaw and powered her legs. Her boots crunched over the uneven ground. Every so often she glanced at the pipes, grateful they had something to follow. But then, a shocking thought hit her. If they followed the pipes, then the people chasing them knew which way they were going too.

And the pipes led to the river . . . a dead end.

Before she'd had a second thought, the noisy beat of the overworked motors thumped through the silence again. A bullet hit a branch to her right, splintering it in half. She screamed and crouched lower. Adrenaline drove her forward.

The clearing appeared out of nowhere, the five motors still spewed equal parts water and black smoke into the air. Carter turned to her, his face a combination of sweat and despair. And fear.

"What do we do now?" she yelled over the din.

"Give me your bag." He reached for the strap.

She dodged away. "No! I'm not letting it go." She clenched her jaw; determined to keep it.

"Jesus Christ. Okay, but I hope you're a good swimmer."

"What?"

"We have to jump."

"Jump? No way! I'm not jumping."

"Yes, you are!" He grabbed her arm.

"What about crocodiles?" Lily stepped back and put all her strength into grounding her feet, so he couldn't drag her to the edge.

"The water's flowing too fast for crocs." The whites of his eyes blazed. "We have to jump, Lily. They'll kill us."

Her chin dimpled. "I can't swim."

"What?" He threw his hands wide. "You've got to be fucking kidding."

She shook her head. Tears stung her eyes. "I can't swim." She spoke through clenched teeth.

A loud crack made them both duck. Sparks bounced off one of the engines.

"Give me your bag." Carter grabbed it, and she couldn't hold on to it this time.

To her surprise, he put the pack on his back. "Listen to me." He clutched her chin, making her eyes meet his. "We're doing this together. Grab my hand and take a huge breath. I promise I won't let go."

Her knees turned to jelly; her body was set to implode. Bile rose to her throat.

The roar of the motors disappeared, and all she heard was her heart thumping to a terrified beat.

"Lily." He clutched her hand in a viselike grip. "I won't let go."

"Okay."

He dragged her to the edge. "Ready?"

She shook her head. *I can't do this. I can't jump.* She turned to him. "Push me. You have to push me. I can't jump."

Carter nodded. "Okay. When you hit the water, kick as hard as you can for the surface. I'll find you, Lily, just get to the surface. Okay?"

She nodded, but at the same time wondered if drowning was how she was going to die.

Another bullet whizzed by, this one just missing her ear.

"Hold your breath."

Lily sucked in a giant gulp of air. Carter gave her an almighty push, and she screamed until she hit the river. Any air she had left punched out of her on impact. Pain ripped up her legs and forearms as they hit the river with a solid slap. She swallowed water. Lots of it. Blackness surrounded her. Her lungs burned. Her eyes stung.

Against all instincts, she forced her eyes open. Everything was blurry, but a bright light called to her, showing her the way. She kicked and clawed with her hands, seeking fresh air.

She launched through the surface and gasped in the freshness, sucking it in with great painful breaths. The water tumbled over her head and rushed her along at a hundred miles an hour, past fallen trees that lined the riverbank. Rocks and hidden branches beneath the water clawed at her legs and back, shredding her skin at every opportunity. But the thing that scared her the most was that Carter was nowhere to be seen.

"Carter!" she screamed.

She heard nothing but the roar of the water. The current smashed her into a wall of rocks that drove up out of the water like a giant blade. Her shirt tore, and her skin sliced on impact. She screamed with the pain.

"Carter! Help!"

At the mercy of the torrent, she tumbled over and over, swallowing mouthfuls as she gasped for air. It was cruel irony after craving water just days ago. She tried to control her direction, but it was pointless.

The fact that she was alive was a miracle. The fact that she could float was yet another. The only other miracle she needed was to find Carter.

"Carter!" She screamed his name until her throat burned. Fighting back the useless tears, she glanced right to left, searching the white caps.

But he was nowhere.

Golden sun blazed upon her, blinding her with its fury. It didn't matter how much she fought the current, the water was relentless, dragging her to an unknown destination. The river widened, and with it came a slight reprieve. The water slowed and the rapids disappeared.

Unable to fight the current any longer, she rolled onto her back and spread her arms. To her surprise, she remembered how to float. Her parents had attempted to give her swimming lessons as a child, but endless ear infections ended the training before she could even master treading water. Floating was the total extent of her swimming skills. She glanced up at the cotton-wool clouds that contrasted beautifully against the bright blue backdrop. A sense of peace enveloped her and she stopped struggling against the water's insistent clutches.

After a while, she glanced to her right and what she saw made her jaw drop.

She blinked and wiped water from her eyes, trying to get a clearer picture. And there it was—a replica of the circular statue that was drawn in her father's journal was carved into what looked like an entrance to a cave.

Before she could really study it, she'd drifted right past. A wave tumbled over her head, covering her in a wall of water. *Am I drowning? Was what I just saw an apparition?*

Her ankle smashed into a giant rock and she howled at the agony. The pain was the jolt she needed to kick her brain into gear.

She lifted her head to avoid smashing into another rock and spied a fallen tree, jutting out from the bank. This was her chance. If she caught it, she was going to hang on to the damn thing like her life depended on it . . . which it did.

The half-submerged tree came at lightning speed and Lily hit it chest-first. She clawed at the branches, desperate for purchase, but the force of the water dragged her down. Her boots and legs sucked beneath the trunk. Her arms and head were the only part of her body above the water.

"Carter!" she screamed.

She clutched at the branches until her fingers bled. Tears blurred her vision.

I'm going to die.

She thought of her brothers. Her friends. Her boss. And her mother, who'd all tried to talk her out of going to the Mexican jungle alone.

"I am not dying, you bastards!" Lily shrieked.

She had two choices.

Let go of the tree, get sucked under, and hopefully pop out the other side and continue floating down the river.

The second choice was to pull her ass up out of the water.

"I can do this." Lily reached for the gnarly remains of a branch. She clenched her teeth and kicked with all her might to haul herself up onto the tree. Inch by inch, she dragged her sodden body from the water. With one final gasp, she flopped onto dry land.

As fresh blood mingled with water and trickled down her legs, Lily burst into tears.

Chapter Seventeen

C arter waited until Lily plunged into the water before he jumped. But he was a second too late. He screamed in agony as a spear of fire ripped through his left hip. As he tumbled into the river, he knew he'd been shot. He hit the water broadside, smashing his legs and the side of his face like he'd smacked into solid concrete. Beneath the turbulence, he struggled to find the surface.

He swallowed water—great bloody mouthfuls of it—and his lungs burned, seeking air that was impossible to get. Around him, the water swirled blood and froth and silvery bubbles that floated upward. His brain kicked into gear. *Follow the bubbles!*

Carter clawed for the surface, fighting bolts of pain in his left hip. He kicked harder, desperation driving him upward. His lungs screamed; his vision blurred. It was an eternity before he shot into fresh air and sucked huge gulps into his lungs.

A giant rock materialized from nowhere and he smashed into it feet-first. His legs bore the brunt of the impact and he howled at the new onslaught. The water was fast, much faster than he'd predicted, and his thoughts snapped to Lily.

"Lily!" Now that he fully appreciated the power of the torrent, his fear for her hit a whole new level. He pushed off the rock, aimed his feet downriver, and allowed himself to be sucked into the middle flow again.

"Lily!" He screamed her name until his throat burned.

With equal intensity, he bounced off hidden rocks beneath the water and exposed ones above. Every collision created a new bruise, and if he didn't get out of here soon, he was likely to break a bone or two.

Lily's pack snagged on something, jerking him back, and allowing volumes of water to crash over his head. Pinned in the middle of the river, he was sucked under. He thrashed and fought against invisible hands that trapped him. The smart thing to do would be to let the pack go, but he couldn't. Whatever was in there was important to Lily, and that made it important to him. With a couple of mammoth kicks, he twisted his torso, fighting to roll onto this stomach. It worked, and whatever he'd snagged on broke free.

The current grabbed and hurtled him along with renewed vigor.

Control was impossible, but he needed to get out of the fast-flowing current and nearer the riverbank. Fighting the agony in his hip, he swam toward the left bank. His only hope was that he'd be able to latch on to something, but with the speed of the water he was already doubtful.

A gnarly shrub clinging to the edge of the bank farther down caught his eye. Rolling onto his stomach, he kicked and swam like fury to grab it before he zipped right on past.

Carter clawed at the rough branches with a vicelike grip. His legs whipped around in the current and speared into the half-submerged bush. Splinters of wood pierced his flesh, but he didn't let go. He climbed up the shrub and heaved his body out of the river.

Crawling through the bushes, he dragged himself from the water's edge and crumbled into an exhausted heap on the rocky ground.

"Lily." Her name whispered off his lips.

His heart shattered into a million pieces as he pictured her caught in that swirling water.

Dragging himself upright, he grasped a nearby tree for support, stood at the river's edge, and screamed her name over and over. All he heard was the relentless rush of water. Searching the opposite side of the river, he begged for a glimpse of her and yet, at the same time, dreaded what he'd see. With the amount of trouble he'd had in the water, he had absolutely no comprehension how Lily would've coped. Tears stung his eyes as he pictured her beautiful face beneath the water, gasping for air.

"Lily! Lily!"

He stumbled along the water's edge, calling out, and every couple of feet he stopped to inspect both sides of the river. Soon his body quivered like jelly, and he couldn't stand a moment more.

"Fuck!" He crumbled to the ground.

He was heading into shock and that wasn't good.

Blurry visions of Lily, the rooster, snakes, and giant trees swirled around him like they were apparitions. In an attempt to steady his thumping heart, he closed his eyes and focused on his breathing.

CARTER BLINKED HIS EYES OPEN. *SHIT! I FELL ASLEEP.*

If his darkened surroundings were any way to judge, then he'd slept for some time. It also meant he was in trouble. *The sun is setting.*

He went to sit up, but the weight of Lily's pack pinned him down. He tugged it off and howled in agony when he rolled to sit.

Sucking in short, sharp breaths, he gasped at the pain. The trees around him set off in a slow spin, and nausea rushed through him like a tidal wave. He splayed his legs out before him and threw up gushes of water and what little else remained in his stomach.

When the queasiness subsided, he wiped his mouth and glancing at his pants, he cringed at the amount of blood staining his left hip. The jagged hole at the center confirmed what he already knew.

I've been shot.

The only good news was it looked like the bullet had gone clean through. He turned toward the water, searching for signs of life.

"Lily." His voice was nothing more than a pained croak. He rolled his tongue around his mouth, trying to produce moisture, but it was futile.

Rolling onto his back, he undid the zip on his pants and peeled them below his hip. His heart lurched. He'd seen bullet wounds before, many of them fatal. This wasn't lethal, but if he didn't do something to stop the bleeding and possible infection, it might become so.

He unclipped the water bottle from the pack and gulped down a few refreshing mouthfuls. His legs were covered in scratches, some as small as paper cuts, some as big as his thumb. He poured the water over the wounds, creating bloody rivers down his calves.

Turning his attention to the bullet wound, he lay on his right side on the dirt, clenched his jaw, and wriggled out of his pants and undies. Craning his neck, he peered over his hip to try to see the entry wound.

His stomach bucked at the sight.

The bullet had gone in high on his buttock and a hole about the size of a button oozed dark blood that trickled in a steady flow down his cheek. The edges of the hole were raised jagged flesh and around that, a red stain seemed to darken before his eyes. The exit wound at his front hip was slightly larger and equally brutal.

He tore his eyes from the blood and charred flesh and panted against crippling nausea. The bullet hole in his shorts was slightly smaller than his wound, and as he poked his finger through the fabric he wondered if any of it had caught in his flesh. He'd seen enough injuries to know that a foreign object in a wound was a sure-fire way to get an infection. He was certain the bullet had gone right through. That was a good start, but he still needed to check that nothing else was trapped in there.

Carter glanced around. Nothing but green surrounded him on his left side, and the river rushed by his right. Other than his camera, whatever was in Lily's pack was all he had. With a bit of luck, the first-aid kit had been put in this pack and not his.

The first thing he removed was the leather-bound journal, and as he placed the sodden book on the ground, he wondered if that was the reason why Lily had refused to let go of her bag. He found it hard to comprehend how it could be worth more than her life.

Shoving the pointless speculation aside, he reached into the pack to tug out clothes, her toiletries bag, a Swiss army knife, the large metal spoon, a small towel, a second water bottle, and a flashlight that he flicked on and off to see if it worked. It didn't.

He found her notebook, now a soggy mess, and at the very bottom was his Tupperware container with his first-aid basics. Without much hope of finding anything helpful for his serious wound, he set the box between his legs and tugged off the lid. Lucky for him the contents were dry.

Despite being fully aware of their inadequacy, he downed a couple of generic-brand painkillers. Anything to dull the ache, even slightly, would be welcome relief. His first-aid kit contained tweezers, scissors, three types of bandages, gauze, gloves, eye patches, and various other bits and pieces to help with cuts, scratches, bites, sunburn, and other minor injuries.

He checked out the medication and promptly swallowed two Ibuprofen as well. The kit also contained antihistamines, diarrhea-relief tablets, a constipation helper, a few other items, and a small plastic tube of sodium chloride.

Based on his experience in Somalia, Carter knew he had to clean and dress this bullet wound before it became infected. The very idea of touching it, though, brought a new wave of nausea that he fought with short, sharp breaths.

A strange sepia color settled over the opposite riverbank, as the sun cast its final rays across the horizon. The sight was the slap he needed to get his brain into gear. He sucked in a deep breath and let it out in one big gush.

"Let's do this."

He crawled to the nearest tree, dragging the pack behind him. Then, as he curled against a giant exposed tree root for support, he rolled out Lily's sopping wet sleeping bag that'd been tied to the outside of her pack. The dark blue padded fabric had a huge rip in the side where the stuffing leached out, and Carter assumed this was what'd snagged in the river.

Upon the sleeping bag, he laid out the bits and pieces he needed. He took a drink of water and popped two more painkillers.

Fighting wave after wave of nausea, he dug into his wound with tweezers, searching for any scraps of fabric that may've been caught by the bullet. The deeper he dug, the more blood oozed down his ass and hip, and the harder he fought a blackness that threatened to swallow him whole.

It was a long, excruciating process, but satisfied there was nothing there, he dropped the tweezers, squeezed his eyes shut, clenched his jaw, and thought about Lily until he'd overridden the urge to pass out.

When his head stopped spinning and he could breathe again, he cleaned the wound with a T-shirt and water, wiping away the fresh and dried blood from both front and back. Once he was done, he stared at the wound, hardly able to believe it was his own flesh. Thankfully, it didn't look as nasty as it had when he'd first started.

As he reached for the sodium chloride tube, he tried to force bravado into his next move.

It's gonna hurt like a bitch!

Carter twisted the top off the little plastic tube.

If I'm going to do this, I need to be quick.

He closed his eyes, clenched his jaw, and released a slow growl in an attempt to psyche himself into it. The excruciating throb in his hip and ass, stung like hell—but it'd be nothing like what was coming up.

Opining his eyes again, he aimed the tube at the bullet hole and squeezed.

A scream tore from his throat as the blazing needles tortured him. The howler monkeys joined in with their own bloodcurdling cries. But he didn't stop. He squirted both front and back, and kept squeezing until all the liquid was gone.

Tears stung his eyes. A sob caught in his throat.

Every single nerve in his body seemed to scream.

He rolled his head back against the tree, squeezed his eyes shut, and tried to push the agony from his mind. His thoughts drifted to Lily and how she'd handled pain the other day when he'd sprayed liquid skin onto her open wounds.

She was strong. She was a fighter.

He had to believe she'd survived.

And come first light tomorrow, he had every intention of finding her.

Right now, though, he needed to get ready for a night alone in the bush.

He placed gauze over his cleaned wound and wrapped a bandage around his hip, butt, between his thighs, and back again. He secured it in place with two butterfly clips he'd found in the Tupperware kit. Deciding to leave his underwear off, he fought the pain as he wriggled his shorts back on.

By the time he stood again, the painkillers had kicked in, dulling the ache enough to keep him moving. He picked up his underpants, and his treasured pouch of SD cards fell out. Collecting them from the ground, he sighed and clutched them to his chest. With a bit of luck, they'd be using these soon to return to Otomi. He tucked the pouch into his shorts pocket, zipped it up, and glanced around.

No matter which way he looked, it wasn't good.

He forced himself to list out the positives. Number one being *I'm alive*. If that bullet had strayed just a couple of inches higher, then he probably wouldn't wake in the morning. The next good thing was the abundance of fresh water at his fingertips, which was a major contrast to yesterday's predicament.

With those two positive thoughts rolling around his mind, he scoured the area for a place to sleep. Like the last four days, he was surrounded by jungle. Trees of all sizes created a cluttered canopy that let in little sunlight. The sky over the river was the only light source and it was getting darker by the second.

He decided to stay near the water rather than venture into the bushes. Where he was, seemed suitable enough. It was flat ground, and once he tossed the loose rocks away, it was relatively smooth. He hooked the sopping wet sleeping bag between his feet and twisted it to remove as much moisture as he could, before hanging it on a nearby by tree.

Assessing the weight of a sturdy stick, it would be his only weapon should a creature come his way during the night. Or a gun-wielding drug runner.

He rolled on Lily's insect repellant, grateful to repel the

mosquitos that'd already begun buzzing in his ears. Lily would have no such luxury. He at least had a pack with some supplies, but she'd gone into the water with nothing. Settling onto the ground, he recalled her skinning the iguana and climbing the tree for the fruits. She was resilient, and if anyone could survive out here, it was her.

He slumped into the curve of the exposed root again and watched the water froth and tumble over a rock that jutted out of the river. Darkness descended with lightning speed and with his full water bottle within arm's reach, along with his make-do weapon, he curled onto his side and willed the night to be over.

Chapter Eighteen

L ily had watched the sun set with tumultuous emotions that swung from being grateful to be alive, to crippling sorrow over Carter's absence. When she'd first crawled onto the shore, she'd spent what felt like hours calling for him. Her only buoying factor was her survival. If she could survive that torrential river when she couldn't swim, then there was every possibility Carter had survived it too.

She'd ignored the painful throb in her ankle, focusing instead on what she had to do to get through the night alone. Her saving grace was the cigarette lighter she'd put in her pants pocket after lighting the fire this morning. It was the only piece of equipment she had.

After stripping out of her wet shirt and shorts and placing her shoes as close as she dared to the fire she'd built, she squatted, near naked, next to the flames and attempted to dry her clothes by holding them on sticks above the blaze. Beyond the firelight, the darkness was complete, no variations, no shadows, nothing but the blackest of black.

Lily pictured her oldest brother, Bobby. Dozens of times on their camping trips he'd drummed into her the importance of carrying a lighter. *It's your most important survival tool. It'll give you fire. That in turn*

will give you sterile water, burn germs off dubious food, give you a signal oppor-
tunity, provide heat, light, a defense mechanism, and most importantly, something
to distract your mind when you're cold and alone.

As she stared into the dancing flames, she realized how right he'd been. The last instruction Bobby had given her before she'd left for this trip, was to buy three lighters at the airport. She had. Fortunately for her, one had been in her pocket when she'd dragged her sodden body out of the water.

Her mind drifted to Carter. For a man who traveled to remote parts of the world, he seemed particularly lacking in survival skills. She imagined him lying somewhere along the river, cold and alone, and in complete darkness. Her heart broke into tiny little pieces at the thought of losing him. She frowned. *Am I falling for him?*

Although she'd initially been annoyed by his cockiness, as each day progressed, she'd found herself wanting to know more about cryptic Carter. There was something about him that she found alluring. It was almost as if he needed saving . . . even before they got lost in the jungle.

She tried to recall what he'd had with him when she'd last seen him. He had her pack, but she couldn't remember seeing the camera on his hip. Her heart squeezed over the possibility of losing all those photos.

Otomi's final resting place was one of them. Without it, there was a possibility they'd never find their guide again. Her mind spun with horrid thoughts, but she dug herself out of that senseless quagmire by focusing on what was in her pack. Provided Carter still had it, that is.

As she flicked an insect from her ear, she cursed herself for not putting her repellant into her pants pocket like she'd done most days. Despite the humid night air, she'd need to sleep close to the fire to keep the bugs away.

Lily's stomach had progressed past growling and into twisted, angry knots that were borderline painful. First thing she'd do at daybreak was find food. Second, was to look for Carter.

Finding Carter wasn't going to be easy, as she had no idea where to search. There was a chance he'd been able to get out of the river quicker than her, especially as he could swim. While she'd been dragged miles downstream, Carter most likely climbed out well before she did.

The obvious choice was to go upriver and hope Carter would be walking toward her. It was also the direction of that cave she'd seen while floating along. Although the sighting was fleeting, she was adamant it was similar to the carved sculpture at Agulinta. Once she and Carter were safe, she *had* to come back and find that cave.

With the decision made to walk upstream, Lily quickly succumbed to overwhelming weariness. Each passing second brought another ache to her body. Her cuts stung, her right ankle throbbed, and her shoulders and neck hurt. There wasn't a part of her body that didn't ache. To top that off, she was exhausted and hungry, and couldn't decide which was worse.

She could do nothing about the latter, but sleep should solve her exhaustion. Deciding to dry her underwear overnight by the flames, she draped them over a stick that she secured with a long branch high over the heat. She tugged on her damp shirt and cargo pants, and positioned herself between a giant tree and the fire. Rolling onto her side to face the blaze, she did a few deep-breathing exercises to calm her mind.

Her heavy eyelids fell, and Lily allowed exhaustion to lure her to sleep.

~

LILY WOKE TO THE SOUNDS OF MONKEYS BEATING OUT A TERRIFYING chorus in the far distance and a faint, eerie light permeated the vegetation. *Huh, it's nearly daybreak.*

Every muscle in her body screamed in protest as she pushed up from her side. She rolled to her feet, yelped, and stumbled backwards. Turning her right ankle side to side, she gasped at the agony. A lump, the size of an egg, bulged over her anklebone.

Shit! That's not good.

Wincing, she rolled her ankle around, assessing how much movement she had. Just the fact that she could move it, convinced her it was just bruising and not sprained or broken. At least that's what she told herself. Her surroundings gradually morphed from the darkness and she welcomed the arrival of dawn with a big yawn.

Lily crawled to the fire and, using a stick, poked at the ashes to reveal the glowing coals beneath. She tossed on a pile of twigs, and then heavier branches that she'd foraged the night before. As the fire took hold, she inspected her right ankle. A blue stain radiated from halfway up her foot to the top of her anklebone, and the bulging bruise made it look as painful as it felt.

"Shit!" She punched the ground. *I won't be able to get my shoe back on.*

Reaching for her still-wet boot, she fully loosened the laces and tugged the tongue out. Wincing, she tried to ease it on, but the pain was excruciating.

"Damn it!" She pegged the boot at the nearest tree.

Lily squeezed her thumbs to her temples and closed her eyes, determined to plan around this new problem. Her grumbling stomach didn't help. Gulping back a few mouthfuls of water, she tried to fool her hunger into submission.

She needed food. Her brain and her body protested in mutual mutiny whenever she was starving. Like now.

Leaning back on her hands, she looked to the trees, searching for something, anything of substance. But it was fruitless. Literally.

She turned her attention back to her foot. She'd need some kind of protection. The thick-barked tree she'd tossed her boot at gave her an idea.

Hopping on her left foot, she went to the tree and attempted to pry a strip of bark from the trunk. It was stubborn stuff and refused to budge. She plucked a stick from the ground and wriggling it up and down, she finally coaxed a portion free. The plate-sized strip was perfect. She gathered her discarded shoe, hobbled back to the fire, and removed the shoelace.

Lily assessed the size of the bark against her sole, and gradually broke off pieces until it was ideal to cover the bottom of her foot. Holding it in place, she tugged her sock on and then, using her shoelace, lashed it all into position.

Happy with the result, she put on her other shoe and stood. It was painful to stand on her right foot, but not unbearable, and the bark shoe was better than nothing. Lily went in search of a branch she could use as a makeshift crutch, and with that sorted, she picked up her right boot and set off upstream in search of Carter and food.

A long-forgotten memory of a camping trip with her brothers tumbled into her mind and she recalled them making whistles out of leaves. Searching for the perfect leaf also kept her mind occupied and she tried several before she hit success.

With the thin, glossy leaf held taut between her two thumbs, she held it to her lips and blew onto the edge. The resulting squeal was piercingly loud. Louder than her voice, and also, though she didn't want to contemplate it, the whistle might not attract the attention of the drug dealers like her voice would. At least that's what she told herself.

Lily eased up to the water's edge, searched both sides of the river, then blew on the leaf whistle. She received no response. The river was flowing very fast and she hoped like hell that Carter's comment about crocodiles not liking fast flowing water was true.

She navigated her way along the bank and decided to count her steps to measure her progress. Every fifty steps, she stopped and blew her whistle. Counting her steps not only gave her something to do, but it also gave her something to look forward to. The stops were the opportunity to rest her throbbing ankle and sip water from the river.

Weaving her way over and around all manner of obstacles, she became aware that the sun was steadily gliding from her side of the river to the opposite side. Once the sun reached the pinnacle of its arc, she'd need to take a rest and elevate her foot for a while.

The monkeys were active at dawn, but now, in the heat of the day, the only sounds she heard were the tumbling water and the occasional bird. Her grumbling stomach added to the noise, as did her ragged breathing.

She kept up the pattern; fifty paces, blow the whistle, fifty paces, blow the whistle.

It was mind-numbingly repetitive. The scenery barely changed too—river on her right, jungle on her left, blue sky above.

A flash of yellow halfway up a tree caught her eye, and she nearly melted at the sight. Papaya hung heavily off a tall, thin plant. With her mouth already salivating, she charged at the tree as fast as her bruised ankle would take her.

The fruit was too high to reach. *That'd be damn right.* The tree was a tall, skinny pole, and impossible to climb and the surrounding trees offered no solution to reach the fruit either.

Furious at the cruel irony, she grabbed the stalk, as high as she could, and dropped her weight. It bent over, and she crawled hand over hand along the trunk toward her meal. A loud crack resonated, and the plant snapped and toppled over. Lily fell to her knees at the fruit, plucked the one with the most amount of yellow skin, and twisted it free. She sniffed it first, inhaling the fresh, tropical lusciousness.

She drilled her thumbs into the outer skin until the fruit split open and after scooping out the seeds, she devoured it in seconds.

Two juicy fruits later, her stomach was painfully full, and she lay on the ground and stared up to the treetops. A light breeze caught the leaves and shimmered them in the filtered sunshine. Raising her right foot, she elevated it on the trunk of a tree. The throbbing in her ankle had become her constant companion, but propping it up did little to ease the painful beat.

She rolled her head from side to side and, attempting to release a knot in her neck, she held the stretch. Her eyes settled on a straight piece of wood in the distance. Easing up on her elbow, she peered at it and gasped as she realized what it was. A cross.

She hobbled over to it.

What the hell is that doing out here by itself? It's in the middle of nowhere.

It was tilted at an angle, rustic and weathered. She knelt down and tried to read the inscription carved into the wood, but nature had obliterated the words.

Her brain went into overdrive. *Why was someone buried in this remote location?* A horrid thought careened through her mind. *If I die out here, no one would bury me.*

Am I destined to become animal food?

She pictured her poor family, never finding out what happened to her. Her quest to the middle of the Mexican jungle suddenly seemed incredibly foolish.

For a fleeting second, she thought of abandoning her search for Carter and continuing on downstream. But as quickly as the idea entered her mind, she dismissed it. She had no doubt Carter wouldn't stop looking for her, and she was determined to do the same.

Saddened by the isolation of the lone cross, she restored it upright. Satisfied it was secure again, she pushed to go and her heart nearly stopped at what she saw. Another cross was just six feet away, also tilted on an angle. This one had a small necklace draped across the middle bar. She limped over and ran her fingers beneath the small turquoise beads that'd been threaded along a leather strap. The necklace was tiny—too small to fit her neck at least. Her heart squeezed as she contemplated whether it was a child's necklace.

Her hand went to her throat as she saw yet another cross to her left. She scanned the area more thoroughly and spied cross after cross, dotted amongst the vegetation.

"What on earth happened here?" The words whispered off her lips as she went to study the next cross. This one had a miniature cross carved into the top of the wood, but other than that, there were no other discernible carvings.

The next one had wire wrapped around the two pieces of wood, holding the cross in place. Each cross was slightly different and were obviously handmade. She found one under the shelter of a large, sprawling tree. It had remnants of flakey blue paint on the cross bar, and as she leaned in closer, she noticed chunky letters engraved into the wood. The paint, trapped in the carving, made it legible.

She deciphered it as *Rosa Maria 4 Augusta 1980.*

"What happened to you, Rosa Maria?"

There were seventeen crosses in total, but only one provided a discernable inscription.

The scene was both creepy and serene. Her mind drifted to

Carter. *He'd love to photograph this.* With that thought, she returned to the river's edge to blow her leaf whistle.

Still no reply.

Lily plucked another papaya from the felled tree, but this time as she ate, she savored every single bite. It was delicious and sweet, and exactly what she needed.

Ready to get moving again, she picked the remaining three papayas, and with no way to carry them, she tucked her shirt into her shorts and fed the fruits down her top distributing them evenly around her torso.

She hobbled to the river's edge, blew on her whistle again, and after listening for a response and receiving none, she continued counting her paces and traveled upstream.

The sun was high in the sky, beaming heat and light upon her with equal intensity. Stifling humidity had sweat trickling down her back and underarms, and she longed to stop and rest along the riverbank, but she pushed on regardless, eating the fruits as she went.

She'd only reached forty paces when the scenery did change. And dramatically too. A river of caked mud had long ago carved a brutal gash through the jungle, bringing with it fallen trees, giant rocks, and anything else that'd been in its path.

Lily climbed onto the dried mud and ate her last papaya as she trod across the rubble expanse. All sorts of bits and pieces had been caught in the mudslide. She found splintered planks of wood, twisted metal, and two coins, both dated 1972. She spied the remains of a mangled pushbike, shredded clothing, and heaps of other objects she didn't recognize. The only item she kept was a bent fork that might come in handy.

About halfway across, the sun, which was now far over the other side of the river, reflected off something on the ground. Her breath hitched as she approached. The sun's rays were bouncing off the side mirror of an old car that was nearly fully submerged. The car's roof was riddled with rust, suggesting that it had been there a very long time.

Were those graves for the people who died in this landslide?

It was impossible to fathom how anybody who'd been swept up in the muddy avalanche would've even been found. The remote location would've hampered search and rescue attempts too.

Lost without a trace. *Is that to be my fate too?*

Casting the rotten thought aside, she stopped to blow on her leaf whistle.

A new sound echoed through the jungle and her heart skipped a beat.

She blew again and the reply was instant.

Yes. Her heart slammed into her chest. *Could it be the men with guns?*

No! It has to be Carter. I know it is!

Chapter Nineteen

"Carter. I'm here." Lily stumbled over in the rush to move forward and fell to her knees. Ignoring the new affront to her flesh, she cupped her hands to her mouth to project her voice, and yelled until her throat burned. "Carter!"

"Lily!"

Tears pooled in her eyes. "Carter. I'm here." She climbed to her feet and waved her arms like crazy. "Carter."

"Lily." He sounded far away. "Lily."

A flash of movement across the river caught her eye and she shielded the sun with her hand. "Carter. Carter, I'm over here."

He stepped out from the tree line and his beaming smile, while welcome relief, failed to mask how pale and weak he looked. "Thank God. You're alive," he yelled across the river.

Something wasn't right. The way he stood, gripping a branch, favoring one leg. *He's in agony.* "You're hurt."

"Boy, am I glad to see you." He ignored her comment.

"You too." Tears tickled her cheeks and she flicked them away and hobbled to the river's edge. "What do we do now?" Just the thought of getting in that water again made her stomach turn.

Carter dropped her pack to the ground, and she nearly crumbled at the sight. She wasn't sure she'd ever see it again.

He cupped his hands around his mouth. "I'll swim to you. Okay?"

His weakened state was as clear as if he'd been standing right before her. "Okay, Lily?"

"Are you sure? It's dangerous."

"I'm a strong swimmer. I'll be fine." He limped to the river, proving her suspicions.

She wanted to beg him not to do it, but at the same time couldn't think of an alternative solution.

"It'll drag me downriver," he yelled across the torrent. "You walk downstream, and when I get there, I'll walk upstream to you. Okay?"

She recalled the swirling water and being hurled along, completely at the mercy of its powerful force. Her heart pounded in her chest. She wanted to stop him but at the same time, they had no choice. "Okay," she finally said.

When he picked up the backpack, her mind screeched to a halt. It was a burden he didn't need. As much as she wanted it, she wanted him more. "Carter?" she yelled.

"Yo?"

"Leave the pack."

He did a double take. "Are you fucking kidding me? I've dragged it this far. It's coming with me now."

She couldn't tell if he was angry or joking. "You don't have to."

"I bloody well do. Now, start walking that way." He pointed downstream. "Go on, I'm watching."

She chuckled at his bossiness. "You sound like one of my brothers."

"Good."

She reached for her makeshift crutch, clutched it with her fingers, and hobbled forward.

"Jesus, Lily, you're hurt!"

"No, no. It's nothing."

"It doesn't look like nothing."

"Just a bruised ankle. I'll be fine."

"Wait there. I'll come to you."

"I'll be okay."

"For God's sake, Lily. Will you just do as you're told?"

She clenched her jaw, and the two of them stared in a Mexican standoff until Lily succumbed to his demands. "All right! But hurry up and get in the water before the sun sets."

Even from this distance she heard him huff. "Okay, Tiger Lily, keep your pants on."

She held her breath as he shuffled to the water's edge. Her heart leapt to her throat when he splashed in. He kicked once and the current whipped him away. Within seconds, he was gone.

Despite his instructions, Lily scurried to follow him, but tumbled to her hands and knees again. Howling at the pain, she forced back the agony, got to her feet and carried on.

Each step was a rushed repeat of the one before, and it seemed like forever before she'd scrambled off the rubble and returned to the rotting jungle floor. She went back to counting her steps, waiting until she hit a hundred before she stopped to whistle each time.

As the sun slipped behind the trees on the opposite riverbank and darkness consumed what little light there was left, a niggling fear that Carter hadn't made it ate at her like acid.

She didn't stop for water.

She didn't stop to rest.

It was just good foot in front of bad foot and repeat.

Suddenly Carter appeared, sodden, pale, and gaunt. She dropped her stick crutch and hopped to him. He dropped the backpack and hobbled to her.

She clutched her arms around him, and he pulled her to his chest. Both of them talked and cried at the same time.

"I thought I'd lost you," he said.

"I was so scared you were gone," she said.

Their mouths met in a heated kiss that said everything. *I want. I need.* She opened her lips and his tongue slipped into her mouth to dance a lustful tango. She tugged at his buttons, undoing them as quickly as her fingers could go. Her hands found his chest, and she glided her palms over his chiseled torso.

He pulled back, distress marring his face. "Sorry. Oh God." His breathing was erratic. His wide eyes looked horrified. "I shouldn't have done that."

"What?" She frowned. "Kissed me?"

"Yes, it's . . . it's . . ."

"It's what, Carter? I wanted it too. We kissed each other."

He blinked. Frowned. Looked completely lost for words.

"What? Tell me." She shoved her fists on her hips, waiting. She thought they had something. Something special. The question she'd asked at Agulinta flashed into her mind. "You're married, aren't you?" She thrust her chin at him.

His shoulders slumped.

"Answer me."

He blinked at her. "It's not that easy, Lily."

"It's a yes-or-no question."

"Please, Lily, I promise I'll tell you. Let's get a campsite sorted for the night and then I'll tell you my whole shitty story."

His candid response and pleading eyes had her rage simmering. "Okay, but you promised."

As he nodded, a pained look rippled across his face. She glanced down to his legs and noticed a dark stain on his shorts. "What'd you do to your hip?"

He cleared his throat, but failed to elaborate.

God damn it, he's debating over whether or not to answer.

She shook her head. "Forget it. You can tell me about that later too. Let's find somewhere to camp." Lily grabbed her pack, flung the strap over her shoulder, turned her back on Carter, hobbled to her makeshift crutch, and limped away.

She would've marched away if she could.

As the monkeys started their howling ritual to announce the onset of nightfall, she settled on an area a couple of feet away from the river. Its flat ground and broad expanse made it ideal. She set about unpacking the contents of her bag and sighed with relief at the sight of her father's journal. It was soaking wet, but intact, and she was confident that once dry, it'd still be legible.

As she plucked items from her pack and laid them around her, she wondered if Carter had looked through the journal, or her notebook. Once he turned up, she had every intention of asking him.

She unclipped the sodden sleeping bag from her pack, unrolled it, and was about to hang it over the branch of a nearby tree when she heard Carter's heavy footfalls. Turning his way, she gasped at the sight of him.

Sweat flooded his forehead, a ghostly hue colored his skin, and the dark stain on his shorts could only be blood.

"Jesus!" She limped to his side and touched his cheek; the fire burning beneath had her gasping. "You're burning up. Come on, sit."

Ignoring the pain in her ankle, she placed her hands on his shoulders and guided him to the clearing. His camera strap lay crossways over his shoulder; she unhooked it and put it down. Glancing around for a place for Carter to sit, she spied the sleeping bag. It was wet, but at least it'd be clean. She spread it out, then placed her hand on Carter's elbow. "Hey, come on. . . sit here."

Tears glistened his eyes and he sucked the air through his teeth as she helped him to the ground. He curled to sit on his right buttock.

She knelt at his side. A trickle of sweat rolled from his temple down his cheek and disappeared into his beard. Carter, however, didn't move.

A monkey screeched right overhead, making her jump. It also made her realize just how dark it was getting. She needed to get a fire going before she couldn't see a damn thing.

She leaned forward and kissed Carter's forehead. "Stay here and rest a bit. I'll get a few things sorted." Handing him the water bottle, she stood.

She gathered a pile of sticks and dry grass and threw a fire together. The flames grabbed quickly and she dragged over a large log and rolled it onto the blaze.

Water was next. Clutching her water bottle, she hobbled to the river and filled it. But even as she pushed the bottle below the surface to fill, she realized she had a problem. Without their saucepan, she had no way to boil it.

She limped back to Carter, checked his forehead, and recoiled at the heat. A fever had taken hold. "I need to look at this wound. Can you lie back? I'll have to take your pants off."

He huffed. "No peeking." He made a guttural sound, but Lily couldn't decide if it was a laugh or a whimper.

She cupped his cheek. "I won't peek. I promise."

After lowering him to the sleeping bag, she spied the hole in his shorts. Her breath caught. "Jesus, Carter, you've been shot!"

He blinked slowly and simply nodded, as if it were an everyday occurrence.

A cold sweat prickled her forehead as she unbuttoned his pants, lowered the zip and peeled them open. Her heart pounded at the sight of the blood-soaked bandage wrapped around his hip and thigh.

As much as she didn't want to, she had to look at the wound to see how bad it was.

She touched his shoulder and their eyes met. The green in his irises had dulled, their usual spark gone, replaced instead with a blaze of fear that drove dread up her spine. "I'm going to take your shorts off now."

"No peeking." His gravelly words sounded painful, and she wondered if he knew he'd repeated himself.

She chuckled, attempting to lighten the mood. "I'll peek if I want to." Her joke went unanswered, and his silence was as loud as if he was screaming.

Hooking her thumbs into the waistband of his shorts, she wriggled them down inch by inch. He worked with her, raising his hips slightly and pushing with his hands. Once removed, she didn't peek as she positioned his shorts over his groin and he put his hand on top, holding them in place. That simple move had her believing he was going to be just fine.

She undid the butterfly clips and unrolled the bandage.

Acid burned her stomach when she finally revealed his bloodied flesh. The wound in his butt cheek was a fairly neat, yet charred circle, as was the exit wound at the front of his hip. Dark purple bruising colored the swollen flesh, marking the trajectory of the bullet beneath his skin.

"Carter, I need to clean this. Do you understand?"

He turned his head her way; his eyes were blank, and he seemed to look right through her. She shuddered and, swallowing back the lump in her throat, she stood.

Upending the rest of the items from the backpack onto the end of the sleeping bag, the first-aid kit was the first thing she saw. She opened it and was surprised to find everything dry. After rummaging through the medications, she popped out two pain-relief tablets.

She crawled to Carter and touched his cheek. "Carter, hey. I need you to take some tablets."

He groaned in response. She tugged him toward her so his head rested on her chest. "Open your mouth." She held the bottle at his lips and when they parted, she popped both pills on his tongue and poured in water. He swallowed loud enough for her to hear. "Good, that's good. Now, lie down. I'll be back in a sec."

He lay on his good side and she tried to ignore the blood oozing from both his buttock and his hip. While she'd never seen a bullet wound before, she'd seen enough injuries while growing up on a farm to know she needed to stop the bleeding.

But how?

Returning to the backpack contents, she hoped for inspiration. The pocket knife was promising, with its selection of knives, minia-ture tweezers, scissors, a nail file, and even a toothpick, but in the end, she gave up on it.

Think, Lily, think!

Carter groaned.

"I'm coming, Carter. Hang in there."

She picked up the large metal spoon. *I could heat water in that.* But it'd take forever to sterilize a decent quantity. Conceding that she had no choice, she poured water to the brim of the spoon and held it over the fire.

It seemed like an eternity before bubbles appeared at the surface. However, as it hit the boiling point, she realized she had nothing to pour it into. She clenched her jaw at her lack of planning.

They had two water bottles. What she needed to do was fill one up with water from the river, and use the other one to hold the boiled water. She placed the spoon of already boiling water onto the sleeping bag, emptied Carter's water into her bottle, and tipped out the remainder.

Securing Carter's bottle between her feet, she picked up the spoon by the handle, but it'd stuck to the sleeping bag. Grumbling under her breath, she tugged at the metal handle and it released, splashing out hot water and the spoon tumbled from her hand and landed on her calf.

"Shit!" She flung the metal off and gasped at yet another injury to her already battered body. The hot spoon had burned a red oblong shape onto her flesh. Tears welled in her eyes and a sense of uselessness gripped her. Her chin dimpled, and when a lump formed in her throat, she let the tears trickle down her cheeks and fall onto her chest.

Through the blur, she looked at the sleeping bag. The hot spoon had melted the synthetic fabric. An idea whizzed through her brain, and she jolted upright. Flicking the tears from her cheeks, she blinked at the melted fabric. It was a sign. Her father's favorite saying, *everything happens for a reason*, raced through her mind.

The hot spoon would be the perfect tool to cauterize the wound. She turned the utensil over in her hands. *Can I do this?*

Lily had branded cattle before. Growing up on a farm had taught her many things that'd required her to step out of her comfort zone. Skinning animals was one of them. But what she planned to do now, was about to hit the top of that list.

Carter moaned, and that was the incentive she needed.

Lily picked the melted plastic off the spoon and washed it. She then held it over the fire. Her heart was set to explode as the flames licked the underside of the spoon. The trick would be to get the metal hot enough that it'd cauterize the wound, but not so hot that it'd burn the nerve endings. Her fingers trembled and she willed them to stop.

In the blink of an eye, the metal changed from silver to red, and aware that she'd taken it too far, she tugged it from the heat. Resting it against a log to cool down, she went to Carter. "Hey, can you hear me?"

If he did, he didn't show it.

"I'm sorry, but I need to cauterize your wounds. It'll hurt a little." She scrunched up her face. "Actually, a lot."

His chin rested on his chest, and his breathing bordered on snoring. *Is he in a coma?* With the amount of pain he was about to experience, that'd be a good thing. The biggest problem she could envisage was getting Carter to stay still when she touched that blazing spoon to his hip. It'd hurt like hell, and even though he looked unconscious, he was sure to snap out of it once the pain hit.

The only way to do it would be to sit on him, pinning him down when she applied the hot metal. It would be like branding cattle, brutal yet necessary, quick and efficient. Touch the skin for one to two seconds, seal the blood vessels, and stop the bleeding. Simple.

Her stomach flipped and burned like acid in a blender, as she went through the process in her mind. Heat the spoon, sit on Carter, touch the metal to his wound, count to two, lift. Done.

A wave of nausea barreled through her. She panted, mouth open, fighting the revulsion and forcing herself to focus.

Once the queasiness subsided, she treated the situation like she did any project—with professional efficiency. Mentally, she pictured the process and repeated it over and over, to ensure she understood the action plan.

As her shirt was the only dry clothing around, she removed it and laid it beside Carter. Kneeling at his side, she placed her hand on his cheek, feeling the fire beneath. "Carter, I'm going to fix you now." Lily leaned forward and kissed his lips. "I'm sorry."

With tears stinging her eyes, she curled his forearm over his chest and rolled him fully onto his side. On the farm, she'd handled many baby calves who hadn't survived their birth. Carter's lifeless body felt the same. Lily shoved that shitty thought aside and gritted her teeth. "You are not going to die."

Carter's eyes were closed, his breathing settled. He looked peaceful. For now.

She stood up and spotted his camera. Her thoughts went to Carter's passion to document everything in pictures. Would he photograph this? She decided he would, and although it sickened her, she lifted the camera, removed the lens cap and water dribbled out. *Shit! That can't be good.*

She fiddled with a few buttons and was surprised when it whirred to life. The display, however, failed to light up. Glancing through the lens, bubbles of water were in the view finger. Unsure if the camera would even work, she still clicked off a series of photos. First shots were of Carter, at a distance, taking in his whole body, and followed by a few close-ups of his hideous wounds. Unable to procrastinate a moment more, she placed the camera aside and, sick to her stomach, she reached for the spoon.

She held it over the flames and counted out the seconds—*one, two, three.* At twenty-one seconds, it glowed red. She pulled it from the fire and poured water over it until it was cold again.

She sucked in a huge breath and let it out in one big gush. "This is it."

With a firm grip on the spoon, she held it on the flames again and counted. *One. Two. Three.* At eighteen, she pulled it from the flames, hopped to Carter, knelt on his back, and pressed the blazing spoon to his flesh.

Carter bucked violently and let out a bloodcurdling scream.

Chapter Twenty

"I'm sorry." The words drifted to Carter like they'd been spoken from a great distance and carried across the wind. His body was heavy, held down by the weight of the world, and yet he felt comfortable, at peace. He wanted to stay right where he was forever. His wife appeared before him, smiling her young, beautiful smile. She tucked a lock of her frizzy blond hair behind her ear in the signature move he loved.

"I'm sorry." The words came to him again, but Penny's lips didn't move. Something touched his cheek—her hand maybe—and when he felt a touch to his lips, he opened them.

He coughed, choking on the liquid that'd been poured into his mouth. His eyes shot open, and he blinked at the darkness. A woman appeared over him; her face shrouded in darkness.

"Hey there." Her words were soft and gentle.

He blinked and blinked some more, trying to make sense of what he saw. For several horrifying minutes, he didn't know where he was, but then it came back to him, every sordid horror. The gunmen. The fear. The pain.

"Are you okay?" Lily touched his arm.

"No." He tried to swallow, but it was like swallowing rusty coins.

"Here. Have some water."

She cupped his neck, and when the bottle touched his lips, he gulped at the cool liquid. After several mouthfuls, he tried to sit, but gasped at the agony. He recalled the pain, the burning fire that pierced his skin, the torture that consumed his whole body. He remembered being shot, and glanced at the bandage wrapped around his hip. But it wasn't the blazing bullet that'd hurt the most —it was something else.

"What'd you do to me?"

She sat back and scrunched up her nose. "I cauterized your wounds."

He did a double take. "You what?"

"I used a hot spoon to stop the bleeding." She said it as if she were talking about a pair of shoes.

"Ummm, wha—" His jaw dropped. "How'd you know what to do?"

She shrugged. "I figured it was like branding cattle."

"Branding cattle?" He jerked back. "What the fuck?"

She shrugged and tilted her head. "It stopped the bleeding."

"Jesus!" Swallowing, Carter glared the bandage. No blood seeped through.

"It worked well, actually." She grinned.

"How long was I out for?"

She shifted on her knees. "Two days."

"What?"

"Two days," she repeated.

His mind spun like a tornado. "I was unconscious for two days?"

"In and out. Yes."

"Holy shit! What'd you do?"

"Looked after your sorry ass." She smiled.

A laugh tumbled from his throat. "I really am lost in the jungle with Lara Croft." He tried to sit up, and both pain and his foggy brain made it an effort.

Lily reached around his back and helped him. His head swooned, and his eyes had trouble catching up. He blinked a few times, trying to get his brain to focus. It wasn't quite night yet, but it wasn't far off. Yellow and orange flames leapt into the air from the nearby fire. He cocked his head at what hovered over the flames. Two forked branches were propped up on either side of the fire and a stick crossed between them like a bridge. Threaded onto that stick was a skinned lizard.

"What the hell's that?"

"Dinner. I hope you're hungry. It took me all day to catch that one."

As his jaw dropped, his stomach growled, and he shared his gaze between the roasting lizard and Lily. "Holy shit! You're incredible."

She nodded, accepting the compliment. "Your timing is perfect. It's nearly ready." Lily strode to the fire and for someone who'd been living alone in the middle of the jungle, she sure looked fresh. Her hair was tied up in a ponytail that curved over her shoulder. Her face radiated health and cleanliness. She looked better than some women he'd met who'd spent the night in a fancy hotel.

In horrid contrast, he was certain the dreadful smell he whiffed frequently was his own body odor.

As she strolled toward the fire, he recalled her injured ankle and the reality of how much time had lapsed while he was unconscious hit home. "Your foot's better."

"Yeah. Still a bit bruised, but at least I can get my boot on now."

He glanced around the campsite, taking in the changes Lily had made. A few items of clothing and one of the bandages hung heavily off branches of a nearby tree, presumably after being washed.

Twigs and branches were gathered in a pile to the left of the fire, ready to toss on when required. A long stick with her pocketknife strapped to the end of it, fashioning a spear, was resting against the tree. "Is that how you caught dinner?"

"No. I caught it in a pit trap."

Carter shook his head. He had some catching up to do.

As Lily removed the lizard from the fire and began carving the meat off it, he pushed up from the ground. Fighting both dizziness and nausea, he stumbled to the far side of the nearest tree to relieve himself.

Returning to the fire, he sat and Lily handed him a large green leaf with another leaf on top that'd been rolled up like a spring roll. "I hope you like it, it's my latest specialty."

"What is it?"

"Iguana and papaya, wrapped in a banana leaf."

Carter had given up being surprised. It seemed Lily was capable of anything.

She sat at his side and, as he ate his first mouthful, he felt her gaze upon him, maybe anticipating his response.

"Yum, Lily. This's bloody delicious." He ate it within seconds, and the two more she made him. They finished off with two small ripe bananas from a bunch Lily had apparently found yesterday.

Soon, he couldn't eat another thing. "I can't believe what you've done."

"Necessity is an amazing motivator."

He turned to her, and for the first time since he woke, he noticed weariness in her eyes. "Most people would've died out here."

Her shoulders sagged at little. "I thought you were going to."

He wanted to wrap his arms around her, pull her to his chest, and hold her there until all the angst evaporated. Her breasts rose and fell with heavy breaths, and for a fleeting second, he considered that she might want the same thing too. "I'm glad I didn't."

Her eyelids closed and opened slowly. "Me, too, because you still have a promise to keep."

He blinked and frowned. "I do?"

"Yep. You promised to tell me your marital status, although it seems you'll do anything to get out of answering my question."

He laughed. "Really?"

She turned to him, shifted her long legs to sit cross-legged, and folded her arms over her chest. "So, come on, I've been waiting for days."

"Now?"

"Why not?"

"Don't we have stuff to do?"

"Nope."

Carter could think of a million things they should be doing, the first being *find civilization*. But, at the very least, he owed Lily his life. And the answer to her question. "I don't suppose you have any coffee?"

She slapped his shoulder. "Stop stalling."

"Okay." He ran his hand over his beard and tugged it at his chin. The last thing he wanted to do was talk about his marriage. He hadn't spoken his wife's name in years.

"Carter!"

"Okay. Okay." He sighed and offered his palms in a peace gesture. "I met Penny at a party when I was seventeen. We were challenging each other to drinking shots." He shook his head at how stupid it sounded. "Anyway, sometime in the small hours of the morning, we went outside, smoked a joint, and the next day, we woke in each other's arms on the beach. Neither of us had any recall of what happened after we reached the sand."

Carter plucked a stick from the fire and gazed at the red coals blazing the tip.

"Nine months later, we had our daughter, Stephanie."

Out the corner of his eye, Lily shifted her position, but she didn't say anything.

"Penny and I married two weeks before Stephanie was born. Both of us had only just turned eighteen. At the time, it was right thing to do."

"Oh, Carter." The sorrow in her voice carved a chunk from his heart.

He sighed. Going all the way back to those years was like sifting through fog. Initially he'd planned on skimming over the details, but for some reason, once he started, he couldn't stop. Maybe it was because Lily was a good listener. Maybe it was because it was good to talk about it. Maybe he just wanted her to know everything about him. It didn't matter why—it just seemed right.

"Penny and I carried on partying. Every night was a crazy concoction of booze and drugs. We moved on from marijuana to heavier drugs, and the days went by in a blur. I was a fully functioning drug addict. I worked as a bricklayer during the day, was captain of my rugby league team, and went home every night to Penny and Stephanie. And the drugs."

He glanced at Lily, expecting to see disgust in her eyes, but it wasn't there. He was confused by what he saw—was it disbelief, or encouragement? He turned back to the fire; certain the disgust would come.

"Penny and I fought endlessly. Jealousy and apathy were the main motivations. Her days were consumed with a crying baby and utter boredom. She was literally going stir-crazy. In the space of a year, Penny changed from a vibrant, sexy, seventeen-year-old bursting with life, to an overburdened, lonely, frustrated mother."

"Poor thing," Lily said. "You were both so young."

He tossed the stick into the fire. "I was nineteen when I was arrested for drug possession. My lawyer had assured me that as it was my first offense, I'd get off with a warning, but the judge had other ideas. I guess he wanted to make an example of me. Father, rugby captain—I had so many reasons why I shouldn't have been doing what I was doing." Carter cringed, recalling the thump of the judge's gavel smashing down on the wooden bench. "I went to jail for six months."

"Oh, my God. That's terrible. What about Penny?"

"She came to see me a couple of times, but it wasn't the place to bring a baby. I told her not to come. We wrote to each other and she sent me photos of Stephanie at all the phases I missed. Crawling. . . her first steps. . . her first words."

He rolled his shoulders, working the stiffness from his neck as he tried to summarise his history. Never before had he told anyone the real story. But right now, in the middle of the suffocating jungle, with the most beautiful woman in the world, the moment seemed right.

No matter what the consequences, he wanted her to know.

He squeezed his eyes shut, steeling himself for her reaction. When he opened them, a sense of calm washed over him and he sighed. "When I was released from jail, I returned home and . . . it didn't take me long to . . ." Pausing, the dancing flames seemed to burn right into his brain.

"To what?" Lily touched his leg and he met her gaze.

Pain pulsed behind his eyes over what he was about to say. "Almost the second, I got home I returned to the drugs. Heavily. Penny and I fought all the time." Carter sipped water. "I was home just seven days when I woke to a screaming baby and a note on Penny's pillow. All it said was *I'm sorry.*"

"She left you? And Stephanie?"

He nodded and stared into the fire. But it wasn't the flames he saw, it was Penny's tear-filled eyes. "Yeah. She vanished and it was my fault. None of her family or friends ever saw her again—or at least that's what they told me. I looked for her for years, before I gave up. I was just shy of twenty when I became a drug-addicted, single dad. So"—he turned to Lily—"to answer your question. I *am* still married, but I haven't seen my wife in decades."

"How could she abandon her daughter like that?"

He shrugged. "Because of me. I don't blame her. We were never meant to be together, never meant to have a child, never should've been a family. Our relationship was poison. But I would never have let Stephanie go, and Penny knew that. Somewhere out there, Penny's living a new life. She doesn't need me turning up and ruining that."

She let her breath out in a big huff. "And Stephanie?"

He smiled as he thought of his beautiful, confident daughter. "She was my motivation to sober up. I gave up the drugs and parties and tried to be the best dad I could. I love her to pieces. She's strong. Incredibly independent. I raised her on my own, and it was the best thing I did in my whole life."

A moan tumbled off Lily's lips. "Where is she now?"

"She's engaged, happy. Living in Sydney. She's an interior decorator and loves it."

Lily frowned, and he anticipated what she wanted to ask. "Steph needed her freedom, but with me hanging around she was never going to get it." He shrugged. "I didn't want her making the same mistakes Penny and I did. I was what you'd call an overprotective parent. So, she tapped into the one thing she knew would set her free. . . my passion for photography. She bought me a ticket to

Rome and told me to go explore the world. I did, and I haven't been back since."

"She sounds incredible."

He nodded. "She is."

The fire crackled as they fell into comfortable silence.

"Thanks for telling me about your wife and daughter."

Once again, a powerful urge to embrace Lily took over, but he fought it. "Is it my turn to ask a tricky question?"

"Nope." She jumped to her feet. "It's time to get ready for the night. The sun's setting."

"Hey, that's not fair."

"Is too." With long purposeful strides, she vanished into the bushes.

"Oh, come on!" Carter raised his arms in protest, and got a whiff of his armpit. The offending stench was enough to make his eyes water. The tumbling river was right there, begging him to slip in.

Lily returned with a handful of twigs and tossed them on top of the pile already beside the fire.

He remembered her toiletries bag in her pack. "I don't suppose you have any soap?"

"Sure do."

His body almost melted at her response.

Lily handed him her wet pack and a towel. "Help yourself."

"Thanks."

After hobbling to the edge of the river, he stripped out of the clothes he'd been wearing for days and unravelled the bandage. The scab over the bullet wound was thick, black, and crusty. The surrounding skin was red and inflamed and the long, swollen bruise that joined the two wounds together was a ghastly purple hue.

After examining it all, though, he realized he was lucky.

It was just a flesh wound. And by the way he could move his leg, he assumed he had no real damage. It hurt like hell, but he was pretty sure once the bruising and swelling was gone, he'd be fine. Thanks to Lily. For the life of him, he couldn't imagine doing what she'd done. He was lucky she had, though, or he might not be here now.

A small eddy at the water's edge was perfect to step into, and he used the soap to scrub away days of dirt, sweat and grime. Ducking his head into the river, he relished the feel of the cold water on his scalp. Rubbing the soap into his matted curls, he tried to finger-comb out the knots, but it was impossible and for the first time in years, he wanted to cut his hair.

Carter gave his clothes a thorough wash but as they were the only gear he had, he wrapped the towel around his hips and shuffled back to the fire.

"Feel better?"

"Like a new man." He returned her toiletries bag to the backpack.

"You smell like a new man too." She grinned.

"Yeah, sorry about that."

"Here." She handed him a large three-pronged branch that'd been resting against a nearby tree. "Place your shorts on this and hold it over the heat. They'll be dry in no time."

Carter stood by the fire drying his clothes, and as darkness gradually consumed them, he tried not to stare at Lily while she fussed about the campsite. "Did you hear any choppers or anything over the last couple of days?"

Lily tossed a decent-sized log onto the fire. "No. Nothing at all."

"Hmmm, what are we . . . four days overdue?"

"Five, I think. Maybe six. I've lost count."

"Would your family be worried by now?"

"They'd be beyond worried. I wouldn't be surprised if my brothers have called the marines, the army, and the president to beg them to look for me."

For a fleeting second, Carter wondered who'd look for him. The answer was easy . . . no one. He'd made a habit of going off the grid. It'd never bothered him, until now. But it wasn't him he was worried about—it was Lily. She needed to get back to her family. "So, I guess we'll follow the river downstream again tomorrow."

She let out a quick breath. "Well, actually . . . there's something

I need to do first."

"Huh? What? Before being rescued, you mean?"

She stood on the opposite side of the fire and the golden glow gave her flawless skin a gilded hue. "The other day, when I was dragged down the river, I saw something."

"Something? What?"

"A cave."

He crumbled to the ground, groaning at the pain in his hip, and sat sideways on the good side of his butt. "There'll be plenty more caves, I'm sure."

She crinkled her nose. "Not like this one."

Carter wished she'd just say whatever was on her mind. Since he'd met her, every time she'd avoided his questions it'd involved that journal. "Does it have anything to do with that leather journal in your pack?"

Anger simmered across her irises. "Did you look through it?"

He glared up at her. "No."

She blinked, as if assessing how much truth there was to his answer. "Oh . . . well."

"Lily, tell me why it's so important. You wouldn't give up your pack, even when the bullets were flying. Was that because of the journal?"

She sucked her bottom lip, then, presumably with a decision made, she went to her pack, which was nestled at the base of a giant tree. Lily returned to the fire with the journal and her notebook, and sat at his side with her long legs stretched out before her. After a deep sigh, she placed her hands on the leather-bound book as though she was drawing energy from it.

"After my father died, Mom and I were sorting through his things and we found a beat-up suitcase at the back of Dad's tool shed. He loved that shed and would tinker around out there for hours. We thought we'd find nothing but rusty old tools and half-finished projects." She sighed. "We'd never seen the suitcase before." As she blinked at him, he had the impression she was fighting tears. "Or the things inside it."

Carter picked up a stick and poked at the fire, trying to remain as casual as possible to encourage Lily to continue.

"Mom and Dad had a whirlwind courtship." She half huffed; half giggled. "They'd been dating just four weeks before he proposed. Can you imagine that?"

Carter shook his head. "Pfft. No."

"Me neither. They were married thirty-five years when he passed away."

"Wow. Must've been made for each other."

"Maybe. Dad was the consummate family man. Everything he did, he did for his family." She lowered her gaze to the journal. "Which is why the contents of that suitcase were all the more shocking."

"What was in it?"

"Besides this, it also had a collection of old photos. The pictures told a story none of my family had ever heard before. If my grand-parents knew, they're denying it."

Carter waited out the silence, allowing Lily to decide when to continue talking.

"Apparently Dad had a wife and daughter before he met Mom, but for some reason he kept their details a secret."

Carter frowned. "Not everyone wants to talk about failed marriages. Especially not with a new wife."

"Mom would've loved him regardless. But the fact that Dad had a daughter that he never mentioned was a brutal secret that Mom still struggles with."

The urge to put his arm around Lily's shoulders and draw her to his chest was so strong he almost ached for it. Instead, he reached out and placed his hand over her forearm. "There can be dozens of reasons why someone would leave their family."

She turned to him and, in this light, her irises were the color of a stormy sky, blue and green struggling against each other. "Not Dad. He'd never do that." Her voice was loaded with conviction. "But we may never know who they were or what happened to them."

Lily ran her hand over the journal, prompting Carter to point at it. "Did any of the photos survive?"

She frowned at him. "What?"

"The water. I guess the photos are all ruined now."

"Oh." Her eyes lit up. "I didn't bring the photos. This's Dad's journal." She unwrapped the leather strap from around the book.

As her delicate fingers undid the knot and rolled the strap off, he wondered how someone so angelic could also be a master at survival techniques. He cast the thought aside as she opened the book and carefully peeled the wet pages over.

"It doesn't look too damaged."

She shook her head. "I think being wound up so tight helped. It'll never be the same, but at least it's still legible." She opened the book about one third of the way in, and then turned a few more pages. Finally, she stopped and held the journal toward him. "Recognize anything?"

"Holy shit! Agulinta."

"That's exactly what I thought the first time I saw it on the news."

He cocked his head. "But how can that be? Agulinta's been hidden for thousands of years. If your dad found it, why the hell didn't he tell anyone?"

"That's what I've been questioning ever since the discovery. Now you know why I wanted to see it for myself."

He nodded. It also explained why she wanted to cling to the journal. It was her only proof her father had discovered it first. "Hey"—he clicked his fingers— "I've got pictures on my camera. Let me grab it."

"Oh, umm." She clutched his wrist. "I'm sorry to tell you this, but the display isn't working."

"Ahhh shit!"

"The camera seemed to work though, at least it did when I took photos of your bullet wounds."

He raised his eyebrows, as he pictured his butt on full display.

"What? I thought you'd be happy about that." She beamed. "Hey, it might win an award."

"Yeah, right, I don't think anyone wants to see my ass."

"It's not all bad." A cheeky twinkle in her eyes confused him.

Blazing heat rolled up his neck and he needed to change the conversation, stat. "Anyway, it's a pity we can't check the photos to compare the real statue with your father's drawing."

"Ahhh." Lily poked him in the bicep. "Lucky for you, then, I did a few drawings myself."

She reached for her own notebook. The pages were crinkled and swollen, displaying significant water damage compared to her father's journal. After peeling over a few pages, she held her book open toward Carter. "See."

She'd drawn a rough outline of the circular structure that stood at the entrance to the site. At the far left, to the top of the circle, Lily had sketched in intricate pencil strokes the carved stone pictures. Her detail was exquisite. "Wow. You're really talented. Just like your father, hey?"

"Thank you."

"I mean it, Lily. Even the way you've drawn this vine and how it's attached to the stone. It's amazing." Carter tapped the sketch. "Hang on a minute. If your father had actually been to this statue at Agulinta, then surely it would've been covered in vines, too."

"Exactly. I wondered if you'd work that out."

He turned to her and cocked his eyebrow. "Oh, really?"

"Yes, really."

She looked very sure of herself, and Carter had a feeling he was going to regret asking his next question. "Okay. I'll bite. What's the significance?"

"Well, you know the cave I mentioned earlier?"

"Yes."

"I didn't get a great look, and I was nearly drowning at the time—"

"Spit it out."

She poked her tongue out at him. "I think the outside of the cave has been carved just like this." She pointed at her father's drawing.

"Let me get this straight. Rather than head toward a rescue, you'd prefer to head toward men with guns, to check out this cave."

"Yep. I knew you'd understand." Lily's grin was magnificent.

Chapter Twenty-One

The charred lizard meat was strangely chewy and crunchy at the same time, but it filled the void in Lily's stomach that'd been throbbing for hours. Carter, however, seemed to be struggling with the food and Lily couldn't decide if he wasn't hungry or couldn't focus. Every move he made was met with a groan or a wince, and each time he looked at Lily he appeared a bit woozy.

The sun had set swiftly, triggering a boisterous cacophony from insects and monkeys in the blackness around them. Carter's silence, though, seemed amplified against the noisy backdrop. He hadn't mentioned the cave since she'd handed him the meal, but she was fairly certain they were in for a heated discussion before sunrise tomorrow.

"How's your meal?" She'd waited until he'd chewed through his final mouthful.

He nodded, but didn't lift his gaze from the fire. "Good, thanks."

"Are you warm enough?" Her question was ludicrous, considering the temperature had barely dropped since night set in.

He cocked his head, indicating he too thought it was a stupid question. "Yep."

She fell silent, conscious that he might need time to himself. He'd been through a lot in the last couple of days, and God only knew what he was thinking. She'd hardly slept while Carter was unconscious, and struggled to keep her eyes open. Carter, however, stared wide-eyed at the fire, and she wondered if he was seeing something other than the flames.

His silence ticked on so long that she was near bursting when he finally cleared his throat and tossed the branch he'd been fiddling with into the fire. "How'd you light the fire, anyway?"

"Oh, lucky for me, I had a lighter in my pocket. My brother made me buy three lighters before I got on my first plane. I'm so glad I listened."

"Your brothers look out for you, hey?"

"Yeah. We're pretty close. Mom had seven babies in seven years, so we all grew up together."

"Wow, that's full on. Raising one child was hard enough."

Lily shrugged. "I guess I wouldn't know any different. We all pitched in where we could, and my brothers all worked on the farm." She stifled a yawn and her head swooned with overtired dizziness. "Sorry. Early night for me tonight."

"I've slept for days, so I'm not even close to tired. Go on, you get some sleep."

The temptation was too good to refuse. "Thanks." She stood and fussed about with their one and only sleeping bag, stretching it out to capacity. One of her T-shirts, filled with leaves and grass, constituted her pillow. After she crawled onto the makeshift bed, her body melted onto the padding. Shuffling around to get comfortable, she finally lay on her side to watch Carter poke another stick into the blaze. The flames danced over his eyes and she wondered what he was thinking. His wild hair and bushy beard framed his face in a messy halo, and she tried to imagine him clean shaven. His features were captivating. Hardened. Handsome. Yet nearly hidden.

"It's good to have you back, Carter."

His gaze met hers, and his eyes were a baffling mix of relief and worry. "It's nice to be back."

She nodded. "Good night."

"Have a good sleep."

As she closed her eyes and listened to the snap and crackle of the fire, she was reminded of one of the most valuable lessons she'd learned during her many camping adventures with her brothers; spending quality time in good company was priceless.

"Hey, Carter?"

"Yeah?"

"I made room for you on the sleeping bag."

He turned to her, blinking. "Oh. Okay. Thanks. Good night."

She closed her eyes, and despite being lost in the middle the Mexican jungle, she felt completely at ease as the serenity lulled her to sleep.

A STRANGE WHIRRING SOUND DRAGGED LILY FROM SLEEP. Flickering her eyes open, it took a couple of moments to comprehend that she'd slept right through to dawn. She sat up, stretched her back, and looked around for Carter. He was off to her left, peering through the camera, which she now realized was the source of the noise that'd woken her.

"Is it working?"

"Oh, morning. How'd you sleep?"

"Perfect. Slept right through."

"Good. I think the camera's okay. Hopefully it's just the LCD that's stuffed. Won't know till we look at the photos."

"Did you sleep?"

"A bit, but that's okay. I wasn't tired."

Lily trotted off into the bushes to relieve herself. When she returned, they had a quick feed of leftover lizard meat, before Lily set about packing up their gear. "You ready to go check out that cave?"

His shoulders sagged. "You're not gonna take no for an answer, are you?"

"No." She chuckled. "I can do this by myself—"

"Like hell. We're sticking together from now on." Despite his overgrown beard, his clamped jaw was evident.

"Okay, but just remember, you agreed to this."

He winced as he stood and dusted off his pants. "Yeah, under duress."

Lily zipped up the pack. "Well, as a matter of fact, I predict you'll be thanking me pretty soon."

"Really?" His sarcasm was obvious.

She hoisted the pack onto her back. "Yep, really." Without a response from him, she set off with the torrential river on her right and the jungle on her left. She kept her pace a bit slower for Carter's sake, and his crunching footsteps were the only indication he was behind her.

She'd counted one hundred and sixty-two steps, before she sighted the little graveyard she'd seen a few days ago. "Here you go." She turned to him and played her hand over the expanse as if showing off an art display. "You can thank me, now."

His brow furrowed, but his eyes followed the direction of her hand and bulged.

"I thought you might like to photograph these. There are seventeen crosses, and look at the one under the tree—it has an inscription."

Carter fiddled with his camera. "Wow. This's so unexpected. What do you think happened?"

"I have a fair idea. I'll show you why next. Go have a look at that one." She pointed under the sprawling tree. "I think they were all buried in 1980."

Carter palmed the tree trunk for support and kneeled beside the small cross. He peered through his lens, and set off a round of clicks. Her only hope, and no doubt Carter's too, was that the camera did these graves justice.

She sat beneath the shady tree, pulled her knees to her chest, and watched him take his time with each and every one of the crosses. His attention to detail was fascinating as he moved around, presumably trying to get the angle and the light just perfect.

It seemed like hours before he returned to her. "This's so bizarre, out here in the middle of nowhere."

She jumped to her feet and slapped his arm. "Come on, then. I'll show you what I think happened." Lily pulled her pack on. "Can you keep up, old man?"

He blinked at her. "Old man!"

"Well, you won't tell me your age, so I assume you're so old that you're embarrassed to tell me."

He rolled his eyes.

She hooked her thumbs into her pack. "Try to keep up."

Giggling to herself, she strode off again. It wouldn't be long before she reached the landslide, so she didn't worry about waiting.

Barely forty steps later, she arrived at the edge of the rubble. Carter was only a few paces behind her. Sweat trickled from his forehead and rolled from his temples. She instantly felt guilty for leaving him. "Here, let me help." She reached for his elbow.

"I'm okay."

"You're not okay. You look terrible."

He waggled his head. "Jeez, thanks."

"I don't mean it like that. You're recovering from surgery."

"Thanks to you."

"Stop whining. I saved your life." She thumped his shoulder. "Come and check this out." Lily stepped up onto the dried mud and tried to retrace her steps to the rusted car she'd found the other day. "See this? I think this landslide may've wiped out a village."

His jaw dropped and he squinted at the wreck. "Holy shit."

"There's all sorts of bits and pieces. I found coins, a bike, utensils . . ."

Carter shielded the sun with his hand to glance up the river of mud that'd cut through the jungle. "Wow, this would've come down the valley a million miles an hour and taken out everything in its path."

"And everyone." She sighed. "So sad."

After a few moments' silence, his eyes flicked her way and he touched her shoulder. "Come on. Let's check out this cave of yours. The sooner we get going again, the better."

She smiled. "Okay. Good plan."

Picking their way across the debris, each of them gathered bits and pieces from the rubble. Lily kept some of the items she found: a few more coins, a necklace with a small heart on it, and a metal plate that might come in handy.

Once across, she stepped right back into dense jungle and, in an attempt to ignore her grumbling stomach, she counted her steps again. It only took thirty-seven steps before she found what she'd been looking for. She couldn't believe how close she'd been to it the other day. Maybe her friend Fate had wanted Carter to be with her. She smiled at that thought.

"Wow. Look at that!" Carter's eyes nearly jumped from their sockets.

His reaction matched hers. "I told you."

"It's in the middle of nowhere."

"I know."

Relief, elation, and curiosity tangled her emotions and she fought back tears. For several days, she'd entertained the notion that what she'd seen while floating on the river had been a figment of her weary mind.

It wasn't.

The cave was exactly as she'd remembered it. It was also exactly like the drawing in her father's journal. With the downward spiral this journey had taken, she'd begun to believe she'd never find the answers she was looking for. Agulinta hadn't provided any, but maybe this cave would.

They stood on the river embankment, and several feet below was the gaping hole that appeared to have been cut into the side of a cliff. The cave entrance was almost a perfect circle, like the end of a pipe. It was recessed back from the river, and angled such that the only way to see it was to either be right on top of it, like they were now, or from the river.

Water oozed out of the cave, giving the appearance of a liquid tongue. It collected in a small, remarkably round pool, before meeting up with the river and catching in the current. Around the border of the cave were intricate motifs, carved into stone, just like they'd seen on the donut statue at Agulinta.

Lily eased to the edge of the embankment, eager to get a closer look and frowned at a few indents carved into the rock wall below her. They appeared to be regular in shape and spacing, and curved down in a steady slope toward the cave entrance, about twenty feet below.

Like a bolt of lightning, she understood what they were. Steps. "Look! I think this is a way to get down to the cave."

Carter hobbled to her side and leaned over the edge. "I think you're right."

Her heart skipped a few beats. "Excellent, let's get down there."

"You're kidding, right? He scowled at her. These steps could be thousands of years old. One slip and you're back in that water." He pointed at the torrent, apparently reminding her it was there.

She swallowed a lump of trepidation. "I'm willing to risk it."

"You're psycho, woman. You know that, don't you?"

But despite what he'd said, the resignation in his tone proved that she'd won that debate. She just hoped she didn't regret it.

"Leave the bag. We'll come back for it."

She cocked her head.

"Lily! It's not negotiable. We're just going *there*"—he pointed down to the cave for effect—"and your pack will still be *here* when we return."

Accepting defeat, Lily shrugged the pack off, wedged it upright, zipped it open, and removed her father's journal, her notebook, and a pencil.

"Really?" Carter scowled.

"I need my notes. Don't worry, I'll carry them."

"Wow, you really are stubborn."

"I like to think of it as determined." She pushed her shirt into her shorts and fed the books down her top. Shoving the pencil into her shorts pocket, she was surprised to find a lighter wedged inside. She must've put it there when she lit the fire last night. For some reason, it made her feel safe, like a little lucky charm.

Although . . . not much of this trip had proved lucky so far.

Carter grumbled under his breath and then, wincing loudly, curled his leg over the ledge and shoved his foot into the first carved nook. "I'll go first."

"Obviously."

He rolled his eyes. "Really? Any other wise-ass comments?"

"Shush, you're ruining the moment." She giggled.

Shaking his head, he gaped at her. "You're impossible, Liliana."

She glared at him. "I wish I'd never told you that name."

"I like it." His grin was magnificent.

"Well, I don't. Stop talking. You need to concentrate."

"Yes, boss."

Once he was halfway along, Lily gripped onto weeds to lower herself over the edge and guided her foot into the first nook. Gripping onto whatever she could, she followed Carter's lead, rock climbing down. It must've taken a miraculous engineering feat to carve these steps into the rock face. Some were no bigger than a foothold, some were as big as a toaster. It was slow going, but with every glance she made toward the cave entrance she knew it'd be worth it.

Soon, she was below ground level, and her cheek brushed against the jagged rocks as she clutched at the wall. It was painstakingly slow, and her legs trembled when she finally stepped onto a rock platform with Carter.

"Lily, this has to be Mayan. Look at these carvings." He glided his fingers over the left-hand curve of the circle perimeter.

"I agree." She eased up beside him and traced her finger over the length of a snake engraved into the stone. "It's very similar to the one at Agulinta."

"Similar . . . I'd say it's the same." Carter tugged at his camera and clicked off a series of photos. "Look at the detail in this carving. See the king's robe? Wow!"

"Yes, I sketched that exact lintel up at Agulinta. The detail is exqui—"

"Shhh." He clutched her wrist.

"What?"

They stared at each other, blinking. Listening.

A regular beat emerged over the rumble of the river. "A motor. We're saved!" She wanted to jump for joy, but Carter's reaction wasn't the same.

In fact, it was the opposite. "What?"

"What if it's not?" His whisper was loaded with dread. "It might be the drug guys."

Her heart stammered. She shot a glance to the river and back again. "What do we do?"

His grip on her wrist deepened. "It's too late to climb up. We have to hide in there."

Her eyes shot to the cave. The liquid tongue. The black hole. The dark pool.

The motor grew louder by the second.

Her stomach twisted at the thought of swimming, but the fear in Carter's eyes was even greater. "We could wait and see."

"We can't risk it. We're trapped like sitting ducks. Now, move."

She froze. Fear ripped up her spine like razor blades.

"Shit, come on! You need to swim. I'll help you."

"I can't—"

He clutched her cheeks, drawing her eyes to his. "Listen to me, you can do this."

"Okay." She swallowed. "Please don't let me go."

"I won't. I promise."

As he grasped her hand, voices drifted over the water. Men's voices. Loud voices. Angry too. Her heart set to explode.

Carter went first; sitting on the edge, he dangled his legs into the pool. "Come on." He patted the rock ledge.

Despite the scream in her head, she followed his lead. There was no time to remove her shoes and the cold water seeped in, filling them up, weighing them down.

"All you have to do is hold your breath and kick. Ready?"

Although she was a thousand breaths away from ready, she nodded.

They pushed off, and she gulped a mouthful of air, just before she plunged below the water. Kicking for the surface, Carter squeezed her arm, urging her forward. "Kick, Lily."

Her mouth alternated between above and below the waterline with each kick and she swallowed equal amounts of water and air.

Pushing against the current, he dragged her into the mouth of the cave, and they slipped out of the sunlight.

With the darkness came a change in temperature, and the cool water had goose pimples tickling her arms. The motor engine grew louder, and the farther they went into the cave, the more it echoed off the walls.

Her heart pounded in her ears as she fought the slight current and struggled to keep her head above the water. To the left-hand side of the cave was a rock ledge, elevated a couple of inches above water. She was nearly out of breath by the time they reached it. When she had her grip, Carter brushed the hair from her eyes. "You okay?" he whispered.

She nodded.

"Good." He held his finger to his lips. "Shhh." The fear in his eyes equally matched her own panic.

Gripping onto the ledge took effort, and she continued kicking, trying to keep afloat. Her boot punted something, and she searched for it again. To her relief, a small outcrop allowed her to place her weight onto it, taking the pressure off her hands.

The motor grew louder, and the voices bellowed over the noise. Their accent was Mexican. They seemed irritated, or excited, or maybe they were just trying to talk over the rumble of the engine. Every sound bounced off the cave walls, amplifying and multiplying them equally. Her pounding heart added to the racket.

At one point, she believed the men were right outside the cave, but then just as quickly, they faded away.

As the seconds ticked by, the fear that'd gripped her dissolved, and she turned her attention to the cave. It was about the size of her one-bedroom apartment. The roof was higher though, and dozens of stalactites dangled from it like gnarly fingers. She followed the line of sunlight filtering through the entrance and her heart just about stopped at what she saw. In a little nook, to her right, two crosses were positioned high on the wall, as if displayed on a mantelpiece. A glint of light captured her attention, and she squinted to see what it was. From this distance, it looked like a necklace curled around the cross.

"That was close." Carter ran his hand over his wet hair and turned to her. "Come on, let's get out of here before they come back."

"Can I have a quick look at those first?" She pointed over his shoulder.

He glanced that way, then turned back to her with fury in his eyes. "You can't be serious!"

"I'll only take a second. Please."

He clamped his jaw. "Jesus! Okay, but be quick."

Using the foothold beneath the water, she put both hands on the ledge and pushed up. But she misjudged the height and cried out as she fell back into the water.

Carter gripped her biceps and dragged her to the surface.

Gasping for air, she clawed for the ledge again.

He chuckled. "What was that?"

Lily spluttered. "Shit."

"Here, I'll help you. Hold on."

Carter launched himself up and out, with an agility that belied both his injuries and days without decent food. He reached for her hand, and using her foothold, she literally walked up the wall and out of the water.

She wiped her hair from her eyes. "Thank you." The books inside her shirt weighed heavily, and she lifted her top to release them. It'd be a miracle if they survived yet another dunking. Her notebook was finished, and with a heavy heart she tossed the sodden mess onto the cave floor. The journal was still wound up tightly with the leather strap, and she resisted opening it, hopeful it'd be okay once it dried out.

Carter placed his hand on her lower back. "Come on, let's see what we've got, and get outta here."

She placed the journal down and together they walked toward the tiny nook.

The crosses were propped up on a couple of rocks that jutted out from the wall. Each cross was unique and just like the other ones they'd found, looked handmade.

A small silver necklace with a crescent moon was draped around the cross on the left, and Lily leaned in to read the inscription. Compared to the ones outside in the weather, this one was easily visible. *Alejandra Maria Bennett.*

Her breath caught. Tears stung her eyes.

She read the next line. *23 Julio 1976–4 Augusta 1980.* A shiver ran up her spine.

"What's wrong?" Carter touched her arm.

"She was just four years old?"

"This other person was twenty-six."

Lily turned to him. "I think they may've been my dad's first wife and child."

His eyebrows bounced together. "The chances of that—"

"Bennett is my surname."

He blinked a few times and his mouth dropped. "Oh. Then . . ." Carter didn't finish his sentence, and Lily turned back to the cross to read the second inscription. "Rosa Maria Bennett."

She frowned at something white wedged beneath Rosa's cross. Swallowing back the lump in her throat, she lifted the wood and her heart leapt to her throat. It was an old photo. "Oh my God, Carter. That's my dad." She pointed at the man in the photo. He had his arm around a woman who wore a long white dress with large flowers decorated across the bottom. Her arms were draped over the shoulders of a little girl who stood in front of her. All three of them were smiling.

"Are you sure? It was a long time ago."

"Some of the photos in that suitcase I told you about must've been taken on the same day. The lady is wearing the same dress in each of them."

"Oh." He sighed.

"I can't believe this. I wonder if they died in that mudslide." Her voice quivered. "Why didn't he ever tell anyone?"

Carter curled his arm across her shoulder and a sob caught in her throat. "It probably hurt too much."

"But what was he doing here in Mexico?"

Carter didn't respond.

Lily flipped the photo over, and there, in her father's distinct handwriting, he'd written *I will love you forever, my beautiful Rose*. Tears tumbled down Lily's cheeks, and Carter wrapped his arms around her. Days of built-up emotion burst, releasing floodgates and, as she cried into his chest, he squeezed her to his body and glided his hand over her hair.

When she could cry no more, she sucked in a shaky breath and withdrew from him. "Sorry, I just . . . I can't believe this."

"No need to say sorry. It must be such a shock. At least he didn't abandon his wife and child."

She nodded. "I feel awful for thinking that."

"Hey, you weren't to know. He was the one who'd kept the photos, but chose to keep their existence a secret."

She stewed over his comment for a moment, then nodded. "I wonder why?"

Lily lifted the cross again and replaced the picture in its original position. "Can you take a photo for me, please?"

"I can try, but my poor camera has just had another swim, so no guarantees." Carter twisted off the lens cap and hissed through his teeth when water poured out. "That's not good."

"I know, but give it a go."

Carter clicked a button and the camera made an odd grating noise. He looked through the viewfinder. "Damn it. The autofocus has broken. I'll have to do it manually and thrust they're in focus." Looking through the viewfinder, he adjusted the lens and snapped a few photos. "Hopefully, they turn out."

He clipped the lens cap back into place and turned the camera to rest on his hip. "Come on." He reached for her hand. "Let's get out of . . ." His eyes darted to the entrance, and he tugged Lily down.

"Shhh." He held his finger to his lips.

The roar of the boat was as sudden as it was loud.

"Shit!" Carter tugged Lily toward the back of the cave.

The engine noise boomed, bouncing off the rock walls. She pictured them right outside the cave and her heart thundered in her chest.

"*Que es eso.*" A man's deep voice reverberated off the rock walls.

"*Se parece a una bolsa.*"

"Oh shit! They found your pack. Come on!" Carter's fingers strangled her wrist as he hauled her around the side of the nook and into the blackness.

"My journal." She wrenched her wrist free and raced to the book. Gripping it like her life depended on it, she raced back to Carter. He seized her hand like she was a naughty child and tugged her forward. There was enough light to see where they were going, but with each step the roof lowered and the walls crept in.

"*Que están en la cueva.*"

"Fucking hell! They're coming." Carter spoke in forced whispers.

They shuffled deeper into the blackness, and with each step it became apparent they were about to run out of hiding space. Hunching beneath the cave roof, Lily shoved the journal back down her top. Soon, they had no choice but to crawl and Lily felt every little rock beneath her already battered knees.

"We know you in there." The heavily accented voice bellowed from the entrance. "Come out and we won't hurt you."

Fear was a nasty vise gripping Lily's chest, as she cowered in the shadows and squeezed Carter's hand in a death grip. An explosion of sound and brilliant flashes lit up the cave as bullets shredded the walls around them.

"Get down!" Carter hurled her to the ground.

Lily hit the floor. Her cheek smashed onto the jagged rocks. She tugged her hands over her ears and squeezed her eyes shut.

The deadly onslaught continued.

Rocks tumbled onto her as bullets ricocheted off the wall just above her head. Something fell on her arm, and she snapped her eyes open. It was the remains of a stalactite.

"Last chance or we come get you." Despite the man's ominous voice, he said it in a singsong manner, as if he were playing a child's game.

"What do we do?" Lily whispered.

Carter turned to her, and when she met his wide-eyed gaze, she knew she was going to die.

Chapter Twenty-Two

C arter had been in terrifying situations before. It was basically impossible to avoid them when traveling to remote places in the world where people were just as likely to cut off an arm for a watch, as they were to welcome you into their homes for dinner. But he'd never been as scared as he was right now.

He knew exactly why—Liliana.

The panic raging in her beautiful blue eyes nearly cut his heart in two.

He'd give his life to save her. And that's exactly what he planned to do.

"Listen to me. I'm going to swim out to those guys. You stay right where you are."

"No, they'll kill you." She clutched his arm.

"No, they won't. I'll reason with them. Explain what we're doing and it'll be okay."

"We'll go together then." The muscles in her jaw clenched.

"No." He spoke in hushed tones. "These are bad men, and bad men do bad things to women."

Her eyes bulged and the panic he'd seen moments ago tripled.

"Just stay here."

She shook her head. "No, I won't let you go." Her bottom lip quivered.

The lump in Carter's throat made it nearly impossible to breathe. He leaned forward to kiss her forehead, but she tilted her head upward and their mouths met. Her tears and whimpers mingled with her soft lips. He clutched his fingers behind her neck and released his lips, drawing her to his chest. "You're going to live. Your survival skills will get you through. Promise me you'll make it back to your family."

She shook her head.

"Promise me, Lily. I need it."

"*Estamos llegando ahora.*" The menacing voice cut through the void.

"They're coming Lily." He put his forehead to hers. He wanted to hold her, to place his body between her and the evil outside. He wanted to tell her how he felt. And, in that moment, he did. "I love you."

Tears pooled in her eyes. Spilled over her cheeks. "I love you too." For a long, heartbreaking moment, neither of them moved.

Suddenly, she pulled back. Her face changed from sorrow to determination. She flicked tears from her eyes. "The current."

"What?"

"The water is coming from somewhere. We can swim upstream."

He blinked at her. "You can't swim."

"I bloody well will."

One of the Mexicans started whistling a melody, as if chasing people with armed weapons was child's play.

"Come on." She slapped his arm.

Wincing at the pain in his hip, he cupped her cheek and leaned in for a quick kiss. "I won't let you go."

"I know."

He reached for her hand and their fingers entwined as if they'd done it hundreds of times before. Rounding the corner, the cave darkened even more. A narrow ledge skirted the side of the stream, but the low roof made it impossible to stand upright. Hunched over, they inched along hand in hand.

"When we get in the water, roll onto your back and kick below the surface, so you don't splash," he whispered.

"Okay."

"You have to trust me."

"I do." She squeezed his hand.

When he couldn't go a step farther, he released her grip. "Stay there." He turned to face the wall, and gradually lowered himself into the water, careful not to splash. With a grip on the ledge, he reached for her. "Okay, in you come."

An explosion cut through the serenity, bullets slamming into the rocks around them, showering them in debris.

Lily squealed and crouched down with her hands over her ears.

Carter reached up to her, desperate to pull her to safety.

She clutched his outstretched arms and then pushed off the ledge. When she didn't falter, he fell in love with her just that little bit more. As instructed, she rolled onto her back. Her whole body trembled, and she held her breath.

"You can breathe, Lily."

She inhaled, and despite the minimal light, terror glistened her eyes. He wanted to wrap his arms around her, to tell her everything would be okay.

Bullets ricocheted above them and a severed stalactite fell from the roof and glanced off his cheek. Ignoring the slice of pain, he hooked one hand under her arm and over her chest, then pushed off the wall. "Kick."

The current was minimal, and with both of them kicking, they were able to move upstream quicker than he'd anticipated.

"*Esperaremos por ti.*" The men yelled their intention to wait for them.

Carter imagined the men sitting with their weapons in their laps, stalking their prey on the little platform near the two crosses.

If this stream didn't play out the way they'd hoped, Lily and Carter were trapped.

With each kick into the darkness, he prayed for a miracle. He'd only prayed once before, when his daughter had hit her head while skateboarding and knocked herself unconscious. It'd worked then— he hoped like hell it worked now.

Every once in a while, gunfire shattered the silence. Each time, they sounded farther away. He stayed close to the ledge, too close sometimes, causing his leg to brush against the rocky, moss-covered wall. Lily's fortitude drove him forward. Her ragged breaths proved how much effort she put into her kicking.

Soon, what little light they had disappeared altogether, consuming them with complete darkness. The men's voices continued to echo around them but, as they faded in the distance, Carter was certain they hadn't followed.

The peacefulness of the tunnel was surreal, like swimming in a dream. Only their breathing and the occasional shout and gunfire from the men broke the silence. The water lapped at the edges in a soothing melody, boosting his spirits. Soon, Carter was entertaining the idea that maybe, just maybe, they'd get out of this alive.

"Do you think they're gone?" Lily whispered.

Carter debated telling her what the man had said. "Not yet." He decided on the truth. They were in this together. "They're waiting for us to come out."

"Shit! Well, I hope this tunnel actually goes somewhere."

"Me too."

Carter used the wall to guide him, and he felt rather than saw the roof closing in on them. His stomach twisted in hunger-pang hell. His bullet wounds throbbed with each kick. The slice on his cheek from the falling debris stung. But he'd do it all over again, if Lily asked. His mind drifted to those four little words Lily had spoken. *I love you too.* With her voice humming through his brain, he wondered if they'd been a knee-jerk response to his proclamation of love. Was it because she thought she was going to die? Dire situations could provoke bizarre actions. He'd witnessed that firsthand in Somalia, and not just once.

"Do you think we can stop for a bit?" Her whisper lured him from his swirling thoughts.

"Oh, sure." Carter reached out and found a rock jutting from the wall for him to hold onto. "Here, hold on to me."

Lily rolled onto her front, reached for his arm, and released a deep sigh. "This's crazy."

"Yeah. Just remember it was your idea."

"Oh, really?" He imagined the surprised look on her face. "Well, don't let me regret saving your ass."

"Is that what you call it?" He chuckled.

"Yep. That's my story and I'm sticking to it."

He curled his arm around her waist and tugged her closer. "Thank you for saving me."

"You're welcome."

It was a long while before their breathing returned to normal and peace returned.

"How long do you think we've been in here?" Lily asked.

"No idea. Feels like hours."

"They're never going to give up, are they?"

"Probably not."

She groaned. "My passport was in my pack, you know."

"We'll get you another passport."

"It's not that, Carter. They'll know my name. What if this is just the beginning? What if they chase us forever?"

Her voice grew shrill and he pulled her to his chest. "It's okay, don't worry, that's not going to happen."

"You don't know that. They could come after my family too."

"Shhh, we can't think about that now. We need to focus on getting out of here first."

Her shaky breath confirmed she was crying, and he squeezed her tighter. "It's okay, babe, we're going to make it."

She sniffed and when she reached up, he assumed she was wiping tears from her eyes.

He'd do anything to keep her safe, but right now, getting out of this tunnel was first priority. "Ready to get going again?"

"Okay." Her voice quivered, but she didn't hesitate to push back from him.

With no choice but to continue into the blackness, he just hoped there was a way out of this mess, or they'd be floating back to certain death.

Ignoring his numerous aches and pains, he kicked off the wall. Lily rolled onto her back, and together they pushed upstream. Little lights dotting the cave roof offered some relief from the black void.

"What are these lights?" Lily asked.

"Glow worms. They use their light to attract mosquitos and other insects."

"They're beautiful."

Soon, the entire roof was full of them, illuminating the blackness like little stars. The cave became a stunning, starry night.

Something brushed Carter's shoulder.

Lily jumped; she'd felt it too. "What was that?" Her voice hit panic mode.

"Not sure."

It happened again and he reached for it, running his hand over the rough, rubbery thread. "It's a tree root."

"Is that good?"

"No idea. I haven't been lost in an underwater cave before."

She huffed. "You're not helping."

"Shhh. What's that?"

A strange clicking noise echoed about them and the hairs on Carter's neck bristled. "Shit!"

"What?" Lily reached for his shoulder.

"Bats, I think."

"Bats!" Her voice escalated a notch.

"Shhh. We don't want to scare them."

"Scare *them*? What about me?"

An explosion of flapping wings filled the air.

"Hold your breath," Carter yelled over the noise. He heard her inhale and pulled Lily below the water with him. With one arm around her, and the other on the wall, he struggled to keep them beneath the surface. Lily curled around, clutched his waist, and although he couldn't see, she must've also grabbed the wall because it became slightly easier.

He counted out the seconds, but soon Lily began to wriggle.

Long before he wanted to surface, she punched his chest, and he had no choice but to let the wall go and resurface.

The bats had gone and the sound of gunfire had Carter imagining the creatures had reached the cave entrance. The gunmen were probably taking pot shots.

A root brushed his shoulder, and Carter jumped before he brushed it away.

"Are they all gone?" Lily asked.

"Possibly."

"I hope so."

A new noise caught his attention, and he squeezed her arm. "Can you hear that?"

"What?" Her voice was high-pitched.

A dull roar rumbled from farther up the tunnel. "I think it's a waterfall."

"A waterfall? But how can that be?"

"Not sure. But let's find out."

With each passing minute, the roar grew louder. Up ahead, a small light appeared like a pinprick and for a couple of heart-pounding seconds, he contemplated that it might be a flashlight. "There's light up ahead."

"Where?" Lily rolled to see over her shoulder. "Oh, yeah."

As it grew, their tunnel brightened, showing the cave roof, barely inches above their heads.

Her kicking increased, and soon the cave was bright enough that he saw every dangling root and the dozens of spiders hanging in their webs.

He couldn't get out of the water quick enough.

As the tunnel lightened, it also grew narrower, and soon it became impossible to swim side by side.

"Lily, roll over and grab my waist."

She did as instructed, and with Lily holding on, they exited the tunnel and entered a large natural well. Squinting against the glare, he made his way to the center of the pool.

Sheer walls rose up twenty feet around them, and on the opposite side, a waterfall tumbled into their pool. Long tree roots dangled down from the surface to touch the water in a lush natural curtain.

"Oh, wow. What is this?"

"It's a cenote," Carter said. "A natural sinkhole. They're dotted all over the Yucatan."

"It's beautiful."

The water was crystal clear and an interesting jade color. Little black fish darted about in front of him, as he made his way to one of the dangling roots. "Here, hang on to this."

Lily let go of him and the two of them clutched at the roots. "What happened to your cheek? You're bleeding."

He touched his cheek. "Got hit by a shattered stalactite." He glanced at his bloody fingers. "It's nothing. Are you okay?"

"Well"—she cocked her head—"other than starving, tired, sore, and scared, I'm fine."

He wanted to press his lips to hers, to feel her flesh against his, to take away all the pain. Instead, he smiled. "Excellent, me too."

He turned his attention to their new dilemma. Scanning the cenote walls for an escape route, Carter had a sinking feeling they were still as trapped as they'd been way back at the cave entrance.

"Let me have a scout around."

"Okay. I'll just hang here then, shall I?"

"Yes." Chuckling, he kicked off and went to the closest edge of the well. The rock wall was a sheer cliff face, rising straight up and offering no footholds. As he swam around, looking for something that'd help them out, he welcomed the sunlight that streamed in like a flashlight beam.

"There are little fish in here." Lily giggled with childish delight.

By the time Carter finished paddling the circumference of the sinkhole, he had two conclusions.

Go up. Or go back.

Neither were good.

Chapter Twenty-Three

L ily was still trying to catch the little black fish when Carter returned to her at the hanging roots. But his worried expression confirmed what she'd already dreaded.

There was no easy escape.

His knuckles bulged as he strangled the roots. "We have two ways out of here. Back the way we came, or climb up these." He shook them for effect.

"Shit." Squinting against the glare, she followed the line of roots up to the surface. "I was hoping you wouldn't say that."

When she'd boarded the plane in Seattle, she'd promised herself that no matter how difficult things became in Mexico, she was determined to enjoy herself. That promise had been broken at least a dozen times since then. This was going to be another one.

Carter watched her; waiting for a response.

Finally, she huffed. "Wow. You sure know how to show a lady a good time."

Carter touched her shoulder. "That's the Liliana spirit."

"Do you want a punch in the nose?"

"Ha, just try it."

"Don't tempt me." She glanced up again. The roots were

thicker at the top and tapered thinner at the bottom. They were rubbery, textured like a carrot, and had little threads jutting out all over them. "So, how do we do this?"

He rattled his lips. "I guess we wrap our legs around and pull up with our hands."

"Do you think they'll hold our weight?"

"Of course."

Undecided if he was lying or not, she cocked an eyebrow. "Okay, off you go then."

"Right."

Carter didn't hesitate. His biceps bulged, his jaw clenched, and groaning, he reached up and pulled himself from the water hand over hand. His legs clamped and released the roots with each move. He was about five feet above her, when he fell.

Lily gasped as he splashed down beside her and she reached for him. "Are you okay?"

He shoved hair from his face. "Of course, I was coming back for you."

"Oh."

"Come on, your turn."

Forcing angst from her mind, she copied him by bundling four roots together beneath the water, wrapping her legs around them, and with all the energy she could muster, she hauled herself up.

It was like dragging a dead body from the water.

Carter matched her progress beside her. "You can do this." His words of encouragement were both welcome and annoying.

Lily was just three feet off the surface when she slipped and tumbled into the water screaming. A surge in the water and flurry of bubbles confirmed Carter had dropped in next to her.

She scrambled for the surface, clutched a root and brushed hair from her eyes.

"You okay?" Carter pushed another strand from her forehead.

She nodded.

"So, that was a good test. Now you know if you fall, you won't hurt yourself."

"No, I'll just drown instead."

He cupped her cheek. "No, you won't. I'll help you."

The concern in his eyes melted her heart. *I can do this. I have to. For both our sakes.*

Tendrils of long, wet hair clung to his face, and little droplets of water trapped in his beard, glistened in the light. His spectacular green eyes studied her. Really, truly looked at her. With no makeup, bruised, battered, and bitten, and hair all over the place, she must look dreadful.

Yet, he seemed to look past all that.

Carter was reaching into her soul.

Her heart fluttered. "Did you mean what you said back there?" The question had been on her mind since the second he'd said it.

His eyebrows drilled together. "Back where?"

"Back when those guys were shooting at us."

He tilted his head, and his features softened with a cheeky grin. "People tend to say crazy things when they're under extreme stress."

His twitching smile had her undecided on whether to be frustrated with him or accept that she'd half expected a similar response anyway. "You didn't answer my question."

He cupped her cheek, and leaning into his palm, she sighed and closed her eyes, feeling the warmth of his palm.

"When you get to the top, I'll give you your answer."

She snapped her eyes open. "You're mean."

"Nothing like a bit of motivation to get you moving."

"Oh, and drowning in a stupid well isn't enough."

"Obviously not. Come on, let's do this."

Steeling herself for another attempt, she clawed her way up. Her fingers bulged with the strain, and with each drag of her legs, coarse knots in the roots grazed her inner thighs. Her bruised ankle throbbed to a painful beat, her fingers screamed in agony, and, after several minutes, she paused, wrapping her arms and legs around the roots. Alternating hands, she released her grip so she could furl and unfurl them, trying to stimulate life back into each finger.

"Come on, Lily. You can do this."

"I can't!"

"That's it. Get angry."

"I am angry. Fucking angry!"

"Good, now use that."

Clamping her teeth, she reached upward. And that was when she fell again. She plunged into the water and came up punching at the surface. 'Shit! Shit! Shit!"

Carter dropped in beside her and she shook the roots like crazy. "This's stupid."

"It's our only way out."

She punched the water again. "Oh, and you don't think I know that? I'm just not strong enough."

He cocked his head. "You're the strongest woman I've ever met, and not just in physical strength. In determination too. I know you can do this."

His faith in her just about brought her to tears again. "My upper body just isn't strong enough."

"Let's take your boots off. It'll be less weight for you, and you can use your feet to grip."

A sob caught in her throat, but she fought it back. "Okay."

Carter brought her right boot to the surface. As he undid the laces, Lily studied the red welts on her hands. Blood oozed from a small flap of skin on her palm. If she didn't get up there soon, her hands and inner thighs were going to be ripped to shreds. She studied the pool edges, searching for somewhere she could at least stand and rest.

There wasn't one.

When Carter finished removing the second boot, she clenched her jaw. *This is it. Time to put everything into this climb, even if my fingers become bloody scraps of flesh.*

Carter tied the laces of her boots together and looped them around his neck. "Now, give me the book."

Lily closed her eyes and sighed. She'd hoped he'd forgotten about the journal. It was her final possession, and having it close to her chest had given some clarity to the insane journey she was on. With a dimpling chin, she conceded she was about to watch her father's lovingly crafted work sink to the bottom of an ancient well.

She reached into her shirt, withdrew the leather-bound journal and tears spilled from her eyes as she handed over.

To her amazement, he undid the top button on his shirt and fed the book down his collar.

Choked built-up emotion, she could hardly breathe. "Thank you."

"Hey." He wiped a tear from her cheek. "You can do this."

She nodded. "I know." She drove conviction into her voice. "I know I can."

"That's my girl."

My girl. She liked that.

Lily curled her socked feet around the root and noticed the difference right away. Not only did she have more grip, but she felt twenty pounds lighter. With each surge upwards, she grew more positive.

"That's it."

"I've got this."

"I know. I know you do, Tiger Lily."

Within minutes, they were halfway. Her stinging fingers begged her to stop, but she clenched her jaw and carried on, determined to make this the last time.

Something touched her hair, and she was shocked to see it was the overhang at the top. "I made it!"

"I knew you'd do it." His eyes glistened with joy and something else. Was it pride, or maybe desire?

She hung there, scrutinizing the thick grass and bushes that curled over the edge. "Now what?"

Carter's fearful expression confirmed he had no idea. "I'll go first. Don't move."

"Okay." He had no worries there; she'd hang there all night if she had to.

Carter unhooked her boots, hurled them over the ledge and they landed with a dull thud somewhere out of sight. Clutching the roots, her breath trapped in her throat and her heart thundered in her chest, as Carter inched over the threshold. Every muscle in his arms bulged and strained as he clawed hand over hand up the final precipice and let out a triumphant roar.

But her jubilation was quickly overridden with trepidation, as she accepted her turn was next.

Carter popped his head out overhead, grinning. "Hey there, what's a girl like you doing in a place like this?"

She rolled her eyes. "Just hanging around."

"Right then, let's get you up here."

Panic riddled her extremities, making her arms and legs tremble. The last two feet of this climb were going to be the hardest of all. If she fell from here, it was guaranteed to hurt.

She met Carter's pleading gaze and nodded.

"You can do this, Lily. Move your feet first, then reach up."

With a clamped jaw, she forced her feet to inch upward and squeezed them around the roots. Secure again, she reached up with her right hand, but the root was wedged into the overhang by her body weight. "I can't get my fingers under it."

"Grab my wrist." Carter leaned dangerously out, offering himself as a lifeline.

With one almighty thrust upward, she latched on to his wrist. But her feet slipped out from under her.

She screamed.

He clutched her forearm; fingers digging in like a vice.

Her heart exploded as she dangled twenty feet in the air.

Their eyes met. Fear blazed in his. "Grab on!"

Her heart thumped in her ears.

"Lily, you can do this." Carter's free hand reached for hers.

A trickle of water rolled down his forehead and caught in his lashes. "Lily. Look at me."

She did.

His eyes drilled into hers. "You can do this."

She clenched her jaw and thrust again. Their hands latched together. Using her feet, she clawed inch by inch, up and over. Carter dragged her the rest of the way, and the two of them flopped onto the ground, panting.

"We did it." Sheer exhaustion had her chin dimpling.

His breathing was erratic as he rolled over and crawled toward her. "I knew you would."

She curled her fingers around his neck and drew his lips to hers. Their ragged breaths mingled and as she closed her eyes, she allowed her body to take over. His lips parted and their tongues met in a delicious dance. She moaned, arched her back toward him, and his hand found her breast. Reaching for his shirt, she fumbled with the buttons to peel the wet fabric from his body and her journal tumbled out with a dull thud.

Revealed at last, she explored his torso, feeling every muscle with her greedy fingers. His nipples were rigid pebbles that she twirled her fingers around. Their kiss grew heated and Carter rolled her over so she was on top. In a flash, she pulled her shirt off, unclipped her bra and flung it aside.

With her eyes trained on his, Lily leaned forward, offering herself, and he obliged by sucking her breast into his mouth. Her wet hair fell forward, cascading about her face. When he moaned his approval across her hardened nipple, her insides clenched. The delicious sensation was something she hadn't felt in a very long time. Too long. She rolled her hips, grinding over the growing bulge in his shorts.

With a groan, Carter pushed on her shoulders, sitting her upright. "No, Lily," he gasped.

"What? What's wrong?"

"This . . . this isn't right."

With a cheeky grin, she glided her hips over his groin. "Feels right to me."

He shook his head. "No, it's not. You're half my age."

Lily feigned shock. "You're fifty-two?"

He rolled his eyes. "No, I'm not, but it's still not right."

Lily covered her breasts with her arm and pushed off him. "Bloody hell." She got to her feet, picked up her bra, shirt, and boots by the laces, and stormed away.

"Where're you going?"

"Away from you."

Chapter Twenty-Four

L ily's wet socks squelched underfoot as she stomped over the vegetation-cluttered jungle floor. Trees as high as skyscrapers towered above her, letting in little light. Her breasts wobbled with each angry step and, without breaking stride, she fished her bra from her handful of belongings and put it on.

She kept up her pace, pushing through giant leaves and tangles of vines that created living bridges between one tree and the next. Her mind slammed to her last boyfriend. He'd been adorable, the perfect catch, up until the moment they'd slept together, that is. From that moment on, she was no longer the object of his desire. He considered her conquered, and had moved swiftly on to his next target. That'd been nearly two years ago, but the wound to her heart was deep.

"Lily, wait. I'm sorry." Carter's voice filtered through the foliage.

A giant spider web, the size of a suitcase, blocked her path. It was perfectly constructed, symmetrical in every aspect and woven with intricate detail. Fortunately, the spider wasn't home. She dropped to her hands and knees and crawled beneath the web, and, as she popped up on the other side, she actually hoped Carter didn't see it until it was too late.

"You don't understand." Carter was still a distance away.

"Damn right, I don't," she yelled into the dense bushes.

"Shit!" Based on Carter's high-pitched cry, she assumed he'd reached the web. "Fucking hell, Lily, will you stop?"

Ignoring him, she put her shirt on and proceeded to do up the buttons. A rock underfoot jabbed her instep but, wincing at the pain, she carried on. Branches in her path were shoved aside and instantly bounced back after she pushed through. A monkey's screech had her looking to the trees in time to see it swing across several branches, following her trek through the jungle.

"Lily!" Carter's fingers wrapped around her bicep, halting her.

She spun to him and saw the fire in his eyes. "What?" Her jaw ached from clamping.

"Will you just stop?"

She put her hands on her hips and tried not to stare at the tangled spider web caught in his beard. "Okay. I've stopped. Now, what?"

He sighed and tilted his head to the side. "I'm sorry. I didn't mean to"—he paused as if searching for the right word—"hurt you."

"Yeah, well I've never been so embarrassed in my life." He reached for her arm, and she snatched it away. "Don't touch me."

"I didn't mean to embarrass you, it's just—"

"Just what?" she yelled. "You feel like a dirty old man."

"Lily, calm down."

She spun on her heel and strode away. "Don't tell me to fucking calm down!" She charged through the jungle, pushing past one plant after the next. Spiky bushes cut her arms and spindly branches whipped back, creating welts along her forearms. She didn't know where she was going, and she didn't care. It didn't matter anyway.

They were lost.

Her feet suffered from her furious pace, and her injured ankle throbbed like crazy. It wasn't long before she had no choice but to slow down.

A fallen log across her path was a blessing. She sat on it and unhooked her shoes from her neck. With the heavy boots on her lap, she alternated glances from the direction she came, looking for Carter, to the knot in her laces that she tried to undo.

She was tugging on her left boot when he appeared from behind the vegetation. His face was flushed, sweat dribbled from his temples, and his heavy breathing showed his exertion.

He eased up to her, sat on the log at her side, and cleared his throat. "Can we at least talk about it?"

She yanked her laces, pulling them tight. "What's there to talk about? You're obviously not interested."

"Oh, Lily, is that what you think? I'm so interested it scares the hell out of me." He fell to his knees and wriggled between her legs. "I've never met a woman like you." He put his hands on her waist. "I love you." His hazel eyes, the color of the churning sea during a storm, pierced hers.

Tears stung, her chin dimpled, but she fought the tempest, certain he had more to say. She swallowed. "But . . ."

He closed his eyes and sighed. "But . . . there's so many buts."

She held her palms open. "So, give them to me."

"We're in a crazy situation that's exposing raw emotions. What you're feeling may not be real." He paused, maybe anticipating her reaction, but she remained deadpan, waiting for him to continue.

"I'm old, a has-been. I have nothing to offer—hell, I don't even have a permanent address. My only asset is my camera, and now that's ruined."

"But you said you love me."

"I do. You're confident, funny, determined, interesting . . . stunning." He blinked up at her. "Do I need to go on?"

"Yes." She clamped her jaw.

He chuckled. "You're resourceful, smart . . . really smart, brave, and you have amazing boobies."

She burst out laughing. "Boobies? Who says boobies?"

"I love your laugh too."

She sighed as the shattered pieces of her heart molded back together. "Carter, we have something special going on here. Why do you fight it?"

"I fight it for your sake."

She melted at his answer. "I'm a big girl. Let me make my own decisions."

He came up from his knees, curled his hand around her neck, and kissed her. It was a sweet kiss—tender on her lips, brutal on her heart. It was a kiss that had her trembling from the inside out. When he pulled back, he reached for her hands and weaving his fingers into hers, he let out a shaky breath. "I love you, Liliana."

She cocked her head. "Why'd you have to ruin a perfect moment?"

He glanced around at the surrounding bushes. "We're soaking wet, covered in injuries, starving, exhausted, and not to mention lost in the middle of a friggin' jungle, and you think this's perfect?"

She nodded. "Yep."

He stood, pulled her to her feet, and when they wrapped their arms around each other, she listened to the echo of his pounding heart. "You're a fascinating woman."

In his arms she felt safe. The world melted away and, as she squeezed his wet body, she didn't want the moment to end. "You know, I don't even know your surname."

"It's Logan."

She eased back and held her hand forward. "It's lovely to meet you, Carter Logan."

He placed his palm to hers. "Likewise, Lily Bennett."

"Good boy. Now, are you going to tell me your age?"

His eyes twinkled. "Guess."

Huffing, she turned to sit back on the log. "Forget it." She grabbed her other boot from the ground and tugged it on.

"Come on. It's a game." Carter sat beside her.

She rolled her eyes. "Not playing." She yanked her laces tight and tied a knot.

"It'll be fun. Go on, guess."

"Okay, sixty-four."

He tutted. "That's not a guess."

"Was too."

Lily took a giant stride up onto the log, sat upon it and slipped down the other side. "See ya."

"Wait, come on." He pushed through the bushes behind her.

She forged farther into the jungle, where every section was a repeat of the previous one. Her already sore feet stung in more places than she wanted to admit. Soon, the pain was too much, and wincing with each footfall, she glanced around, searching for an area to rest.

It was at least another five excruciating minutes before an ideal location presented itself. The area was no bigger than her ten-seat dining table back at home on the farm. She eased to the ground and lay back. Every muscle in her body fought against her. The trees above swirled, as if caught in a blender, and when the spinning continued, even after she closed her eyes, she couldn't decide if it was starvation or exhaustion causing it. Probably both.

Carter crawled in beside her and let out a loud moan.

"How are those knees of yours, old man?"

He chuckled. "Not as bad as the blisters. I reckon they're as big as New York City."

"Mine too. It's the wet socks."

"Yeah. That's what I figured."

She cleared her throat. "I'm sorry I got us into this mess."

Carter rested his hand on her forearm. "What're you talking about? It's not your fault."

"Yes, it is. If I hadn't forced us to check out that cave, then none of this would've happened."

"Oh, yeah. That *is* your fault."

She laughed and propped up on her elbow to look at him. "Are you always this incorrigible, Grandpa?"

"Oooh, nasty." He eased up onto his elbow too. A cute smile curled at his lips and he brushed a loose hair off her chin and tucked it behind her ear. "It's not your fault. We could never have predicted those guys rocking up right then."

"I know. I just feel bad."

"Well, don't. We've only survived this long because of you. If it were up to me, we would've died back there with Otomi."

With everything that'd happened, she'd forgotten all about Otomi and his unfortunate family, who would never see him again.

Or Pompa. That silly bird had meant so much to Otomi that he'd included the rooster in his dying wishes. But they'd failed him. Lily made a silent promise that if they made it out of the stupid jungle, she'd compensate Otomi's wife somehow. She sighed. "Poor Otomi."

He cupped her cheek. "I agree. Don't worry, we'll make sure he's buried with his father."

"We have to escape this jungle first."

"That's where you come in. You need to get those survival skills firing and find us some food."

She studied Carter, seeing both strength and tenderness, despite the chaos. His free spirit was a refreshing change from the stiff suits she worked with every day. And his lovely, expressive eyes were almost capable of telling stories on their own. If she didn't make it home, she was grateful to be sharing her final days with such an incredible man. She mentally slapped herself at the depressing attitude. They were going to make it, both of them. She'd make sure of it.

"Hey, speaking of firing." Lifting the Velcro flap on her pants pocket, she pulled out her lighter. "Look what I have."

His eyes lit up. "Holy shit. You're amazing."

"You can thank my wacky family for this survival tip."

"I think I'm in love with your family."

She sat up. "Wait until you meet them before you make that judgment."

He screwed up his face.

"Jesus, Carter, I'm joking. They're not that bad."

He sat up and tugged at his laces. "It's not that."

She copied his lead and untied her boots, yet he failed to elaborate on his comment. "Well, tell me, or do I have to slap it out of you?"

Wincing, he kicked off his shoe. "You know I've been to jail, right?"

"Yeah."

"Well . . . your wonderful country won't let me in with my drug conviction."

Lily turned to him, blinking. "Really?"

"Uh-huh."

"So, you've never been to America?"

He shook his head. "Nope."

"Oh."

"That's another one of those *buts* I should've mentioned earlier."

Chapter Twenty-Five

Lily sucked air through her teeth, forcing back the pain as she peeled off her sock. Placing her foot onto her thigh, she inspected the damage. "Owww." Her foot was red raw, and several blisters on her sole had not only burst—they were bleeding.

"Oh, Jesus Lily. Why didn't you stop earlier, you crazy woman?"

"There wasn't a decent place to rest."

He shifted to his knees with a groan and lifted her other boot onto his thigh. "Let's get this one off. You need to dry your feet out."

Lily allowed Carter to remove her shoe and sock. She refrained from looking at her second foot; the expression on his face was enough to know it wasn't good.

"Okay, you stay right there."

She gave him a salute. "Yes, boss."

"Oh." He stopped and turned back to her. "I brought your book." He plucked her father's journal out from down his shirt.

Her chin quivered; she'd thought it was long gone. A lump sprang to her throat at his thoughtfulness. "Thank you."

"You're welcome." He gathered their socks from the ground and hung them over a nearby branch.

Without even unwinding the leather strap, she knew the journal was ruined. A tear tumbled down her cheek, and she squeezed her eyes shut, trying to quell her emotions.

"Hey." Carter's touch on her shoulder was like a soft blanket. "You okay?"

She shook her head; certain words wouldn't form.

Kneeling down, he thumbed a tear from her jaw. "We might be able to save it." He motioned to the journal in her lap.

"I don't think so. It doesn't matter."

"Like hell it doesn't matter. We've lugged it this far. It's going to make it all the way."

She chuckled at his assertiveness.

"Here, let me put it in the sun." He plucked the journal from her hands and placed it in the one and only ray of sunlight that pierced the canopy. "There, it'll be dry in no time."

"Thank you."

"No worries. Get some rest." He strode off to her left and she lay back to study the tangle of vines that hung above her in a living macramé. The spear of sunlight that hit her journal had her wondering what the time was. It didn't matter, though. They had much more important things to worry about. The pains in her stomach were at the top of her list. If she didn't get food soon, she'd likely pass out.

Carter made trips back and forth with armfuls of twigs and branches, while she studied the trees around them, searching for anything edible. But even once he'd amassed a huge stack, she'd found nothing.

"Want to help me get this fire going?"

"Sure." She rolled onto her knees and crawled forward. Just the thought of standing was enough to keep her off her feet. With a handful of leaves on the bottom, she added small twigs, alternating their direction to create a crisscross pattern. When she fished the lighter from her pocket, she found the pencil too. She'd forgotten all about it.

As she touched her finger to the lead point, she wondered if it was strong enough to double as a weapon. Placing it aside, she lit the fire and within a minute or so, the fire was substantial enough that she eased back and tossed on a couple of larger branches.

Carter arrived at her side, carrying a forked branch with her socks draped across it. "Here you go."

She smiled up at him. "You're a fast learner."

"Taught by the best."

She held it over the flames and he left her again, returning moments later with his own forked branch. He sat beside her, and they both held their damp socks over the fire.

"Any idea about food?" he asked.

"Not yet. We need to watch the monkeys again. Whatever they're eating is good enough for me."

"They don't usually get active until sunset."

"True. Any idea what the time is?"

He looked up to the canopy, and she followed his gaze. A spear of light cut through a break in the canopy. It was angled enough to confirm it wasn't the middle of the day. "It must be afternoon. Maybe three or four o'clock."

"I'll go with whatever you say." He shoved a loose curl from his eye.

A breeze rustled the vegetation, and Lily shuddered as the air swirled across her damp shoulders and back. Her stomach growled loudly, and she was torn between searching for food and planning a way to keep warm overnight. The jungle temperature dropped dramatically once the sun went down, and their damp clothes were a problem. Acknowledging that she had no choice, Lily placed her sock-covered branch aside, stood, and began unbuttoning her shirt.

Carter raised his eyebrows. "Hello . . . did I miss something?"

"We need to get our clothes dry, or we'll freeze. Come on, your turn."

She peeled her shirt off her shoulders and squeezed out the excess water.

Shirtless, she grabbed a nearby branch, but it wasn't sturdy enough. "We need to find a way to secure these over the fire, or we'll be putting on wet clothes again tomorrow."

He grinned at her. "You just want to get me naked."

"Maybe." She grinned back. "I'm serious, actually. Come sunset you'll get cold, and by morning you'll have sores everywhere. Believe me, I know." She recalled one particularly rainy camping trip as a kid, where she'd suffered so badly that her father had declared she'd never do it again. Of course, he didn't win that declaration.

"Right." He whipped his shirt off and Lily cast her eyes over his body. A flush of heat blazed through her at what she saw. Carter might look unkempt, with long hair and a shaggy beard, but there was no hiding the steely abs lining his torso.

Dragging her eyes away, she pushed through the stinging in her feet to scour the area for a long branch. A vine would be ideal too, but it might be difficult to remove from its host tree without a knife. She didn't feel uncomfortable walking around in just her shorts and bra, and, at every opportunity, she snuck glances at Carter, trying to take in more of his surprising physique.

Working together, they rigged up a contraption that held their shirts, shorts, and socks over the flames. Once their clothing was sorted, her grumbling stomach begged for attention.

"We have to find food."

"I know. But where?"

Lily shook her head and looked to the trees. "Let's look around while we still have a bit of light."

"Okay, but make sure we can see the fire at all times."

"Ahhh," she said. "Who's the survival expert now?"

He tapped her bottom. "Learning from the best." He reached for her hand, entwined her fingers in his, and, glancing to the trees, they stepped from the fire. Every tentative step was agony, but she didn't complain, aware that Carter would be feeling the same.

After a while, her neck grew stiff from looking upward. She tilted her head side to side and spotted a strange plant that half clung to an enormous tree, as if it was too heavy to hold itself there. At the end of each sinewy tentacle grew a large pink bulb. Each bulb was covered in flaps that stuck out like triangular ears. "Hey, Carter, check this out."

Carter arrived at her side. "Pitahayas! Good stuff." He twisted one off, tore it open, and bit into it.

She copied his move. The white flesh inside was dotted with hundreds of tiny black seeds and its consistency was similar to a pear, but it was very bland, almost tasteless. She cocked her head. "Is it ripe?"

Carter had already devoured half of one. "Yeah, I'd say so."

"But it doesn't have a taste."

"That's normal."

"Oh, okay. I hope it fills me up."

"From what I've seen, nothing fills you up."

"That's true."

After eating one more each, they plucked off a few handfuls and carried them back to the fire. She'd eaten two more before her stomach pangs subsided.

As the air cooled, the monkeys started their evening ruckus, and the minimal light they had faded at lightning speed. Soon, they were surrounded by complete black. She couldn't even see stars.

With the darkness came the cool air, and Lily shivered in response. She stood and reached for her shirt hanging over the fire. It was dry and she pulled it on. Her shorts weren't ready though, and she left them there. Carter did the same, and she was a little disappointed when he was dressed again. Her boots were still damp, and she turned them around and nudged them closer to the fire.

As Lily stifled a yawn, she contemplated where they'd sleep. When she was a kid, she'd learned the hard way that sleeping on the ground was not a great move. Damp could seep up from the earth, allowing hypothermia to set in. "We need to build a layer between the dirt and our bodies to sleep on."

"Okay. What do you suggest?"

"For starters, let's bunch up these dead leaves and put them into that area between those exposed roots." She pointed at the base of an enormous tree. The roots keeping the tree upright bulged from the ground like retaining walls. One of the roots was as high as Lily's thigh and curved in a way that was perfect for what she'd planned. She was annoyed that she hadn't thought of their bedding earlier, or she would've made the fire closer.

Together, they scooped up handfuls of leaves and tossed them toward the tree base. Even after they'd collected all the leaves visible within the firelight, only a quarter of the exposed root area was covered. "We need more."

Grabbing a thick branch from the fire, she used it as a torch to scan beyond the tree. A mass of ferns, tightly knitted together, caught her attention. The tops of the ferns were lush green, but the lower branches were dry and brittle. Exactly what they needed. "These are perfect." She tugged one and it came away freely. "Grab the dry ones."

Fortunately, the dried fern leaves were in abundance, and soon they had an ideal bed set up.

"It looks positively cozy," Carter said, upbeat.

"It'll do the trick, that's for sure." Lily tossed the branch back into the fire and sparks floated into the air and disappeared. She crawled onto the leaf pile and sat facing the fire. Her body ached all over, especially her shoulders, and she rolled them, wincing at the stiffness.

"Sore, huh?" Carter kneeled behind her and gently massaged the knotted muscle at the base of her neck. Moaning at the pleasure, she rolled her head from side to side. "Oh, that feels so good. How's your wound? You must be in loads of pain."

"Yeah, some."

His thumbs applied pressure and she groaned at both the bliss and agony of it. "It's okay to admit you're in pain."

"Oh, pot, kettle, madam."

"What?"

"Even when I can see you're in pain, you refuse to admit it."

Her stubbornness was born from years of sibling rivalry. "I guess so. I learned pretty early on that I needed to be tough to compete against my brothers."

He eased forward and placing his legs either side of hers, wrapped his arms around her waist, and rested his chin on her right shoulder. "You were amazing in that cenote today."

She shook her head. "If I was amazing, I would've done it on the first go."

"That's what made you amazing. You didn't give up."

She huffed. "The prospect of dying is a great motivator."

"So is the determination to live."

Lily leaned her head back to rest on his shoulder, and as she stared at the glowing coals on the underside of a log, she ran her hands along his forearms. "Do you think we're going to make it?"

"I know we are." He squeezed her to his chest.

With nothing else to do but pray for an uneventful night, Carter lay down with his back to the exposed root, and when he patted the leaves in front, Lily crawled in beside him.

He nestled in behind her, his chest to her back, and as she stared into the dancing flames, sheer exhaustion had sleep beckoning. She closed her eyes, and breathing in long, deep breaths, she thought about her family. They'd be going out of their minds looking for her. Her thoughts jumped to her passport, which was now in the hands of the drug runners, and wondered if her blind determination to come to Mexico to find answers had now put her entire family in danger. She'd never be able to forgive herself if anything happened to them.

Carter's breathing grew deeper, and when he squeezed her, it was like he could sense her troubling thoughts. The warmth of his flesh, nestled up against hers, made her feel complete and she knew that no matter what happened, Carter would protect her.

In an attempt to force all the uncertainty from her mind, she focused on her breathing, determined to get some sleep.

Sometime during the night, the mosquitos came, attacking every inch of her exposed skin with cruel hostility. They buzzed in her ears until she was driven stir-crazy. They stung her arms, her legs. They stung her face too.

She tugged her collar up, did up the top button on her shirt, put her hands over her ears, and prayed for the night to be over.

Chapter Twenty-Six

Screeching monkeys dragged Carter from sleep. He blinked his eyes open, and was surprised to see orange coals still glowing in the fire and sunlight spearing its way through the jungle.

Lily scratched her chin and he couldn't decide if she was still asleep or not. He reached for her hand.

"Don't," he whispered.

"It's itchy." She sounded groggy.

Carter propped up on his elbow. "Your fingernails are dirty. If you break the skin, you'll get infected."

Lily whimpered and rolled to sit up. Carter swiveled around to sit beside her. "Crappy night, huh?"

She nodded. "Just a bit."

He leaned over to kiss her forehead. "We'll have a better day today. I'm sure of it."

"I hope so."

Carter stood and reached for her hand. "Come on, let's eat something and get going." He launched her upright and she winced the moment her feet touched the ground. "You okay?"

"My feet hurt." She pouted her lip and it was equal parts cute and heartbreaking.

"Do you think you can walk?"

"Yeah." She didn't hesitate, and his heart just about burst with pride. Many people would've crumbled into a mess by now.

"Hungry?" he asked.

"Always."

He handed her a pitahaya and, as he ate, he noticed dozens of bites on Lily's legs, arms, and some on her face. His were the same and he wasn't sure if he could stand another night like that. Some of Lily's spark seemed to have trickled away too.

He needed to keep things upbeat. "Lucky we found these." He pointed to his half-eaten fruit.

"I'd rather have a steak any day."

"Me too. Hopefully, we'll be eating one before sunset." He reached for his boots to feel inside. They were still a bit damp, but they'd have to do. He handed Lily her socks and boots.

Ready to get going again, Lily gathered her father's journal and hesitated with it in her hands. Her lips pulled into a thin line and her eyes were loaded with sadness. Turning to the fire, she tossed her journal into the embers.

"What're you doing?" Carter launched at the book, trying to save it from the heat before it took hold.

She wrapped her fingers around his arm. "Leave it. It's ruined."

"Are you sure? It might dry out."

"I'm sure." As she gripped his hand in hers, the book burst into flames. Even if she'd changed her mind, it was too late now.

They watched it burn until little gray puffs of ash floated into the air and, within minutes, there was nothing left of her father's notes but the charred leather binding.

He squeezed her hand. "Come on, let's grab some more pitahayas and get going."

By the time they had several fruits secured in their shirts, the sun was permeating the vegetation enough that they could see where they were going. Not that it helped. "I don't suppose you have any tricks to tell us which way to go?"

"Sure," she said. "Find me a patch of sunlight, and I'll identify east and west."

"Oh, okay." But, as they continued walking, finding a decent patch of unfiltered sun was like finding scents in the air. The occasional rays of light that pierced through the canopy were nothing but a tease.

The blisters on his heels and the balls of his feet were agony. He imagined Lily was the same and had no idea how she was continuing. Twice they stopped to eat fruit and take a quick break, but each time, it was Lily who announced it was time to carry on. His tongue was as dry as leather, and although the fruit helped, he'd give anything for a gallon of water.

Carter was on the verge of calling for another stop, when suddenly the claustrophobic jungle vanished, and a huge mound of rubble spread before them.

"The mudslide!" Lily squealed and stepped up onto the dried mud.

He followed her lead and climbed onto the avalanche of debris that'd cut an impressive gash through the jungle.

After a few steps, she bent down. "Look, a fork." The handle was bent out of shape, but the tines were intact. "We can use it as a weapon."

"Not against me, I hope."

A cheeky smile lit up her face. "No, silly. Iguanas."

The sun beat down on him with ferocious intensity and as he squinted against the glare, sweat dribbled from his temples, armpits, and down his lower back. They had two choices—follow the landslide up, toward where it originated, and hope to find civilization, or follow it down toward the river.

The water was too tempting, and the decision was made both quickly and unanimously.

Once they'd stepped from the shade of the jungle, heat attacked from every angle. It beat down from above, rose up from the caked dirt, and the breeze that floated over the mud gateway was like a hot, hideous breath. His feet grew heavier with each step. His lips cracked, and when he tasted blood, he licked at it, grateful for the little moisture it provided.

They gathered items from the debris. In addition to several

gnarly-looking utensils, Carter found a rusty hammer, and they unearthed a pot that was buried so deep that only the handle was showing.

The sun was still high in the sky when they reached the water. After a quick scan up and down the river to ensure they were alone, Carter tossed his assortment of salvaged equipment down, stripped to his underpants and flopped into the water. The river was instant relief, and casting caution aside, he drank several mouthfuls of the unsanitized water.

Remaining submerged to his shoulders, he watched Lily offload everything she'd collected and strip down to her underwear too. His breath caught at the sight of her gorgeous body. Lily had the physique of an athlete. Svelte, yet toned. Golden skin that looked even more golden in this sunlight. And long, tanned legs that he'd dreamed of having wrapped around his waist. She tugged out her hair and stepped into the water, allowing her long, dark tresses to tumble over her shoulders.

I have officially died and gone to heaven.

His heart pounded to an erotic beat as she tilted her head back and lowered into the water. Running her hands over her forehead, she smoothed her hair and stood again.

Unable to deny himself a moment longer, he reached for her hand.

She turned, their eyes met, and anticipation sizzled between them. He drew her toward him and, as she neared, she placed her hands on his shoulders, and when she curled her legs around him, his dreams came true. Desire simmered in her eyes, and from the second their lips met, all sense of control was gone.

Their tongues explored, as did his hands. He found the clip to her bra, undid it, and took the weight of her breast into his hand. His manhood sprung to life, throbbing and growing, until it hurt from the constraint in his jocks. Gripping his hair, she deepened her kiss and a slow moan tumbling from her throat.

She pulled back, their eyes met again, and something passed between them.

A suggestion that they'd crossed a line. . . possibly.

An acknowledgment there was no turning back. . . probably.

Confirmation that they each wanted this as much as the other. . . absolutely.

Their second kiss was heated, wild. All constraint was gone. He needed her, and if her impassioned moans were a way to judge, she needed him too. He uncupped her breast and wove his hand into her pants. Her lips found his neck, trailing kisses from his shoulder to his ear lobe. Concentrating solely on bringing out her pleasure, her gasps took him to another world. Her nails clawed his back and she cried out, tightened her legs around him as her body shuddered in climax.

His rock-hard manhood commanded attention.

With his hands around her bottom, and her legs squeezing his waist, he carried her from the water. A lush patch of grass was like a welcome mat, and he laid Lily down. She pulled the already undone bra from her shoulders and flung it aside.

Carter's breath was short and sharp as he tugged his jocks down and flicked them off. As he stood naked before her, his body throbbed to an erotic beat. He wanted to ask Lily if she was certain of this, yet, at the same time, if she'd said no, it would take all his might to pull back.

Maybe she saw his hesitation, because she put her thumbs into her pants, rolled them down, and flung them into the bushes. With her eyes on his, she spread her legs.

It was all the invitation he needed. Carter fell to his knees between her thighs and easing forward, he placed one hand at her side for support, cupped her breast with his other hand and leaned in to taste her. As he sucked her nipple, drawing the delicate bud into his mouth, his manhood reached bursting point.

Lily wrapped her legs around him and as he sucked air in through his teeth, he glided into her, savoring every ounce of her body. Her face was the epitome of sexy; eyes nearly closed, mouth half open.

With each tempered thrust, she writhed beneath him. Her eyes opened, but her glazed look implied she wasn't seeing. Her tongue flicked out over her lips, leaving a glint of moisture in its wake.

He slowed down, determined to draw the exquisite moment out as long as he could. With each thrust, her breasts bobbed as she clawed at the grass. Arching her back, she gasped and a flood of heat inside her took him over the edge.

Carter cried out and drove into her over and over, until he couldn't thrust anymore. He fell to her chest, and as he listened to her thumping heart, she trailed her fingers up and down his back.

It was a long moment before he rolled off and lay beside her. She wriggled in so her head slotted into the crook of his shoulder. Lily placed her right arm and right leg over his body, trapping him, as she curled her finger around his nipple.

He closed his eyes and savored the throb of post-sex glory.

After a while, she shifted up onto her elbow, and opened his eyes.

"I'm glad you didn't stop that time."

He smiled. "I couldn't even if I'd wanted to."

Her eyebrows lifted. "Did you want to?"

"Hell, no."

She put her head back down on his shoulder. "Good."

Carter could've stayed right where they were all day, but the ticking clock in his head urged him to keep going. "Come on. Let's get moving before the sun sets on us again."

Groaning as they stood, he cupped her cheeks to kiss her; just a brief kiss of reassurance, that said so much more. There were so many things he wanted to say. At the very top of his list was *I love you.*

But he resisted.

Although both of them had already said it, in the back of his mind he couldn't help but wonder if Lily would run away, shaking her head in confusion, the second they were rescued. He wouldn't blame her if she did, but he didn't want additional confessions of love, making her decision more difficult.

He reached for his underpants and removed the pouch he'd bought in Peru.

"What's that?"

He tugged on the string to open it. "I bought it from a market stall in Peru. I keep my SD cards in here." He pulled one out to show her.

"You keep them in your underpants?"

He nodded. "Safest place in the world. No one ever goes in there."

She tugged on her bottom lip. "I just did."

"Momentary lapse in concentration." He grinned.

"Really?" She picked up her bra, and he ogled her glorious breasts before they were concealed again. Time stood still as she slowly put it on. A cheeky smile lit up her face.

"You're a tease, Tiger Lily."

She chuckled as she fitted her breasts into position. Then, she gathered their final reserve of pitahayas, handed one to him, and they sat cross-legged on the grass.

"So." Carter wriggled his brows. "After that incredible sex, now that we've found water and snacks, all we need is to be rescued and it'll be a perfect day."

She nodded and appeared thoughtful. After a while, she snapped her fingers. "Remember I found that banana tree near the graveyard? Maybe there'll be more."

"Hopefully." He stood, helped her to stand and they gathered their new collection of mangled belongings. "After you."

Lily strode on ahead, and if her feet were giving her any trouble, she gave no indication of it.

They arrived at the graveyard much quicker than he'd antici-pated, but after barely a cursory glance, they continued on. Their next place of interest was where Lily had nursed him back from unconsciousness. Again, they didn't stop.

Carter's hunger pangs howled like dogs and were impossible to ignore.

They hurt like hell too.

Lily squealed and he jumped. "There! Look." She strode toward a tree boasting a huge bunch of bananas, fifty at least.

But, in another cruel irony, they were all green.

"Come on, help me." Lily had her fingers around the trunk and was trying to pull it over. Carter put his hands above hers, and together they wrestled the tree to the ground, until it snapped. They each twisted off a couple of bananas.

"Can you eat them green?" Carter asked.

"Of course." She struggled to pull back the rubbery peel. When she bit into it, she screwed up her mouth as she chewed. After she swallowed, she poked out her tongue. "Ewww, it's powdery." White bits caked her tongue.

"You make it sound so enticing."

"Shut up and eat." She peeled another one and handed it to him.

With each disgusting mouthful, he hoped his wish from this morning would come true. But, as he glanced ahead at the endless jungle, he knew there wouldn't be a big juicy steak waiting for him at the end of today.

Chapter Twenty-Seven

After Lily had forced down two more bananas and ensured Carter did the same, they plucked as many as they could carry and set off again, following the river downstream. She tried to ignore all the aches and pains in her body, from the itchy mosquito bites to the dozens of scratches on her forearms and calves, to the blisters on her feet.

All of them were bearable; however, her hunger was not.

The bananas had filled a void, but the lack of a decent meal had her both dizzy and slightly nauseous. It also meant she had no energy and had to stop more frequently.

A flat grassy knoll at the river's edge became their next resting place. She tossed everything onto the ground and crumbled to the grass. Laying back, she wiped sweat from her brow and studied the fluffy white clouds swirling above her.

Carter crawled to her side. "You okay?"

"Yeah."

"Liar." He kissed her forehead. "We need you to catch another one of those iguanas."

She rolled to him, trying to assess if he was serious. "That takes time, you know."

He nodded. "I know, but without decent meals we're getting weaker, which is only making us slower anyway."

The prospect of meat, even lizard meat, had her insides jumping for joy. "If you're serious, I'll set up a trap right here."

"I'm serious, babe. Go work your magic."

Babe. She liked that. Lily gave him a quick kiss and crawled over to their eclectic collection of salvaged utensils. She selected the four-pronged fork. The two outer tines were thicker than the two inner ones. She handed it to Carter. "Do you think you can bend back these two prongs?" She pointed at the two middle ones.

"Sure." He took the fork from her, and she turned back to their things and fished out the other two forks and gave them to Carter too. She grabbed a tin cup and a metal spoon, and searched for a spot where the ground was soft enough to dig a hole.

She chose an area away from the trees, so she wouldn't risk hitting roots, knelt down, and using the spoon and cup, began to dig. It didn't take long before the ground became as tough as rubber.

Once again her hands suffered, and soon the blisters and scabs started bleeding, but the thought of food kept her going.

Carter came and took over. He removed his shirt, and she watched, mesmerized, as the muscles in his back bulged and flexed with each attack he made on the dirt.

While he was digging, Lily rubbed the ends of sticks on a rough rock, fashioning each one to a point. It worked, but it was slow going. It seemed like an eternity before the hole was large enough for her trap and she'd made five sticks into spears.

Carter rolled onto his back, his chest rising and falling with ragged breaths. Every inch of his exposed skin glistened with sweat.

"You okay?"

"As okay as I can be."

"We're nearly finished. Just need to position these facing upward in the hole."

With a collection of small rocks in the bottom, Carter secured four of her miniature spears upright and eased back from the pit. "How's that?"

"Good." She covered the opening loosely with twigs and leaves, concealing the hole beneath. When she stepped back to examine their trap, she hoped it'd work. And soon. "Time for a swim?"

"Hell, yeah."

The sun was a white fireball over the river when they stripped naked and stepped into the cool water. Lily dunked her head under, and when she stood up her breasts bobbed at the surface. It was delightfully wicked, yet utterly heavenly.

The sunlight caught in Carter's beard, highlighting the red tinge through it, and she wondered what he'd look like clean-shaven. She couldn't see any gray hairs in his beard or hair.

"You still haven't told me your age, you know."

"Guess?"

"This game is getting a little old."

"So, play."

"It's okay, I don't need to know anyway. But I do wonder if you're afraid to tell me."

"Why would I be afraid?"

"Because you think you're too old for me."

He tilted his head, and the sunlight shining through his green irises had them shimmering like highly polished emeralds. "Okay, then, I'm forty-two."

"Hmmm, that's what I thought."

"You thought I was forty-two?"

"No . . . I thought you were old." She splashed a wave of water over him. He laughed and pushed his hair off his face, and by the cheeky look in his eyes she knew what was coming. She squealed and made a dash for dry land.

Carter grabbed her waist. "Oh, no you don't." He picked her up in a bear hug and dunked them both. She giggled and screamed, and when she came back above the water, Carter was laughing too. It was the first time she'd heard him truly laugh. It was a wonderful, infectious sound, and she found herself chuckling along with him.

She wrapped her legs and arms around him.

He pushed a lock of her wet hair from her cheek. "So." He waited till their gazes met. "What do you think of my age?"

Rolling her eyes to the sky, she feigned thoughtfulness. "Oh, I don't know. You're really old."

She squealed as Carter dunked her again. They came up laughing and their lips met, gentle at first, but as she drove her fingers through his hair and pulled him toward her, it intensified. Wrapping her legs around him again, and their breaths became feverish.

Delightful shudders rolled through her, drawing her nipples out, until they ached. As if he knew, Carter rolled her unrestrained bud between his thumb and finger with just the right amount of pressure.

Raw lust shimmered in his eyes and his penis felt enormous between her thighs. She wove her hand down between them and as her fingers wrapped around him, he grew thicker and longer beneath her touch.

The desire to have him in her . . . deep, deep inside her, couldn't be ignored a moment more.

She guided him to her opening, but he paused there; kissing her, touching her, and drawing out the anticipation, until she was ready to burst. Their mouths released and she gasped as he filled her. His tongue lashed out to wet his lips, and as she studied every exquisite detail of his face, she knew she was making love to the most handsome man she'd ever seen.

Slowly, slowly, they made love.

It felt so right, so complete, like the last piece of a puzzle finding its home.

She squeezed her legs, holding position, as he repeated his movements over and over. When his eyelids flickered open, the raw passion in his eyes made her insides blaze with delight. As her climax built to monumental heights, she turned her attention to his neck, trailing kisses up and down from his ear to his shoulder.

His moans matched his movements. His thrusts grew faster, harder, pounding something deep inside her that begged to be pounded. With her arms around his neck, she hung on as he squeezed his fingers into her hips and drove himself into her over and over. They worked together, drawing out each other's pleasure, as if they'd done it a thousand times before.

She felt incredible. Alive. Oh, so alive.

Glorious shudders rolled through her and Lily let out a cry. Carter froze, his entire body stiffened. He was at the point of no return. Releasing a primal groan, he plunged deep inside her. He repeated the move, three times, and more, before he slowed. Finally, he wrapped his arms around her and clutched her body to his as if she was saving him. Maybe she was.

She waited until their erratic breathing returned to normal before she released her grip on him and smiled. "Wow. For an old man, you still got it."

He laughed, loud and hearty. "You're cheeky."

"I know." She reached for his hand, wove her fingers into his, and then kissed him. It was just a brief, tender kiss that said so much more. But her grumbling stomach couldn't be ignored any more. "I'm starving. You ready to help me catch dinner?"

"You bet."

As Lily stepped out of the water, Carter cupped her bottom. "Are you all right there?"

"Yes. Just helping you out."

She giggled. "Really?"

She used her shirt to dry herself, and as she picked up her underpants, she had second thoughts. "I think I'll give these a wash. In this sun, they'll be dry in no time."

"Good idea. My jocks could just about walk on their own too."

"Ewww, too much information."

"Oh, and yours aren't like that?"

Just as she was about to step into the shallow water, she froze. "Stop!"

"What?"

She pointed toward a rock that protruded above the water. "A fish, near that rock. See it?"

"Oh yeah, it's a big one."

Lily had an idea. "Did you bend those forks?"

"Yes." Carter followed her back up to the grassy knoll.

"I need a spear." Naked, she headed toward the trees, searching for a long stick and found one quickly. *Rope. I need rope.* She collected her bra from the grass and, as luck would have it, the straps were removable.

Sitting on the grass, Carter sat to her side, and although she found his nakedness incredibly distracting, the thought of getting that fish up on the riverbank drove her on.

"I need a small, flat rock, about the size of a coin," she said.

"I'm on it." The muscles in his bottom glided up and down as he walked away and she had to drag her eyes away from that wonderful spectacle.

Holding a fork beside the stick, she wrapped her bra strap around it twice. Then, she held the second fork on the opposite side and repeated the move with the strap.

Carter handed her a rock. "Will this do?"

"Perfect." She pushed the rock between the two forks, wedging them apart, then wrapped the rest of the elastic around and around and tied it in place. The finished weapon was a four-pronged spear.

"That's fantastic. Remind me never to get on your bad side."

She giggled. "Hopefully it works. Do you want to do it?"

"No way, you're the Tiger Lily."

Holding the spear in her hand, she assessed its weight. "It'll be a miracle if this works."

"I've already seen a couple of miracles in the last week, so I'm betting it will."

Lily returned to the riverbank, and to her surprise there were now two fish swimming near the rock. Easing up to the edge, her breath trapped in her throat. She held the spear above her head, then using all the energy she could muster, drove it at the fish. An explosion of water erupted near the rock.

She squealed and dived for the stick. When she pulled it above the water, a fat, foot-long fish writhed on the end. "Holy shit, I got it!"

The fish flipped from side to side as she brought it up onto the grass.

Lily stared openmouthed. "I've never caught a fish that way before."

"You're amazing."

She put the fish on the grass, salivating by just looking at it. "I can't believe that worked."

"I can. Now, we need a fire." Carter trotted to the tree line and began gathering wood. She dressed, no longer bothering with washing her underpants, and then set about building up the kindling.

Within minutes, the fire was blazing and the fish had stopped moving.

"Do you know how to gut a fish?" she asked.

Carter shook his head. "Sorry. Never had the pleasure."

"Okay." She reached for the butter knife she'd found in the mud slide. "I wish we had a sharper knife, but this'll have to do." She ran her thumb over the blade. It was completely blunt. "Can you find me a couple of large leaves, please? As big as you can get."

She waited until he returned before she tugged the fish off the prongs and placed it onto one leaf. As she began cleaning the fish, she was reminded of her father. After her mother had insisted that Lily join her brothers on their quarterly camping trips, or maybe because of her mother's persistence, her father had demanded that she learn how to catch, kill, and prepare her own food.

Never in her wildest dreams did she imagine that those lessons would save her life.

Maybe his unwavering commands were because of what happened to her father's first wife and child.

"What're you thinking about?"

She jumped at Carter's voice. "Oh, umm." She cleared her throat. "My dad. Do you think it's weird that he made me learn survival skills?"

"I'm bloody grateful he did."

"Yeah," she sighed. "I am too, but I was just wondering if he had other reasons for doing it."

"Like what?"

"Well, maybe he was lost out here with his wife and child. It'd explain why he gave me such a hard time about learning them."

"Maybe."

She shoved the unanswerable questions aside to concentrate on dinner.

After scaling, gutting with the blunt knife, and skewering the fish onto two sturdy sticks, it was slightly mangled, but still looked mighty tasty. "Dinner is ready to cook."

Carter rubbed his hands together. "Yum, I can't wait."

She handed the sticks to him. "Hold it over the flames, but don't let the stick burn."

"Yes, boss." Carter beamed as he sat naked by the fire, following her instructions.

While her hands were bloody, Lily divided the fish remains into smaller portions on the additional giant leaves. She carried one of the leaves to the pit they'd dug earlier, and carefully positioned it over the twigs on top of the trap. With a bit of luck, something would sniff it out, and they'd have red meat very soon.

Lily returned to the fire and put the three other bundles of fish guts high up in a tree branch. Other than ants, which seemed unavoidable, she hoped no other creatures would find their bait.

By the time the fish was cooked, the sun had begun its slide down behind the trees on the opposite side of the river. As Carter divided the fish between them, her mouth watered from the delicious aromas. Even though it was steaming hot, she couldn't wait, and scooped a chunk of white flesh into her mouth. "Oh, my God. This's so good."

"Sure is." Carter had the leaf up to his mouth and scooped the fish in by hand. His eyes rolled and he moaned as he swallowed.

"We'll have to get ready for the night after this." Lily didn't want a repeat of last night's insect attack and would make sure their bed was closer to the fire this time.

"I'll be ready for anything after this."

By the time they finished the meal and had a cozy bed made of dry fern leaves, the sun had disappeared behind the trees. Sunset had been a magnificent display of reds and purples, and was promptly replaced with a near full moon that lit up the night sky.

Carter lay down on the crunchy leaves, and Lily eased in next to him, turning her attention to the fire. She sighed deeply and he draped his arm over her. "This's nice."

"Mmmm. Who'd have thought we'd be this comfortable?" He trailed his finger up and down her arm.

"Food helps."

A loud crack echoed about the trees and Lily jumped. Carter squeezed her wrist, indicating he'd heard it too. *Crack. Crack. Crack.* Several more rounds split the silence.

"Gunfire! Shit!" Carter launched to his feet. "Put the fire out." As he tugged the nearest log from the fire and dragged it toward the river, Lily grabbed the tin cup, scooped the water and tossed it onto the flames. She repeated the move at a frantic pace, tossing cups of water, until only minor coals glowed in the bottom. The fire hissed and smoke spiraled upwards, but the flames were gone.

Exhausted, she went to Carter, and as he wrapped his arms around her, they eased back against the large tree. A light breeze drifted off the water, rustling the leaves around them. Monkeys howled somewhere in the distance, and more animals continued their usual nightly chorus, but, other than that, everything seemed normal.

"You sure it was gunfire?" Lily's heart thumped an urgent beat in her chest.

"I'm pretty sure. What'd you think?"

More loud cracks ripped through the stillness. They seemed closer this time.

"That's gunfire," she said. "Do you think it's those guys from the cave?"

Carter's grip tightened around her waist. "No idea."

"What do we do?"

As she listened to his breathing, she heard something else. "Is that music?"

"Oh, yeah. It sounds close."

Clutching his arms around her shoulders, she strained to hear.

The music echoed through the jungle as well as shouts and laughter. "Sounds like a party."

"It does." It was a long moment before he shifted. "I have an idea. But you might not like it."

She turned to him, but could only just make out his shape in the filtered moonlight. "Try me."

"There's a chance it may not be them. It could be just a farmer or villager or something, right?"

"I guess so."

"I think we should go look. While it's dark, we have the upper hand. We can sneak up on them and see exactly who we're dealing with. What do you think?"

As much as it terrified her, it was an opportunity they shouldn't miss. "Okay." She squeezed his hand. "Let's do it."

But as soon as she said it, dread shifted in her stomach like a ball of scorpions, twisting, turning, stinging, and adding a whole new level of torture to her battered body.

Chapter Twenty-Eight

C arter shoved a couple of bananas, the tin cup, and a spoon down his shirt, but not the hammer. That he clenched in his fist. The weight alone made him feel safer. With Lily clutching her four-pronged spear behind him, he led the way toward the music. The moon was a bright beacon high in the sky, providing enough light to make out shapes in the landscape ahead.

With the river remaining their constant companion on his left and the virgin jungle on his right, Carter forced himself to keep moving. A barrage of gunshots shattered the serenity and they dove for the ground. After a couple of thumping heartbeats, whilst they confirmed the bullets were not aimed at them, they stood again and kept going.

With each tentative step toward uncertainty, his mind raged with a debate. Were they the men who'd chased them into that tunnel? Or were they farmers celebrating a bumper crop? Were they walking toward a rescue party? Or certain death? Once they were rescued, would Lily go back to America and he'd never see her again? Or would they stay together . . . forever?

The last two questions dominated his thoughts. He knew, without an ounce of doubt, that he'd fallen in love. Deeply fallen.

Head and heart. He'd never been in love before, not even with the mother of his daughter. What he felt for Lily was so powerful it hurt. And given their radical situation, that was a miracle.

Once they were rescued, if she ran back to her family, although he wouldn't blame her, he was set to be a shattered man.

"Hey, Carter?" Lily's whisper interrupted his troubling thoughts.
"Yeah?"

"No matter what happens, I want you to know I've had a wonderful time."

It took all his might not to laugh out loud. "I think you're delusional."

Her fingers curled around his arm, and he turned to her. "I know it's been crazy and dangerous, and we've nearly died a couple of times, but"—she ran her hand up his arm—"I found you."

He pulled her to his chest and stroked her hair. "We found each other."

She leaned back to look up at him, and the moonlight glistened in her eyes. "I love you." The words crossed her strawberry lips in a breathless whisper and his heart just about burst.

He curled his hand behind her neck, gliding his fingers over her flesh. "I love you too."

Carter felt like he could walk on water. The doubts he'd experienced, moments ago, vanished, replaced instead with a fierce determination to live.

No matter what, we are going to survive.

He leaned in and kissed her. It was a kiss that said it all—I want, I need, I love. He hugged her to his chest and closed his eyes, feeling the warmth of her body against his.

They remained embraced until a burst of gunshots shattered the moment. He squeezed her body to his, wedging her between him and a tree. The gunfire was over as quickly as it started.

He kissed her forehead. "Come on, let's go check this out."

As the moon crawled its way above the open expanse of the river, they wove around and through dense jungle, carefully assessing every step. It was slow going, and fear was like hundred scorpions scurrying up his back, keeping him rigid.

The music had become loud enough that lyrics were noticeable. Occasionally, he heard people talking. They spoke in Spanish, but he couldn't quite hear their full conversation, and the echo about the trees made it confusing.

Carter smelled smoke, and at the scent of something cooking. His stomach twisted in protest. Maybe the people were actually friendly.

His gut told him otherwise.

But it wasn't just the gunshots triggering that feeling; something else was wrong, he just couldn't pinpoint what.

A distant light caught his eye. As he batted a buzzing insect away from his ear, he stared at the spot. There it was again. Flames flared in the distance. They were closer than he expected. Grasping Lily's hand, he pulled her down to crouch with him.

"Look." He pointed ahead. "See the fire?"

"Oh, yeah."

"We have to be really quiet now."

"Okay."

He toyed with the idea of making her stay there while he checked it out, but she'd refuse. She was that kind of woman. . . another reason why he'd fallen in love with her.

As they inched forward, the flames became more prominent. It was a decent-sized fire, at least three times the size of the ones Lily had lit over the last week. He still couldn't see any men, and the music had died down somewhat.

The fire was set back from the river by at least fifty feet, and was centered in a large clearing. Carter crouched down behind a shrub with his fingers strangling the hammer. To the right of the fire, a thatched hut came into view. It was big enough to be permanent. *Is that someone's home?* This was their first sign of civilization in days, but it didn't produce the amount of elation it should have. In fact, it did the opposite.

The dense shrub provided ideal cover, and as he lowered to his hands and knees behind it, Lily crawled in beside him. His eyes adjusted to the firelight allowing him to see another building to the left of the first. This one was also thatched and had a small verandah that ran the length of the front, with a couple of steps centred in the middle. It looked cozy and inviting, and Carter had to resist stepping into the clearing and cheering for joy.

A distinct smell had his back straightening and his mind racing. Marijuana smoke. It was an odor he'd never forget . . . from a time in his life he'd prefer to erase from his memory.

He clutched Lily's arm. "Smell that?"

She nodded. "What is it?"

"Marijuana."

Her eyes bulged. "Are you sure?"

"Absolutely. We have to get out of here."

"What? No! We only just got here." Her lips drew to a thin line.

"Yes, and now we're going."

"Not yet." She spoke through clenched teeth. "They can't see us. Let's just wait and see what happens."

Carter grumbled at her stubbornness, but returned to his hands and knees at her side. After a couple of minutes, they still hadn't seen anybody around the fire, and he couldn't work out where the music was coming from. Neither of the huts had lights on inside. *Maybe they're asleep.* But that wouldn't explain the marijuana smoke.

Someone is smoking it right now. But where?

Looking for the telltale sign of a glowing cigarette tip, he focused on the far right of the area, where the clearing met the jungle, and panned his gaze slowly toward the left. *There, between the two huts.* First one circular glow, then two more. He studied the spot until he made out the shapes of three men in chairs.

"Oh, my God!" Lily clutched his arm.

"It's okay. They can't see us."

"No, look." She pointed to the far side of the left hut, beyond the fire. "My pack."

His jaw dropped. Her pack, with its distinctive orange blaze down the side, was on the dirt, like it'd been tossed over the railing. "Shit. Now we *know* who they are. Let's go." Carter pushed back.

"No! We have to get it. My passport's in there."

"Lily!" He bulged his eyes at her.

"If anything happened to my family because of me, I couldn't live with myself."

"Nothing's going to—" Carter clutched her arm pulling her down lower. "Shhh." He pointed forward. A man walked between the fire and the hut on the right.

The firelight ensured there was no mistaking the rifle slung over his shoulder. He stopped at the edge of the clearing and parted his legs. *He's pissing into the bushes.*

Once finished, he adjusted the rifle position and walked back around the fire, returning to his two mates. He must've dialed the volume higher as the music got louder.

"Now, do you see why we need to go?" He spoke in a forceful whisper.

"I'm not going without my pack." Her eyes narrowed. Her lips pursed.

He shook his head, gearing up for a fight.

She squeezed his forearm. "I'm doing this with or without you."

"Lily, this's fucking stupid. They have guns."

"I don't care. If I don't get it, I'll spend the rest of my life looking over my shoulder."

He clenched his fists and racked his brain for inspiration to convince her otherwise. "You watch too many movies."

"I'm not joking, Carter."

"Neither was I. Besides, your passport may not even be in there."

"It's hidden in a zipper that's hard to see, so I'll take my chances."

"Lily . . ."

"Look, we have two choices," she hissed. "Go now, while those men are busy, or wait until they sleep."

"Lily," he pleaded.

"You won't talk me out of it." She plonked her fists on her hips.

He believed her. If there was one thing he knew about Lily, it was her dogged determination. He reached for her hands and she clutched her palms to his. "Getting your pack could get us killed."

"We've lived so far."

"That doesn't make us invincible."

"Will you stop, please? I'm getting my bag. You can stay here."

He sighed. "You know I won't do that."

"So, help me figure out how to get it."

Clenching his fists, he glanced at the fire. "This is stupid."

She reached for his hand and squeezed. "Thank you."

"Thank me once we have the damn pack."

"I'll do more than thank you."

He tilted his head. She was sexy as hell. Even with mosquito bites dotted on her cheeks, and her hair in a scrambled mess.

Carter turned back to the clearing. "Let's think this through."

"Okay."

Obstructing their view of the whole clearing were the two huts and the men were seated between them. In the middle, the fire gave enough light to see the front of both huts, but not much else. The river was down to the left. "We could skirt the riverbank and come up the other side."

"That's what I thought."

"Really?" he said, sarcastically. "What else did you think?"

She blinked up at him. "I think you're wonderful for helping me."

"Or bloody stupid."

"Awww, don't be like that."

Ignoring his chilling instincts, he turned back to the clearing. The men were still in their chairs, smoking, and the music was loud enough that maybe they'd go unnoticed. That was a big fucking maybe. Everything they'd been through, every injury they'd overcome, it might all end here. But Lily would do something stupid if he didn't help. Of that he was certain.

He had to do this, for her sake.

Chapter Twenty-Nine

Carter's heart galloped as he seized Lily's hand. "Stay down."
Leading Lily, he left their viewing spot and aimed toward the river. A dense patch of wiry plants made the direct route impossible, so they backtracked a bit before they reached the water again.

The moon reflected off the flowing river as slivers of shifting light and a slight breeze drifted over the water, licking the sweat off his forehead yet it failed to cool him down. At the water's edge, Carter knelt down and pulled the bits and pieces from his shirt. "Let's offload anything that's not essential, and finish off these bananas."

He handed her a banana, and as they munched away on the dense fruit, he tried to formulate a plan. "Okay, when we get there, you're going to stay by the river and I'll sneak up and grab the pack."

Her eyes squinted, and he sensed her looming objection.

"If you want my help, this is it. If anything happens, you need to run. Lily, I mean it—promise me you'll run."

She closed her eyes, inhaled a deep breath, and then opened them again. "Okay."

Carter cupped her cheeks. "Promise me, Lily."

It was a long moment before she nodded. "I promise."

He touched his lips to hers, then wrapped his arms around her and squeezed her to his chest. Each time she was in his arms, he felt like he was home, and despite days lost in the jungle, she still had a delicious scent.

Carter eased back. "Okay, so once I get the pack, we'll carry on downstream. With this moonlight, we should be able to walk for a few hours. Agreed?"

"Yep. Agreed."

The plan was stupid. One hundred percent idiotic. But he'd seen determination written all over her. The fire in her eyes. The way her mouth drew to a thin line. Her clenched fists. If he didn't help her, she'd do it without him.

And that was more stupid.

Lily grabbed her four-pronged spear, Carter clutched his rusty hammer, and they set off along the riverbank again. Compared to some of the jungle they'd traversed so far, the trek was relatively easy. The ground was fairly flat, and they didn't have giant boulders or shrubs to navigate.

The river tumbled along relentlessly. Insects droned monotonously in his ears and the occasional bird added to the chorus. Music still floated through the air, as did the occasional waft of smoke, but, other than that, everything appeared safe.

And that's what scared the crap out of him.

A strange shape in the water caught his eye, and he just about cheered at the sight. He crouched and tugged Lily down with him. "Boats, Lily, look."

"Oh, my God."

"This's it. We're getting out of here."

"With my pack."

"Are you serious?"

"I'm not going without it." Her eyes darkened; her beautiful mouth twitched with resolve.

She was impossible. His stomach twisted. His head pounded.

Armed with rage, he raised his hammer and edged forward.

The boats were against the shore, courtesy of the current. They were bigger than he'd first thought, about twelve feet long and five feet across at their widest points. He spied their motors and fist-pumped the air. *Yes! This is definitely our ticket out of here.*

Something wrapped around his throat.

Carter gasped and swung the hammer.

It was a couple of frantic heartbeats, before he realized it was a rope. He jerked it away, furious that he'd overreacted. The rope was securing the boats to a nearby tree. Nothing more.

"Fucking hell," he hissed, through clenched teeth.

"Are you okay?"

He let out a gush of air. "Yeah, damn rope got me." His thundering heart drowned out the music and his head spun from both anger and exertion.

He ducked under the rope and squatted at the water's edge. In the moonlight he made out a pair of oars positioned across two seats.

"Okay, can you untie the ropes?"

"I'm not going without—"

"Lily!" He shot her a furious glare. "Untie the fucking ropes."

She planted her feet. Anger seethed in her eyes.

He hadn't meant to swear. Confusion, insanity, anxiety, and most of all fear, were hijacking his emotions. Clenching his fists to stop the trembling, he forced calm to his body. "We're not leaving without the pack. Okay?"

Her shoulders relaxed, and with one hand on the rope, she followed it up to the tree. Carter's heart thumped in his ears as he leaned over and clutched the side of the boat as the ropes slackened.

Lily returned. "I'm sorry I made you mad." Her voice quivered, but he chose to ignore it. He had to keep moving before his resolve shattered.

"It's okay, come on, let's get rid of this boat, so they can't chase us, and we'll keep the other one for us."

Together, they manipulated the first boat so the back end was nudged against the shore and the front pointed downstream. They gave it a shove and it glided out toward the middle, and, within seconds, it caught in the current and disappeared from view.

He tugged Lily down and they listened in silence.

Satisfied they'd gone unnoticed; he wrapped his hand around her wrist. "Stay here, I'm going to take another look."

"I'll come—"

"Lily!"

"Two pairs of eyes are better than one." Her clenched jaw was noticeable in the moonlight.

"You're one of the most stubborn women I've ever known."

"Thank you."

"It's not a compliment."

"Well, I think it is."

He huffed out his frustration. It was clear she wouldn't relent. "Stay beside me."

She saluted. "Yes, boss."

Ignoring her sassiness, he clutched her arm, and side by side they climbed the small embankment. If there was some kind of track up from the river, they'd obviously missed it and, as he pushed through the bushes, he tried to commit the way he was going to memory.

At the crest, they crouched amongst the shrubs, and the flames centred in the middle enabled him to orientate himself. The music seemed to bounce from every angle, but he couldn't hear the men. Peering beyond the fire, it was impossible to see if they were still seated between the buildings.

"Oh, my God," Lily whispered. "There's Pompa." She pointed to their left, about fifteen feet away. "We have to get him."

A jackhammer pounded in his brain. "Like hell we do."

The rooster was halfway between them and the fire. His cage was on its side, yet Pompa was roosting, seemingly unfazed by his toppled cage.

"We have to. Think of Otomi. Think of Otomi's wife."

"It's a fucking bird!"

"A bird that meant a lot to Otomi's family. We have to rescue him."

Carter clenched and unclenched his jaw. "You're being irrational. Besides, he doesn't look like he needs rescuing."

"They're probably getting ready to roast him on that fire."

"Lily, we're not getting the fucking bird and that's not negotiable." He spoke through clenched teeth.

The anger blazing in her eyes, seemed enhanced in the filtered light.

"I'm not risking our lives for a bird, but trust me, I'll make sure Otomi's family is looked after. Understand?"

"Okay." She huffed out a sigh. "Okay."

"Good, let's get the boat ready." He eased back from the crest and marched through the bushes toward the river. A crack of gunfire had them both diving for the ground, but laughter in the distance quickly followed. *Thank Christ! those bullets weren't aimed at us.*

He stood again. "Let's turn the boat around." They repeated the move they'd done on the first boat, positioning the craft for a quick getaway. Carter could barely breathe, yet Lily appeared calm, as if they were about to take a romantic paddle.

He handed her the rope. "Here's what's going to happen." He waited until she met his gaze. "I'll grab your pack. While I'm gone, you get ready to jump into the boat, the second I return. I'll throw you the bag, and then push the boat out and jump in. Hopefully, we'll get away unnoticed. Got it?"

"Got it." She clutched his arm, her fingers like a vice. "Be careful." Her eyes were hauntingly beautiful in this moonlight, and if he'd had his camera, this would've been the shot of the day.

With a clenched jaw, he grabbed the hammer, then took one last look at Lily before he spun away and charged up the embankment. By the time he reached the top, his breathing was ragged and loud, too loud, and he took a moment to pause, crouch down, and settle his nerves.

I am not cut out for the hero shit.

Yet here I am. Fetching Lily's pack. The absurdity of it had him choking back laughter.

His mind filled with the image of the moon reflecting in Lily's pleading eyes. He'd do it for her. Hell, he'd do anything for her.

The loud music bounced around the bushes, but other than that, everything seemed quiet. Except for his thumping heart. And his tortured breathing. He closed his eyes, counted to ten, clutched the hammer, stood, and carried on.

Utilizing the cover of the bushes, he crept to the left of the fire and paused again, listening as he scoured the clearing. Everything was calm.

From this angle, he couldn't see the men, but every once in a while, a puff of smoke indicated they remained seated between the two huts.

That was a good sign. From that angle, they wouldn't be able to see him.

Carter inhaled, long and deep, and let it out slowly. Holding out his trembling fingers, he willed them to stop.

This is it. The point of insanity has arrived.

He glanced around. Everything was still. A thumping drum solo erupted from the shadows between the huts. He couldn't have asked for better cover. Now or never. He sucked in a deep breath. Dug his toes into the ground.

And dashed across the clearing.

He grabbed the pack, spun to sprint away, but tripped over the strap and fell to his knees. Something in the pack clanged and the sound was as loud as gunfire.

His brain hit panic mode.

The next sound Carter heard set his heart to explode. *Dogs.*

He pushed off the dirt and ran. Fast. The pack swung in one hand. The hammer clenched in the other. With every stride, the barking dogs grew louder. He hit the bushes at breakneck speed, jumped into the darkness, and kept on running.

The dogs sounded vicious and huge, and Carter pictured at least fifty of them. They crashed through the bushes behind him, gnashing teeth, and growling like the devil.

An explosion of gunshots rang out, as did angry shouts. His damn knees threatened to buckle beneath him as he launched down the embankment.

"I'm coming, Lily!" he screamed. "There's dogs. Get ready."

He launched onto the riverbank, pain ripped across his knees, and a big black dog landed at his side. Carter tossed the pack into the boat and, to his horror, Lily charged at the beast with her spear.

A glint of steel flashed in the moonlight.

The dog howled.

Carter grabbed her hand. "Get in the fucking boat!"

She did, launching her long legs over the side in one swift move.

He pegged the hammer at a snarling beast and when it hit the dog behind the ear, it howled and scampered away. Carter pushed the boat from the shore and dove over the side. But he mistimed it. His chest hit the side. His feet hit the water. He glanced back. Two dogs were menacing nightmares at the river's edge, barking and baring teeth, barely inches from his feet.

Lily clutched at his shirt, and he scrambled up the side of the boat and flopped into the bottom.

He launched to his feet, shoved an oar at Lily. "Paddle!"

She grabbed it, sat down, and dug the blade into the water. Driving his oar in too, they aimed for the middle of the river.

In the middle of the boat was the birdcage. He couldn't fucking believe she'd saved Pompa. Fury and dismay merged as one over her actions. Nothing could justify risking her life to save the stupid bird. Nothing.

Seconds after leaving shore, the current took over, and they eased away from the riverbank. With their element of surprise gone, there was no need to keep quiet. Carter launched at the motor. The white handle was easily visible against the black engine.

A load crack had Carter's already racing heart exploding.

"Fuck! They're shooting. Get down."

As bullets thumped into the wood around them, Lily dove to the floor and pulled the cage down. The boat's siding was saving their lives, but out on the river, they were sitting ducks.

Keeping his head down, Carter gripped his fingers around the handle and gave an almighty pull. A puff of black smoke erupted, but that was all as the rope zipped back in.

He tried again.

It sputtered. And died. Nothing more.

Strangling the plastic, he clenched his jaw and yanked again.

Each time the motor rattled a little more than the previous time. "Come on!" he screamed, and wrenched again.

Bullets splintered the wood, barely missing his ear. "Fuck!"

More desperate attempts to start it. More deadly bullets.

Terror clawed at his throat. Lily glanced at him and the alarm in her eyes nearly crippled him. *This is it. Do or die.* And he had no intention of dying.

Not today! Not here!

Carter stood. Yanked the rope with everything he had. The engine sputtered once, twice, then roared to life.

He grabbed the tiller, hunkered down, and steered them into the fast-flowing water. Within a heartbeat, they barreled downstream, putting distance between them and the gunmen.

It was a long time before Carter could breathe again. It was even longer before he felt safe enough to sit up on the seat.

"Are you okay?" he called over the motor.

Lily crawled onto her seat too. "Yes. You?"

"I'm okay. But I can't believe you saved the fucking bird."

She smiled. No, it was more than that, it was a broad beam of triumph and elation. Lily began to giggle, and soon both of them roared with laughter. After yet another brush with death, their hysterics made them seem insane.

Maybe they were.

Lily met his gaze. Her eyes shimmered as if she'd been crying. "Thank you for getting my pack."

"Stupid thing nearly got us killed," Carter grumbled.

Lily crawled over her seat to him, clutched her arms around his neck and wept. "I love you."

And that made the whole terrifying experience worthwhile.

Chapter Thirty

Lily wiped her eyes and returned to her seat. Sheer exhaustion racked her body.

What they'd done was incredible . . . and incredibly stupid.

Her insistence nearly got them both killed. But it was like she'd been possessed. She'd never be able to rest knowing those men had her name and all her passport details. And there was no way she could leave Pompa in the hands of those madmen. It would've been like leaving Otomi all over again, and she just couldn't do it.

She turned Pompa's cage upright. The bird had his tongue out, panting, and his normally fluffed up feathers were flat, lifeless. "There you go, mate." She wished she could release him from the cage and hold him, let him know he was safe. If he died of a heart attack or something after all that, she'd be devastated.

Carter adjusted the engine down a notch and she turned to him, frowning.

"Lily, move up front and watch for rocks."

"Okay." She climbed over her seat and eased down into the bow section.

The motor had them barreling over the water at breakneck speed. During the day this would've been okay, but in this minimal moonlight, it was downright dangerous. Lily could barely make out the dark shapes of larger rocks in the water, often only when they were they were about to hit them. "It's really hard to see. Maybe we should stop."

"Not yet." He was difficult to hear over the roar of the motor.

The blackened jungle whizzed by, and she scanned the river, clutching the rim of the bow, desperate to remain onboard, should they hit something hidden beneath the water.

The engine sputtered, and she turned to Carter. Ethereal moonlight highlighted his distress. The motor coughed, spewed black smoke, and died completely, plunging them into eerie silence.

"Shit!" he screamed to the heavens.

After a deep breath, he tugged on the handle and pulled the ignition rope several times, frantically attempting to restart the engine. Eventually, he sighed, crumbling to his seat. "I think we're out of fuel."

They were at the mercy of the river.

"Grab an oar, babe."

Lily pushed up onto the seat and reached for her oar. Carter moved to sit beside her. "What do we do now?" she asked.

"Try not to crash."

"Very funny. I'm serious."

"Me too. We need to stay in the middle."

Clutching the oar, she hooked her feet under the seat, and strained to see the rocks before they hit them.

"Watch that rock! Paddle!" Carter used his oar to push off a giant boulder on her right.

"Do you think we should pull into shore?" she asked.

"Maybe." Carter dug his oar into the water to avoid another rock. "We'll keep going a bit more."

White water frothed at the bases of rocks, making them a little easier to see, but it was the ones hidden beneath the boat, of which they'd already crunched over several, that concerned her the most. If they hit one, there was every chance they'd smash a hole in the boat and sink to the bottom of the river.

She had no intention of getting back in the water again.

The moon was nearly all the way over to the left side of the canyon. They'd be in complete darkness soon.

The boat lurched to a halt, slamming her forward. Metal squealed, loud and torturous, and the bow raised out of the water.

"Shit!" Carter leaned over the back. His muscles bulged as he strained against its weight.

The motor was caught on something. Water tumbled into the boat.

"Oh shit!" She crawled to the back to help him.

The merciless torrent drove the boat under, keeping the engine wedged against the rock.

"We have to lift it!" Carter's panic scared her as much as the water flooding in. "Grab on and help me."

She copied his lead and leaned over the back of the engine. With water cascading over her arms and lower body, she gripped her fingers onto the motor. "I'm ready."

A groan released from her throat, matching Carter's cries of exertion. The motor didn't budge at first, but then, as if something snapped, it flipped up. The bow plunged onto the water and they both fell forward.

The current caught again, carrying them on downstream.

"Holy shit!" Carter eyes were as sharp as ice picks. "Are you okay?"

"I thought we were going to drown."

"Yeah, me too. Let's pull into shore." Carter tugged wet hair from his eyes. "We need a spot to hide."

They bounced off several more rocks, both above and below the water, before she pointed to the right, farther up the riverbank. "There. That tree."

"Perfect. Paddle." Carter dug his blade into the water, as did Lily, and after a couple of frantic strokes they pulled in behind the fallen tree. About a quarter of its trunk sprawled across the river.

Carter clutched at a branch protruding from the water, and using more branches for leverage, moved them closer to shore. "Can you get out?"

261

"Okay." Leaning over the bow, she looked down, but it was impossible to see where the water stopped and the riverbank began.

"Here, hang onto this rope."

A rope draped across her shoulder and she grabbed hold. Climbing over the side, the water rose up to her ankles, and she stepped from the boat and trampled coarse shrubs to get up the riverbank. "I'll pull you in."

Carter tossed her pack ashore with a dull thump and, seconds after a splash, he was at her side. He put Pompa down and the bird made clucking noises, as if happy to be on dry ground too. She reached for her bag and groaned. *It's soaking wet.* Hopes of finding dry clothes evaporated. Blindly fumbling around inside, she searched for something that would make their situation better.

But there was nothing. The clothes were wet. The toiletries bag was useless, and she already knew they'd exhausted most of the supplies in the first-aid kit. And if all that wasn't bad enough, her insect repellant was gone. The roll-on that was usually within easy reach in a side pocket must've fallen out.

"Shit," she grumbled.

"Don't tell me your passport isn't in there after all that."

"Oh, hang on." Curling her fingers under the hidden flap at the back, she tugged at the zipper. She reached into the padded pocket and sighed with relief. "Yes! It's here."

"Thank Christ."

"I told you it would be." It was water damaged, but it didn't matter. To have it back in her hands was a huge relief. Her Amex card was there too, and her small stash of cash. It seemed they didn't find this hidden pocket at all.

"That's good, babe." He leaned in and kissed her forehead. "I don't suppose there's any food in there?"

"Oh, I wish."

As Carter fussed about, securing the boat to a nearby tree, Lily scanned the surroundings. Behind her, she struggled to make out anything in the darkness. In front, the river reflected the moonlight and slithered past until it disappeared in the distance like a sleek black eel. The fallen tree's branches jutted from the water like desperate fingers and water tumbled over it with relentless repetition.

Lily leaned against the trunk on the riverbank and was surprised it still emanated warmth from the day's sunshine. With a bit of luck, it'd keep them warm enough through the night.

"How're you going?" Carter touched the small of her back.

She was wet, tired, cold, exhausted, and hungry. But there was no point mentioning any of them; he'd be the same.

"I'm okay. I'll be better once the sun comes up."

"Yeah. Me too."

She sat on the grass with her back against the tree trunk, and the second she became comfortable, a mosquito droned in her ear. Groaning, she flicked it away.

Carter crawled in beside her. Their legs and shoulders touched, and just being next to him made her feel safe. It was impossible to understand how a man she'd known for just days could make her feel so complete. But he did. Her heart was open to him and she was ready to let him in. As he trailed his hand up and down her thigh, she knew she already had.

The insect returned, relentlessly buzzing in her ear. Every time she flicked it away, it came back.

Raw emotions bubbled to the surface. Tears pooled and spilled from her eyes. Discreetly wiping them away, she sucked in a shaky breath.

"Hey." Carter ran his hand over her hair. "Don't cry."

"Sorry, I can't help it."

"No need to say sorry."

"This's so crappy."

He wrapped his arm over her shoulder, tugging her closer. "I know."

A wave of utter helplessness engulfed her. Lily's chest heaved and tears flowed. Carter wriggled around so that she sat between his legs, and had her back to his chest. He held her in his arms, smoothing her hair and whispering words she didn't hear. It felt good to cry.

She cried for her father and what he'd endured decades ago.

She cried for her mother, who'd become a widow, too young.

She cried for her family, who'd be frantically searching for her.

She cried for Otomi, whose life was cut short so brutally.

And she cried over the cruel irony of finding the man of her dreams, yet they might never make it out of the jungle alive.

She sucked in a shaky breath, forcing away her sorrow. "I'm guessing a fire is a bad idea?"

"Yeah. Sorry, babe, I don't think we should." He flicked at an invisible insect. "Those guys might come looking for us."

Drying her eyes with the back of her hand, she nodded; she'd expected his response. With wet clothes, buzzing insects, and excruciating hunger, she was about to experience one of the worst nights of her life.

Nothing could get worse than this.

At least that's what she hoped.

"Come on." Carter wriggled out from behind her. "You lie next to the trunk and I'll lie beside you."

She allowed him to move her into position, and when he crawled in beside her, their faces were inches apart. He kissed her lips, just a brief kiss of reassurance.

"I don't know how much more I can handle." Lily rolled into the crook of his shoulder.

He draped his hand on her arm. "This'll be our last night. I'm sure of it."

His steady heartbeat was as soothing as the warmth of his body next to hers, and she was surprised at how comfortable she was.

Her mind drifted to her family. They'd be beside themselves with worry. "What are we going to do when we get there?"

"We'll go straight to the police, report Otomi's death, and ask them to call your family."

She tried to picture how that conversation would go. She imagined lots of tears and lots of *I told you so*'s.

But they'd be wrong.

Despite everything that'd happened and nearly dying several times, she had survived. She had the pictures to prove it.

"Hey, what happened to your camera?"

"I left it back at the sinkhole."

"What? Why?"

"It was ruined. It doesn't matter, it's insured. Besides, I have the SD cards—they're much more important."

She glided her hand over his chest, feeling the muscles beneath. "I hope the pictures turn out."

"Me too."

They slipped into comfortable silence, and soon Carter's breathing became deep and steady. As he drifted off, Lily tried to curb all the unanswerable questions running through her mind so she too could fall asleep.

Chapter Thirty-One

Lily must've slept, because when she blinked awake there was enough light to see Carter lying next to her. His eyes were closed and his lips were slightly ajar, inhaling long, slow breaths. Carter was handsome in a rugged, outdoorsy way. His long, dark lashes rested on his upper cheeks. His nose was cute and straight. A ray of sun caught in his hair, highlighting both blond and whiskey colors in the knots.

"You know that's rude, don't you?"

She jumped. "What?"

He opened his eyes. "Staring."

She giggled. "I thought you were asleep."

"How can I sleep with your beautiful eyes drilling into me?" He kissed her forehead and groaned. "Oh, man, I feel like I've been hit by a Mack truck."

"Yeah, me too." She lifted her head.

He rolled his arm out from under her neck and flexed his fingers. "Pins and needles." He flicked his hand, obviously trying to work the blood back in.

"Sorry about that."

"It's all good. Did you sleep?"

She nodded. "I must have."

"Good. Come on, let's go." He crawled to his feet. "I reckon we'll be eating steak for lunch today."

Lily moaned. "Stop teasing." She stood and stretched, manipulating the pain from her shoulders.

"Shit, Lilly! Look at your legs."

She didn't want to look, but couldn't help it. Sometime during the night, ants or mosquitos, or possibly both, had feasted on her legs. Hundreds of angry red dots marked every inch of her skin. From the second she saw them, the itching attacked. She wanted to claw her nails up her shins, her thighs, her ankles.

"Don't." Carter must've seen that urge because he grabbed her hands.

Squeezing her eyes shut, she forced the new affront to her body from her mind. "This had better be the last day of this fucking shit." She opened her eyes and Carter met her gaze.

He burst out laughing. "All right then, Tiger Lily, let's get moving."

While Carter untied the boat, Lily went into the bushes to relieve herself. Just the thought of being rescued and using toilet paper again had her moving faster.

Every step was agony, but she had no intention of removing her wet socks and boots. She'd never get them back on. Carter put Pompa's cage into the boat, along with her pack, and then helped her aboard. She slushed through the ankle-deep water to the front seat, sat, and reached for the oar.

Carter jumped in, pushed off, and they floated downstream.

Unlike last night, the river seemed peaceful, almost serene. Rays of sunlight pierced the trees on the right-hand side of the ravine and shimmered off the water like dazzling stars. Small butterflies danced about in a spectacle choreographed by nature. If it weren't for her hunger and aching body, she'd have loved every minute.

Even the boat behaved itself today and maintained course down the river, almost of its own accord. Only on the odd occasion did they need to steer it back into position.

Pompa showed no signs of distress and flapped his wings,

soaring on the morning breeze. They rounded the first bend in the river and Pompa crowed long and loud, ruffling his feathers.

Carter huffed. "Lucky we don't eat you, crazy bird."

Lily snapped her eyes to him. "We will not!"

He did a double take. "I was joking."

She turned back toward the bow and pretended to study her battered hands. Her aggression had been uncalled-for, and she instantly regretted it.

"Lily?" Carter said it as a question. "What's going on? Why's Pompa so important to you?"

She turned back to him. "I didn't just want to save him for Otomi's sake."

"I'm sensing that."

Closing her eyes, she inhaled deeply, and let the air out slowly. "When I was twelve, I had a pet rabbit called Fluff Bomb. He was cute and mischievous and constantly escaped from his cage. Dad told me if I didn't fix his pen, he'd put Fluff Bomb into our next stew."

She could still picture the fluffy rabbit sitting in her lap, flicking his ears back and forward while she tickled his pink stomach. "Anyway, one night he got out again and ate mom's entire snow-pea crop. My dad loved his snow peas more than my rabbit." Her fingers trembled as she covered her eyes. She clenched her teeth, determined not to cry.

"Come here." Carter wrapped his hand around her wrist, pulled her to him, and she rested her chin on his shoulder, forcing back the tears.

"It was my fault she was killed."

"It wasn't your fault." He pulled back, his eyes darkened, drilled with concern.

"It was."

He tilted his head, and a small smile curled at his lips. "Well, I think what you did for Pompa makes up for it."

Nothing could ever make up for it, yet she nodded.

Pompa crowed and flapped his wings and Carter chuckled. "See, even Pompa agrees."

The boat bumped off a rock neither of them had seen and she scurried back to her seat and clutched the oar.

It was already warm, despite the sun still hiding behind the trees. The occasional fish jumped from the water, making Lily's grumbling stomach grumble even more. With each curve in the river, it widened slightly. This, in turn, had the current diminishing. When the sun finally peeked over the top of the treetops, Lily fought the glare with squinted eyes.

"Carter!" She pointed ahead. "There's people."

"Where?"

"Over there. It's a jetty." Lily shielded her eyes from the sun. "They're kids." Her heart thumped. "They're fishing."

"Yes. *Hola!*" Standing, Carter waved both hands above his head. "*Hola.*"

The two children waved back.

"Paddle, Lily. We're saved."

Tears pooled in her eyes. A lump in her throat made it impossible to breathe. Every muscle ached. Yet, she sliced that blade through the water, driving toward salvation. The two children continued waving, and soon Lily heard their giggles. They wore only brightly colored shorts, and their welcoming smiles were a brilliant contrast to their dark skin.

"*Hola necesitamos ayuda.*" Carter cupped his mouth, projecting his voice. "*Es que la madre o el padre en esta lista?*"

"*Sí. Sí,*" one of the boys called back.

"*Se puede conseguir que por favor.*"

The children ran off like a fox was on their tail.

Lily frowned at Carter. "What'd you say?"

"I asked them to get their folks." Carter put his oar into the water to slow their speed.

The second they reached it, she leaned over and clutched at the pylon. Carter launched onto the rickety platform to tie them up. She handed Pompa's cage and her pack to him, and then he helped her from the boat.

She fell into his arms. The realization they were saved reduced her legs to jelly. Carter hooked one arm around her waist, picked up

Pompa's cage with his other hand, and she grabbed her pack. Together, they headed toward the little cottage in the distance.

Through tear-filled eyes, Lily spied a buxom woman waddling toward them. *"Oh Dios mío. ¿Estás bien? ¿De donde vienes?"*

Lily only recognized one phrase—*oh Dios mío*. Oh, my God. One of her friends from college was Mexican, and this was her favorite saying. Lily agreed with it wholeheartedly.

The woman arrived at Lily's side, clutched her elbow, and led her toward the cottage. Lovely aromas wafted from the building.

Have I died and gone to heaven?

Her aching body convinced her otherwise.

The woman and Carter carried on a conversation Lily couldn't understand. She switched off trying to comprehend and allowed them to look after her. The giggling boys grabbed Pompa's cage and her bag, and raced ahead with the rooster bouncing between them.

After a couple of steps inside the cottage, Lily was seated at a small table with four wicker chairs positioned around it. Within seconds, a glass of water and a small bun were in front of her. Lily gulped down the water, and then bit into the bread roll. The outer crust cracked to reveal a slightly chewy, vanilla-colored center. Never before had anything tasted so good.

Carter sat at her side and he too was treated to food and water.

He placed his hand over Lily's. "We made it."

She nodded. "We did."

He grinned. "I'll see if Teresa has a phone."

"Discúlpeme, Teresa, ¿tiene un teléfono?" Carter held his hand to his ear, mimicking his question.

"No. Sin embargo, nuestros vecinos hacen." Teresa shook her head and Lily's heart sank. The conversation continued between Teresa and Carter, and, as if a starter gun had sounded, the two boys shot from the kitchen and raced out the front door.

Carter turned to her. "Teresa doesn't have a phone, but her husband's working at a farm nearby. The boys have gone to get him, and then he'll take us into town."

Lily nodded. *"Gracias, Teresa."*

"Está bien."

After the small bun came a bowl of curry. It was hot, both in heat and spice, and brimmed with meat and vegetables. Lily scooped large spoonfuls into her mouth and was full much sooner than she'd expected. She couldn't even finish the meal.

Carter too had stopped.

Lily put her hands together as if praying. "*Gracias, Teresa. Gracias.*"

The Mexican woman turned, wiping her hands on a towel, smiling.

"Please, sit with us," Lily said, and Carter translated and indicated a chair.

As Teresa leaned over to sit, a small silver cross dangling around her neck swung forward and Lily's mind flashed to the necklace in the cave.

"Carter, can you please ask Teresa if she knows about the mudslide?"

He turned to Teresa, and Lily watched their hands and facial expressions, trying, but failing to follow their conversation.

As their discussion continued at length, Lily grew more confident that Teresa could help.

"What was your father's name?" Carter asked.

"Malcom Bennett."

When he repeated the name, Teresa's expression grew grim as she spun her finger around her ear and said, "*Loco.*" Lily recalled Otomi's reference to the monkeys being *loco* and wondered who Teresa was referring to.

Finally, Carter turned to her, and the look in his eyes drove a spike into her heart.

He placed his hand over hers, preparing her for what she was about to hear. "Like we'd already figured, the mudslide was in 1980. An entire village was wiped out, killing everyone."

"Did she know my father?"

He nodded. "He was a missionary—"

"Ahhh, I don't think so." Chuckling, Lily shook her head. "Dad never went to church. He didn't even believe in God."

"Let me finish." His eyes drilled into her. "He worked as a

272

missionary around this area for about a year before he met his wife. They worked together, travelling among the small communities, talking about God and religion. Even once he had his daughter, they continued."

Lily tried to picture her dad doing this, but couldn't.

"When the mudslide hit that village, he and his wife and child were in a car. They were swept away. He survived, but couldn't get his family out of the mud in time. Apparently, he held on to his wife's hand until she died."

Lily's chest burned at the horror of it.

Carter cleared his throat. "Your father stayed with them for three days before he finally let go. Apparently, he walked through the jungle for a week, surviving on just water and berries, and by the time they found him he was a little crazy. Nobody even knew of the mudslide until he told them."

Lily covered her mouth. "Oh, my God."

"Teresa says after the accident, your father stayed around for a few months, but one day he just disappeared."

Lily blinked at Carter and Teresa, and tried to picture her father walking from the jungle, exhausted and starving, like they'd just done. It was difficult to believe, and yet it explained much of her father's actions. It answered why he didn't believe in God and didn't want any of his children married in a church. It explained why he was insistent on his children learning survival skills. It might also explain why he'd continued having children until a daughter was born.

The pain he'd suffered would be the reason why he never mentioned his first wife and daughter again.

A flush of warmth radiated through her body, bringing a sense of relief. Her father was still the family man she'd always known him to be, and not someone who'd willingly abandoned his wife and child. It appalled her that she'd thought any different.

Finally, she had answers to the questions that'd brought her to Mexico, and she was confident this knowledge would help her mother's grieving.

It made every painful step worthwhile.

Chapter Thirty-Two

The two children came bounding into the kitchen, followed by a middle-aged Mexican man with graying hair and a scraggly beard. Carter stood to shake his hand and introduce themselves.

"Hola, mi nombre es Carter, esta es Lily." Carter informed Pedro of their situation and asked to be taken to the police.

"Sí, sí, te llevaré a la policía."

After Lily hugged Teresa and said goodbye, she and Carter squeezed into the front of Pedro's beat-up old pickup. Lily's pack and Pompa's cage were put into the back and the two squealing children jumped in too. Carter asked the date, and was surprised to learn it'd been eleven days since they'd left Corozal. He relayed the information to Lily.

"Feels like so much more."

"I agree."

"We're a week overdue. I wonder if my brothers are here."

"We'll find out soon enough."

Bumping along the winding road, leafy trees brushed against the side of the truck and the kids giggled in the back. Pedro asked many questions, and Carter had just as many of his own.

"*Hombres muy malos.*" Pedro's eyes bulged with apparent fear. "*Hombres muy malos,*" he repeated shaking his head.

"What's he saying?" Lily asked.

"I was telling him about the guys who chased us, and he says they're very bad men."

She huffed. "I could've told him that."

It was more than an hour before they arrived at a police station. The squat orange building with peeling paint and no windows didn't portray any semblance of authority. Out front were two horses and two motorbikes.

Pedro pulled to a stop, Carter jumped out, and Lily winced as he helped her from the pickup. He put his arm around her waist and aided her into the building.

The police were as efficient as the boxy computer on their desk, but they made up for it with their friendliness. Lily and Carter were treated to more food, and at the insistence of the two overweight officers, they posed for photos that Pedro willingly took. It seemed like hours before they'd explained everything. Several times, Carter noticed Lily had closed her eyes, and he wondered if she'd fallen asleep.

"*Por favor,*" Carter said. "We need a hospital."

"Ahhh, *sí, sí, sí.*"

Lily and Carter were whisked out the back of the station and loaded into a beat-up old Jeep that was caked in red dirt from the wheels to the roof. The birdcage and her pack were shoved onto the back seat and the rooster crowed, as if in protest. Lily leaned on Carter's shoulder, and before they'd even travelled through the small town, she was asleep.

It was several hours before they reached another town. This one was much bigger than the last. They cruised down the main street, and when they arrived at an intersection, Carter was shocked to see the ocean. Golden beaches lined the shore and azure water stretched to the distant horizon.

Barely five minutes later, the police officer pulled to the curb next to a giant, red, Perspex cross announcing the emergency entrance to the hospital. Carter put his arms beneath Lily's knees and around her back, and carried her up the pebbled path. The police officer ran at his side, shouting commands in Spanish, before they'd even reached the doors.

Two glass panels slid open, flooding him with cool air. "*Ayuda. Ayudame por favor.*" Carter called for help, and two women in white uniforms came running forward.

He placed Lily's limp body onto a trolley and briefed the nurses of their situation. Lily's bloodshot eyes opened. Her cracked lips parted, but no words came out. He wove his fingers into hers and squeezed, but she didn't respond. His chest tightened at her overwhelming weakness. Carter ran alongside the trolley, clutching her hand while they wheeled her along a fluorescent-lit corridor.

"What's happening?" Lily's voice was a broken whisper.

"It's okay, baby, we're at a hospital now. Close your eyes and rest."

She squeezed his hand, and her eyelids fell.

Hospital staff pulled her trolley into a room with cables dangling from all manner of equipment. The nurse tugged a white curtain around them, and a stout man with a stethoscope around his neck approached Lily. He checked her pulse and his frown drilled his bushy eyebrows together.

The doctor barked orders at the nurses. An IV drip was attached to Lily's forearm. One nurse studied the wounds on her hands. Yet another began removing Lily's boots. When her socks came off, the nurse winced at the sight.

Carter watched on, fighting exhaustion that threatened to crush him. The room began to swim. Unable to stand a moment more, he tugged a chair to Lily's side and placed his hand on her arm, hoping she knew he was there.

Another man in a white coat hooked his hand beneath Carter's elbow to lift him up. "*Vamos, señor, tenemos que mirar a sus lesiones.*"

"I'm okay. Just look after Lily."

"She's in good hands." The man spoke perfect English. "But you'll be no help to her if you pass out."

Carter had trouble focusing. His eyes burned. His body shook. The man helped him to stand. "I want to see her at all times." Carter wasn't sure if he'd actually spoken the words.

The man pulled open the curtain. A bed was there. The soft mattress was too much to resist. Carter shuffled over, climbed onto the white sheets, and groaned when his head molded into the soft pillow.

"You can see Lily from here. Okay?"

He smacked his lips together, trying to get moisture. In the end, all he could do was nod.

The doctor who'd been with Lily appeared at his side. He placed his fingers on Carter's wrist, checking his pulse. "Where are you hurt?"

"Everywhere." Carter didn't recognize his own voice.

The doctor smiled. "Okay. Let's get an IV drip here too."

"I have a bullet wound." Carter reached for his hip, and the doctor's eyebrows shot up. He clutched at a pair of scissors and came around the other side of the bed.

"But it's okay now. Lily cauterized it."

The doctor laughed. Maybe he thought Carter was delusional.

Carter watched for the doctor's expression, as his shorts were cut from his body. The doctor leaned in, his eyes concentrating on the scars. "Good Lord, it *is* cauterized. Who did you say did this?"

Carter pointed at the adjacent bed and grinned at the memory of her relaying what she'd done. "With a spoon."

The doctor shook his head. "Well, it looks like it's healing."

After a nurse shoved a needle into the back of his hand and connected it to a tube, she went to his feet to remove his shoes. He braced for the pain he knew was coming. She peeled off his wet sock. Carter howled.

The room swam, darkness crept over the light. He sucked in short, sharp breaths, then everything went black.

∽

CARTER WOKE TO THE SMELLS OF ANTISEPTIC AND ROAST CHICKEN, and the sounds of laughter. He blinked back grogginess, and turned to the people milling around the adjacent bed. Lily was propped up by pillows, dressed in white, and with her dark hair cascading over her shoulders, she looked like an angel.

"Well, hello, sleepyhead." She smiled at Carter and reached over to touch his hand. "How are you?"

He cleared his throat and his tongue was as dry as leather. "Okay. How about you?" Clutching a metal triangle over the bed, he tried to sit.

"Billy, help him sit up," Lily requested.

A man in a checked shirt, with broad shoulders and an equally broad smile, strode to Carter. As Billy fiddled with buttons on the remote control to the bed, Carter frowned at Lily.

"Carter, I'd like you to meet my brother Billy. And this's Danny." She indicated the second man at her side.

Billy held out his hand, and when Carter gripped it, he tried not to wince at the man's strong embrace. "Thank you for saving my sister."

The bed raised and Carter adjusted the pillows behind his head. "Actually, Lily saved me. A few times."

"So we heard." Danny shook his hand too.

Carter frowned. "How long have I been asleep?"

"You've been dozing on and off for two days."

"Two days? Really? What'd I miss?"

Lily smiled. "Well, my brothers arrived, the police came several times to ask more questions. Oh, and a *Sixty Minutes* interview."

He crinkled his nose at her. "Did not!"

"Yeah, they did. They interviewed me yesterday, and they're coming back to interview you later." The smile fell from her face. "They're with a police helicopter now, trying to locate Otomi."

At the memory of taking photos of Otomi, Carter felt for his jocks, but he was naked beneath the white gown. "Shit." He sat up and searched the room.

"What's wrong?" Lily reached for him.

"My SD cards. They're gone." He tried to get off the bed, but his head spun.

"Calm down, it's okay," Lily said. "The nurses found them when they undressed you. I asked Danny to look after them."

He sighed with relief. "Thank God."

Danny reached into a drawer at Carter's side and handed over the little pouch.

Carter clutched it to his chest, closed his eyes, and inhaled a few calming breaths.

"Want my computer so you can look at the photos?" Bill asked.

"Oh, no thanks." He'd look at the photos in private. Seeing his snapshots for the first time was something he treasured. Rarely had he shared that moment with other people, and he wasn't sure he was ready to break that tradition with Lily's burly brothers hovering around, especially as hundreds of photos were sneaky ones he'd taken of Lily.

He had no idea what she'd told them about him . . . about them, and he didn't want to be the one breaking the news. Not until he spoke to her first.

"Aren't you going to look at them?" Billy asked.

Carter sighed. "Not yet. I hope you understand."

"Ahhh, no, not really." Billy was gruff with his response.

"Leave him alone, Billy." Lily came to his defense, and when he turned to her, their eyes met. Her intensity indicated she understood his reluctance, and if it was even possible, he loved her even more.

"Hey, guys, can you tell the nurses Carter's awake?"

"Yeah, sure." Billy nodded at his sister, and the two brothers eased away from the beds.

"Oh, and tell them I'm starving." Carter couldn't ignore the roast chicken aroma a moment more.

"Me too." Lily grinned.

"You're always starving."

She reached for his hand again. "I told you I have a bottomless stomach."

He wove his fingers into hers, and slotting their palms together had his pulse racing. Their connection wasn't just physical, though; Lily had truly touched his soul.

He was in love.

Their gazes met and he wondered what she was thinking.

She'd had two days to rethink their situation.

He just hoped this wouldn't be the last time he lost himself in her stunning blue eyes.

Chapter Thirty-Three

Four days after they'd stumbled from the jungle, Lily and Carter were discharged from the hospital. Lily's feet still hurt, but the pain was bearable. The scabs and blisters on her hands looked hideous, as did the dozens of mosquito bites dotting her body like a disease.

But she didn't care.

She was alive, and so was Carter.

That in itself was a miracle.

She glanced down at his shorts and giggled. The knee-length, blue pants were covered in bananas, some whole and some half peeled. His multicolored shirt added to the spectacle. Billy must've gone out of his way to find the ugliest clothing for Carter.

"What?" Carter rolled his eyes.

"Nice pants."

He huffed. "Your brother has a mean sense of humor."

"And he's the nice one."

They walked hand in hand out of the hospital, and Lily's brothers met them out front in a red Dodge Nitro that they'd hired more than a week ago. She didn't miss the look of worry on their faces. They'd both expressed their concern over her relationship with Carter.

When she'd told them about her feelings for Carter, he'd been asleep in the bed beside her. As they'd alternated their glances from her to Carter, she'd had to admit, Carter looked as scruffy as some of the homeless people on the streets of Seattle. But they didn't know Carter like she did. Hell, she didn't even know him very well.

But she did know she wanted to learn everything about him.

It took her three days to convince her brothers that she'd be all right and they could go home. Now, walking to the car, she just hoped they'd kept good on their promise and booked their flights for today.

Carter opened the car door for her, she climbed in, and he shut the door. When he wriggled onto the seat beside her, she had a flashback to the first time they'd shared a car together. It was difficult to believe how much her impression of him had changed since then.

"Where're we going?" Carter rubbed his hands together.

Danny put the car into gear and accelerated away from the curb.

"To your hotel. We've booked you two rooms."

"Thank you." Lily stifled a grin. They wouldn't be needing two rooms. Carter wriggled his eyebrows, and by his cheeky grin she figured he was thinking the same.

Billy twisted to look at her in the back seat. "We've paid your hotel for a week's stay. Your replacement passport should be here by then."

"Oh, okay." Although she'd rescued her passport from the drug runners, the water damage had rendered it useless. But replacing it was the last thing on her mind.

"We've also arranged a cell phone so you can call us anytime." Billy handed a box over to her.

"Thanks."

Lily turned her attention out the window and was surprised to see the ocean. "Where are we?"

"Tequila Bay," Billy said.

"It's beautiful." Lily couldn't remember the last time she'd visited a beach. At least a decade or more. She wound down the window and breathed the fresh ocean scent. Small waves crashed into the shore and a flock of seagulls squawked overhead. Closing her eyes, she inhaled deeply.

She'd never felt so alive in her whole life.

Ten minutes later, Danny pulled the car onto a stamped concrete driveway. He parked in the shade, and the four of them climbed out. Her brothers led the way, bypassing reception, and heading straight for the elevator. They hopped in and Billy pressed the buttons for the second and the fourth floor and handed a room card to Carter. "You're in room 207."

"Cheers, thanks for organizing this. I can't wait to have a proper shower."

The elevator pinged open and after a fleeting glance at Lily, Carter stepped out and the doors closed.

"You could be a bit nicer to him, you know."

"You barely know him, Lily." Her older brother glared down at her.

"I know he saved my life."

The elevator doors reopened and she followed Billy down the breezy corridor. "What you've been through has made you—"

"You guys have no idea what I've been through. That man saved me in more ways than you'll ever know."

Billy pushed on the door to her room and she walked straight to the large double glass doors beyond the lounge, and opened them. Stepping outside, she clutched the railing and a gentle breeze drifted up from the ocean, embracing her.

Billy and Danny flanked her and hooked their arms across her shoulders. Side by side, the three of them looked out to sea.

"I really like Carter."

"We know, but we're worried about you," Billy said.

"I've just survived a week lost in the jungle. I think you can stop worrying."

"We're your older brothers, that's what we do," Danny said.

She squeezed their waists. "I know. But this is my decision. Go home to Mom. Please. I promise I'll ring you every day."

Billy tried to tickle her waist. "Promise."

Giggling, she ducked away. "Yes, I promise."

"Are you ready to call Mom now?" Danny asked.

She sighed. "I guess so." The moment Lily woke up in the hospital she'd called her mother. But she hadn't told her the full story. She wanted to wait until she felt human again. It didn't feel right doing it over the phone, but she had no idea how long it'd be before she returned.

It was time.

Her mom answered after the third ring. The dark cloud of mourning still dampened her usual chirpy voice.

Lily answered her mother's questions about her health and waited until there was a pause in the conversation.

"Hey, Mom, there's something I need to tell you. It's about Dad."

Her mother's breath hitched. "Go on." Lily could picture her mother's trembling hand hovering near her mouth, ready to choke back tears.

With her mother on speakerphone, so that her brothers could listen, Lily told her all about what happened to her father's first wife and child. Lily's heart broke at the sound of her mother sobbing. Out of the corner of her eye, she saw Danny wipe a tear off his cheek.

Her mother and brothers were skeptical, as they had every right to be, and asked dozens of questions, most of which she had answers to. Even though it was extraordinary, Lily believed it was true. Her only hope was that Carter's photos survived to reinforce the story.

Her mother's sadness switched to anger as she asked why her husband had chosen to keep such an important aspect of his life a secret.

They went around in circles over that question, with the four of them tossing out suggestions, but unfortunately, it was a question they were never likely to have answered.

Saying goodbye to her mom was hard, and Lily felt physically drained by the time she ended the call.

Her brothers spent the next two hours going over the story again. Their expressions confirmed how unbelievable it was. Their time to leave arrived, and they turned their attention to ensuring Lily had documented all the details about her passport replacement, emergency contacts, and how to use her new phone. It was after lunch when they finally said their goodbyes.

Danny gave her a handful of Mexican pesos and kissed her forehead. "Be careful, baby sis."

"I will."

Finally alone, Lily sat on the bed, picked up the hotel phone and dialed room 207. Carter answered on the second ring.

"How was your shower?" she asked.

"The best, and you?"

"I haven't, yet. It's taken me this long to get rid of my brothers."

He laughed. "Okay, take your time. I've got to sort out some money and my passport, so how about I meet you in one of those deck chairs on the beach at say three o'clock?"

She sighed. "Sounds perfect."

After hanging up, she stripped out of the colorful dress Billy had bought her to wear from the hospital and headed for the shower. The warm cascade was a slice of heaven, and she took her time washing her hair, scrubbing her nails, and shaving her legs.

Feeling like a new woman, she made her way downstairs and headed for the resort-wear shop she'd spied on the way in. Twenty minutes later, she headed back up to her room with a new bikini, a sarong, glasses, a big floppy hat, and another dress.

Just before three o'clock, she made her way back down to the lobby, and passing through reception, the front page of the only English-language newspaper caught her eye. A small photo in the bottom corner of the *Herald* showed a coffin being lowered into the ground. A crowd of mourners surrounded the coffin and despite her obvious distress, Lily recognized Renata among them.

In the top corner were two pictures of herself. One she recognized as her staff photo at More to Explore, and the other must've been taken while she was in the hospital, though she couldn't recall when.

Lily bought the paper and strolled across the terracotta lobby. She stepped down onto the sand, made her way to the water's edge, and slipped onto a padded deck chair beneath a thatched umbrella. Tequila Bay was a giant horseshoe-shaped beach with golden sand and small waves that crashed delicately onto the shore. Several hotels dotted the shoreline, but it still retained a quaint, untouched feel about it. It was peaceful and therapeutic—exactly what she needed.

After a long moment admiring the exquisite view, she removed her sarong, adjusted her bikini, and lifted the paper onto her lap.

A lump formed in her throat as she read of Otomi's burial in the plot next to his father. Yet, as sad as it was, it was also comforting to know his dying wish had been honored.

Lily turned the page to a picture of a police officer handing a rooster to a woman who looked like a thinner version of Renata. Her expression was a baffling mix of grief and relief, and it made that stupid dash to rescue the bird all worthwhile.

The next five pages detailed raids on marijuana plantations and the subsequent arrest of sixteen men. There was a brief mention of attempted murder and how a renowned photojournalist from *National Geographic* had been shot in the hip while trying to escape the gunmen. She chuckled at an entire column dedicated to Lily's surgical skills and why cauterizing wounds could be dangerous.

A man carrying two red cocktails, with small umbrellas and sliced pineapple balancing on the brim, sat beside her. She lowered the paper. "I'm sorry this seat is—"

Her jaw dropped. "Carter?"

The man at her side was freshly shaven, showing off a couple of dimples that punctuated his cheeks, and, after a moment's pause, a cheeky smile lit up his face. "Yep. That's me." His delightful manly scent drifted over her.

She tried to take all of him in. His distinct cheekbones. His strong chin. His stylish haircut that had several curls bouncing about his forehead and around his ears.

"I, ummm . . ." Lily was lost for words, and when he licked his lips, butterflies fluttered in her stomach. Carter was more handsome than she ever could've imagined. But, even as she studied his striking features, she knew this man was so much more than just good looks. Carter had the courage of a lion, the compassion of a true friend, and a wicked sense of humor. And she had every intention of learning everything else there was to know about him.

He handed her the cocktail, and in an attempt to absorb every inch of his exquisite features, she sipped on the sweet liquid while admiring him.

He sipped his drink, then set the glass on the table and held out his hand. "Hi, I'm Carter Logan."

Giggling, she put her glass down too. When their palms met, her stomach did a little happy dance. "Hello, Carter. I'm Lily Bennett."

A cheeky expression dazzled his eyes. "It's lovely to meet you, Tiger Lily." He pulled her onto him.

Squealing, she straddled his hips and poked his chest. "My name is Lily. Just Lily."

"I know, but Tiger Lily suits you. Brave and beautiful." He reached up, curled his hands around her neck, and guided her lips to his. She melted into his touch and savored a realm of new sensations, his exquisite manly scent, his minty breath, his clean-shaven face. It was a long moment before she eased back and looked into his inquisitive eyes.

His warm hands glided up her bare thighs. "So, what do we do now?"

She frowned. "Now . . . as in right now?"

"No. As in once we leave here and go back to our lives, our jobs."

"Well, we don't have to worry about my job. I quit a few days ago, before you woke up in the hospital."

"You did?" His brows thumped together.

"Yeah, my asshole boss was shitty at me because I wouldn't give him an exclusive to our story. I told him to make a bid for it, like *Sixty Minutes* had."

"You *sold* the story? I didn't know that."

"Sure did." She grinned. "A hundred thousand dollars should make its way to Otomi's widow in the next day or so."

He huffed. "Wow. Well done. So, rescuing the bird wasn't enough, hey?"

She crinkled her nose. "Nope."

Carter sighed and paused with his hands on her knees. "Lily, you know I can't go to America, remember?"

"I know." She curled her lip into her mouth. "I guess I'll just have to come and explore the world with you instead."

His eyes sparkled. "But what about your family and your home?"

"I always hated my apartment, and my family will be content just knowing I'm happy. Besides, wherever we go, they can come visit."

He blinked at her with a glorious smile. "Are you sure?"

"I've never been more sure about anything in my life." It was true. Fate had brought them together, and she had every intention of keeping them that way.

A cheeky grin crossed his lips. "Then our first destination should be Australia. I'd love you to meet my daughter."

"Oh Carter, that would be perfect."

He pulled her down to him and when their mouths met, the little butterflies dancing in her stomach fluttered through her body.

Lily had found more than she'd hoped for in the Mexican jungle . . . she'd found the man of her dreams.

THE END

DEAR FABULOUS READER, THANK YOU FOR FOLLOWING LILY AND Carter along this incredible journey of survival. Are you ready for another action-packed romance featuring a strong willed woman and the rugged hero who steals her heart? Try EXTREME LIMIT or ZERO ESCAPE today, these are the other two books in the Maximum Exposure series and you can read these in any order.

Turn the page for more details, or for more thrilling books by Kendall Talbot.

But before you go, would you like a FREE ebook? I'd love to share my crime thriller Double Take with you. Double Take is set in my home town of Brisbane, Australia and it's a thriller that will have you guessing to the very end. And if you sign up, you get it an ebook copy for FREE **https://kendalltalbot. com.au/doubletakefree.html**

Thank you and happy reading,
Kendall Talbot

Two lovers frozen in ice. One dangerous expedition.

Holly Parmenter doesn't remember the helicopter crash that claimed the life of her fiancé and left her in a coma. The only details she does remember from that fateful day haunt her—two mysterious bodies sealed within the ice, dressed for dinner rather than a dangerous hike up the Canadian Rockies.

No one believes Holly's story about the couple encased deep in the icy crevasse. Instead, she's wrongly accused of murdering her fiancé for his million-dollar estate. Desperate to uncover the truth about the bodies and to prove her innocence, Holly resolves to climb the treacherous mountain and return to the crash site. But to do that she'll need the help of Oliver, a handsome rock-climbing specialist who has his own questions about Holly's motives.

When a documentary about an unsolved kidnapping offers clues as to the identity of the frozen bodies, it's no longer just Oliver and Holly heading to the dangerous mountaintop . . . there's also a killer, who'll stop at nothing to keep the case cold.

Will a harrowing trip to the icy crevasse bring Holly and Oliver the answers they seek? Or will disaster strike twice, claiming all Holly has left?

Extreme Limit is action-packed romantic suspense full of drama, danger, and passion, featuring a fiesty heroine

and the rugged-yet-mischievous hero who steals her heart. Head to the Canadian Rockies and get ready for the adventure of a lifetime, with a happily ever after guaranteed

Zero Escape

To survive, Charlene must accept that her whole life was a lie.

For twenty years, Charlene Bailey has been living by the same mantra: pay in cash, keep only what you can carry, trust no one and always be ready to run. That is until her father is brutally murdered in New Orleans by a woman screaming a language Charlene doesn't understand. When police reveal the man she'd known all her life was not her biological father, Charlene is swept up in a riptide of dark secrets and deadly crimes.

The key to her true identity lies in a dangerous Cuban compound run by a lethal kingpin, but Charlene can't reach it alone. After a life of relying on herself, she'll have to trust Marshall Crow, a tough-as-nails ex-Navy man, to smuggle her into Havana.

The answers to Charlene's past are as dark as the waters she and Marshall must navigate, but a killer in the shadows will stop at nothing to drown the truth.

Zero Escape is action-packed romantic suspense full of danger, mystery and passion. It features a determined heroine and the rugged ex-navy man who steals her heart. Get ready to head to Cuba for the adventure of a lifetime, with a happily ever after guaranteed

Lost In Kakadu

WINNER: Romantic book of the year.
Together, they survived the plane crash. Now the real danger begins.

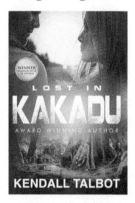

Socialite, Abigail Mulholland, has spent a lifetime surrounded in luxury... until her scenic flight plummets into the remote Australian wilderness. When rescue doesn't come, she finds herself thrust into a world of deadly snakes and primitive conditions in a landscape that is both brutal and beautiful. But trekking the wilds of Kakadu means fighting two wars—one against the elements, and the other against the magnetic pull she feels toward fellow survivor Mackenzie, a much younger man.

Mackenzie Steel had finally achieved his dreams of becoming a five-star chef when his much-anticipated joy flight turned each day into a waking nightmare. But years of pain and grief have left Mackenzie no stranger to a harsh life. As he battles his demons in the wild, he finds he has a new struggle on his hands: his growing feelings for Abigail, a woman who is as frustratingly naïve as she is funny.

Fate brought them together. Nature may tear them apart. But one thing is certain—love is as unpredictable as Kakadu, and survival is just the beginning...

Lost in Kakadu is a gripping action-adventure romance set deep in Australia's rugged Kakadu National Park. Winner

of the Romantic Book of the Year, this full-length, stand-alone novel is about a woman who needs to find herself, and the unlikely hero who captures her heart. Lost in Kakadu is an extraordinary story of endurance, grief, survival and undying love.

Sunken treasures. Dangerous enemies. Action-packed romantic suspense.

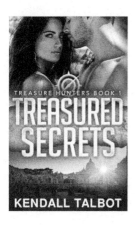

When Italian chef Rosalina Calucci finds a clue to an ancient treasure, she makes the mistake of bringing it to rogue treasure hunter Archer Mahoney, a dangerously sexy, frustratingly irresponsible, Australian millionaire. Something she knows all too well since he's also her ex-fiancé, a man who would rather keep his secrets to himself.

Archer Mahoney, will do anything to drown out his painful past; breaking up with the irresistible, smokey-eyed, woman of his dreams is proof of that. But his talent for finding lost treasure is almost as good as his talent for finding trouble and his feisty ex is just the beginning.

Rosalina's clue could be the key to locating an ancient treasure that's haunted Archer for years. But some treasures are buried in blood, and a deadly nemesis will stop at nothing to keep a sinful secret contained. Can they mend the ocean between them, or will Rosalina's quest for answers be just the beginning to Archer's nightmare?

Get ready for the adventure of a lifetime, with a happily ever after guaranteed.

Treasured secrets is book one in the thrilling romantic suspense Treasure Hunters series, full of drama, danger, and passion. It features a strong-willed heroine and the rugged-yet-mischievous millionaire who steals her heart.

A grieving detective with nothing to lose.
A dying town with everything to hide.

After the shocking death of his daughter, suspended detective Edge Malone who seeks oblivion in a bottle and plans to photograph a rare blood moon in isolated Whispering Hills, California. But his night takes a deadly turn when a high-tech drone is shot from the sky—and a ruthless gunman murders an innocent bystander who dares to visit the crash site. Driven by instinct, Edge seizes the drone and escapes into the woods.

Now being hunted, Edge unwittingly thrusts Nina Hamilton into the chase—a street-smart beauty who is no stranger to men with dangerous motives. But when the drone data leads them to a shocking discovery, they quickly learn that no one in Whispering Hills can be trusted. The truth of the small town is anything but quiet, and the price of secrets runs six-feet deep...

Get ready for the adventure of a lifetime with Jagged Edge, a full-length, stand-alone thriller featuring a kick-ass woman and a jilted man who needs to find himself again.

Prepare for a cruise like no other.

When an electromagnetic pulse (EMP) strikes Rose of the Sea, the pleasure cruise becomes a drifting nightmare. Powerless and desperate, the eleven hundred passengers and crew must face their new reality: No one is coming to save them.

The First Mate. The EMP destroys the captain's pacemaker and when he dies, Gunner McCrae is thrust into the top position. But no amount of training could prepare him for the savagery of desperate humans and an unforgiving ocean.

The Anchor-woman. Gabrielle Kinsella is known for bringing shocking stories to the world. She should be reporting on the headline of the century. Instead she's fighting for her children's lives.

The Acrobat. Held captive by a predator as a child, Madeline Jewel found freedom as the ship's acrobatic dancer. But being trapped in an elevator brings her worst fears back to life.

The Gambler. Zon Woodrow, notorious gator hunter, won his ticket in a poker match. But that isn't the only pot he's looking to score. With the ships security system obliterated, Zon turns his attention to the casino's vault. And this time, the house won't win.

As resources dwindle aboard Rose of the Sea, the body count continues to rise. Will ordinary people survive an extraordinary disaster? Or will human nature drown them in darkness?

Find out in this gripping survival thriller. FIRST FATE is book one in the Waves of Fate series.

A crime of love. The chance of a lifetime.

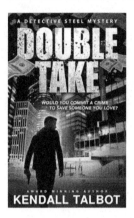

Jackson Rich is at risk of losing the love of his life, and he'll do anything to save her. Even if it means robbing a bank. So it's time to call in a few favors from his old gang because they owe him. Big time.

Gemma's spent her entire life doing the right thing. Now doing the wrong thing could be the best decision she's ever made, if she's brave enough.

When Detective Steel gets a tip-off of a planned heist, he doesn't know where the robbery will be. Only that it's going to take place during the famous horse race that stops a nation—the Melbourne Cup. And when it goes down, he'll be ready.

Except what happens next, only one of them sees coming. And for the others, it's suddenly no longer about the money. It's about retribution.

Get ready for a heist thriller that will have you turning the pages all night long. Double Take is a full-length, stand-alone bank robbery mystery featuring a desperate man, the burley cop hell-bent on bringing him down, and a crazy woman with a mission of her own

What readers are saying about DOUBLE TAKE:

"This story is so well planned and well written, it was as if it had actually happened! I was riveted to my chair while reading the twists and turns. If I could give it 6 stars, I would." ★ ★ ★ ★ ★ Multi-Mystery fan.

Made in the USA
Monee, IL
11 November 2021